A Different Truth

ANNETTE OPPENLANDER

First published by Oppenlander Enterprises, LLC, 2016
Second Edition
www.annetteoppenlander.com
Text copyright: Annette Oppenlander 2016
ISBN: 978-0-9977800-1-7

Library of Congress Control Number: 2016910838

Design: Brian Kotulis

For my husband and best friend, Ben, his undaunted support and valuable insight into living at a boys' military prep school, and for my children, Brian, Ethan and Nicole.
I also owe much gratitude to my writing buddies, Dianne, my friend and advisor, Susan and Dave who've been tirelessly critiquing my work for years. And to Brian Kotulis, an amazingly gifted art designer who created the beautiful cover.

OTHER NOVELS BY ANNETTE OPPENLANDER

Escape from the Past: The Duke's Wrath (Book one)
Escape from the Past: The Kid (Book two)
Escape from the Past: At Witches' End (Book three)
Surviving the Fatherland: A True Coming-of-age Love Story Set in WWII Germany
47 Days: The True Story of Two Teen Boys Defying Hitler's Reich (Novelette)
Everything We Lose: A Civil War Novel of Hope, Courage and Redemption
Where the Night Never Ends: A Prohibition Era Novel
When They Made Us Leave: A Novel about Hitler's Mass Evacuation Program for Children
A Lightness in My Soul: Inspired by a True Story
Boys No More (Short Story/Novella Collection)

GERMAN NOVELS
Vaterland, wo bist Du? Roman nach einer wahren Geschichte
47 Tage: Wie zwei Jungen Hitlers letztem Befehl trotzten
Erzwungene Wege: Historischer Roman
Immer der Fremdling: Die Rache des Grafen

"No event in American history is more misunderstood than the Vietnam War. It was misreported then, and it is misremembered now." —Richard M. Nixon

CHAPTER ONE

They came for me in the night, evil shadows that chased away my dream.

"Get up!"

The voice, cold and demanding, makes me open my eyes. Only I can't see a thing because in that instant the beam of a flashlight hits my face. Before my fuzzy brain can figure out what to do I'm yanked out of bed. I shiver, less from the cold, but from the uneasy feeling that's creeping up my spine.

Hushed sounds like suppressed grunts filter into the room. The corridor beyond is plunged into darkness. Heavy boots stomp around me. I search for a familiar face, someone I recognize, but the harsh light remains glued to my eyeballs. I'm about to shout, demand an explanation when they force back my arms and my shoulder blades begin to throb.

"Move." The speaker's voice sounds deliberately deeper, a bad actor's attempt to disguise his identity.

"What's going—"

My head and question disappear under a hood. I spit to keep the fabric from entering my mouth. It smells rancid as if someone has wiped their armpits with it. Gagging, I open my eyes wider... nothing.

I'm blind.

My chest heaves as I suck hard to find enough oxygen under the cloth, and resist the dizziness that wants to engulf me. I urge my sluggish brain to come up with an idea when a shove sends me staggering forward into the hall. Too late.

I notice mumbling, suppressed groans and staggering feet. There are others like me. Someone squeezes my wrists and pushes me onward at the same time. It's like a bad movie scene, except I'm in it. Suddenly I'm fuming mad, a burning in my stomach that works its way up to my throat. And there is a flicker of something else—fear.

"Walk!" comes the order from farther away. I twist my hands, but the iron grip holds. My body feels clumsy in the darkness. Now my wrists are being tied. Fingers made of steel clamp down on my biceps and guide me around a corner. I'm trapped.

I try remembering if I missed an announcement, something that would explain this bullshit. Nothing comes to mind. All I can think of is my heart pounding in my neck and the stinky cloth on my face.

"Stairs," someone hisses.

I step down, feel the momentary void before my foot hits the next tread. The cover shifts and I can see my toes. Somehow it feels comforting. This whole thing reminds me of Boy Scouts when they led me into the forest to make a fire and find my way back. Except this—whatever this is— seems really hostile. The voice of dread inside me whispers louder.

Somewhere ahead a door bangs. We must be going outside. A moment later I feel gravel under my bare feet, shooting darts of pain up my calves. I stub my big toe and suppress a groan. I'm not the only once because cries and grunts erupt all around me. I'm confused and clueless, getting angrier by the second, imagining how I smack these guys in their fat noses.

We keep walking, turning corners until I lose all sense of direction. Since my arrival at the academy two weeks ago, I've learned to march everywhere. I was sort of proud of knowing my way around so quickly. Until now, when the stuffy blackness in front of my eyes is playing tricks as if my head is stuck in a barrel of ink.

How long have we been out here? Palmer's campus spreads across hundreds of acres. I imagine being hauled into the woods and left to find my way back. Somehow that seems too easy.

By the time I'm yanked to a stop, my mouth is dry with a mix of panic and rage. Straining my ears I hear nothing but muffled whispers, impossible to understand or identify. Hundreds of cadets live here and I've got trouble just remembering the guys on my floor, Barracks B, one of six dorms. Not to mention the battalion and company officers who all look the same with their buzz cuts and uniforms. What a bunch of jerks. The voice of warning nags louder.

An arm wraps around my throat and forces me to the ground, followed by a blow to my stomach. Lights explode behind my eyelids. Struggling to breathe, I ignore the stinging in my ribs. I'm used to getting beat up in football, but this is cheap. This isn't a fight, it's slaughter.

Anger constricts my throat and makes it even harder to get air. Damn hood. Another punch lands, higher this time into the chest. Are they going to kill me? I didn't ask to come to this stupid school in the first place. What if I pretend to pass out? *But how would they know with your face covered up*, the voice in my head gripes. *They'll simply pound you to mincemeat, conscious or not.*

I've got only one choice, to stay calm and look for an opening. My fingers constrict as I receive another jab. More throbbing joins the angry burn in my gut. *Think*, I order myself. *Concentrate.* The cries around me are distracting. So is my aching body. I wait for another strike, but nothing happens. For a moment I feel suspended like I'm floating. It's worse than the attack because now I hear the thump-thump of other guys being pummeled.

I manage to roll on my side and yank on my ropes. One hand comes free. I rip away the hood and gulp air. Better, though it's still too dark to see anything.

The knock to my stomach comes out of nowhere. I pull up my thighs to protect my belly, watching the shadows that move like liquid smoke. Cries mix with the sound of punches as the attackers hover above their prey. The air boils with agony.

I'm on fire now, a volcano ready to blow. The chicken shit closest to me looks like he's taking aim. Instead of turning away to shield myself, I jolt forward and wrap a foot around his ankle. Then I yank. The scumbag grunts and collapses to the side. When I roll to my knees everything turns red. I punch in rapid succession until the guy quits moving. *One down.*

Ignoring my churning gut, I stand up. The fighting around me continues, flashlights dance, illuminating bits and pieces of an eerie battle. I've got to get away, hide some place. I'm not bad running sprints, but they outnumber me and my feet are raw. Maybe it's best to stay low and crawl off into the darkness.

By the time I notice the shadow sneaking up behind me it's too late. A kick to my knees sends me flying. Landing on my side, I want to spit with disgust. What worms. The scumbag I've hooked earlier sits up and holds his middle. Serves him right.

I swing a fist, but the blow lands on the other mugger's thigh which is hard and smooth as a medicine ball. It's the last punch I manage before my arms are forced down, and somebody sits on my legs. No matter how I writhe and kick, my attackers stay out of reach. I feel like a turtle lying on its back. More blows pelt me until a whistle sounds. Like ghosts, the thugs vanish.

I lie unmoving. My feet ache, my middle cramps and my head pounds in unison with my heart. Above me the moon cuts a thin crescent into the sky, the stars cold and distant—indifferent. I'm alone. A lump appears in my throat and I swallow it away. I didn't cry when my parents dropped me off and I'm sure as hell not going to cry now. I don't notice the dampness until I begin to tremble. My back has turned to ice. When I straighten to stand, my stomach twists as if I've eaten rocks and I slump back on my knees.

Somewhere to my right I hear moans, soft cries like suppressed weeping. I inch toward the sound. The sliver of moon makes it hard to see who is lying there. Some still wear blindfolds and have their hands bound. I grope in the dark to untie them and pull off their hoods. I recognize one of them by his high voice. Markus Webber, a freshman who lives in the room next to me. Markus is fourteen and looks twelve. He's crying. New fury bubbles inside me. Lousy rotten cowards, beating up a mere kid.

At least I'm sixteen, I think grudgingly. Not that it does any good. Like Markus I'm a plebe, a new cadet at the beginning of my 'career', that's what my dad calls it, at Palmer Military Academy. I'm scum. Dirt under the oldmens' shoes, fair game to be yelled at and made to service my superiors until I've learned the rules. I'll pay my dues for an entire year until I advance to oldman status and earn the right to torment the next generation of plebes. Who comes up with this stuff?

"You okay?" I ask, my voice strange in my ears.

Markus curls into a ball. "My stomach."

I crawl closer and grab his arm. "Better get up. You'll freeze."

Markus wipes his face and shifts onto his knees. "Thanks, man."

Around me boys stumble to their feet. When I hear another groan, I make my way toward the noise. It sounds familiar.

"Tom?"

My knee strikes something hard. The flashlight fires a sharp beam across the lawn as I grab it. Tom is lying on his back, his knees bent and sticking up like two extra-long twigs. I yank away the hood and untie his hands.

"Shitheads," Tom grumbles. "Nothing like a warm-welcome hazing in the second week."

We met the first day. Tom stood near the entrance to our dorm, looking out of place like a mismatched shoe. He's tall and skinny with black hair and brown eyes that zoom into your face not missing a thing. I liked him immediately.

I plop down to inventory my pajamas. "Did you recognize anyone?"

My pants are wet and stained with blood and grass. Several buttons are missing from my shirt and the right sleeve and arm stick to my skin. My mother's stern voice echoes through my head, "Andrew, be careful with your clothes, everything costs money." Andrew, that's me, though everyone but my mom calls me Andy. At the time I swallowed the comment of why they were sending me to this posh school, if it was so expensive.

Supposedly it's to help me study, but there is something else. Something they haven't expressed in words. I know they're unhappy about my grades and resent my rebellion. I draw a rattled breath.

Tom stares at me. "You okay? You look as if you've seen a ghost."

"Nothing." I try a smile though I can tell Tom isn't buying it. "Looks like they got you pretty good."

"Couldn't get the stupid hood off."

"They had to be oldmen. Some were definitely from the football team, too damn strong. I mean I punched this guy in the thigh and it felt like cement. Who has legs like that?"

"I guess you'd know best, playing with them every day," Tom says with a crooked grin. "Let's go, my arms are turning to icicles."

I scan the three-story building, its windows like black eye patches. The flashlight beam fades somewhere along the second floor.

"We're behind the faculty dorms. I bet they know." Most of the single teachers live here while professors and military personnel with families stay in houses near campus. The building is strictly off limits, though I don't have the faintest idea why any of us would want to step inside.

"Probably happens every year," Tom says.

"Did you notice they avoided our faces? Not to leave marks you'd see tomorrow." I rub my chest as if I can rid myself of the soreness.

"Might hurt their precious reputation if someone from the outside found out," Tom says. "On second thought, my father would probably thank these wackos for teaching me a lesson." His voice drops into a jeer. "The school trains young men in discipline, how to protect the country. None of that peace-loving hippie bullshit." Tom's voice returns to normal. "I think he even believes it himself."

"How is being beaten by cowards teaching anything? Cocksuckers." It comes out much louder than intended and I hear a few giggles behind me. I grin despite the soreness. It's forbidden to curse. Most everything is forbidden, certainly the things I've enjoyed doing before I got here. I grimace. At least one guy has a stomach ache right now.

"Wonder if we'll figure out who did this," I say aloud.

"Doubt it."

The cheerfully bright entrance of our barracks appears, its hallways deserted. I push away the thought of what other surprises await us, like how I'll make it through two entire years. Tom holds open the door, his face tweaked into a sarcastic grin despite the bruise swelling on his collarbone. I grin back.

At least I've got a friend.

CHAPTER TWO

The six a.m. bugle echoes down the corridor. "Sirs, reveille has sounded, Sirs," the call boy yells.

I roll on my side. In my dream, my father handed me the key to a brand-new '68 Ford Shelby Mustang, all shiny chrome and black, something that would never happen in a million years. Not when you've got two brothers and two sisters and your father is an assistant professor. Not when your mother buys five loaves of bread for a dollar to create endless lunches of peanut butter and jelly sandwiches.

With a groan I sit up only to slump back down. A wave of nausea clogs my throat. I remember the beating last night, the evil shadows dragging me outside. Something is definitely wrong with this place. I move my injured shoulder which immediately begins to throb. At least football practice won't be 'till afternoon.

We train every day, two hours of wind sprints, one-on-ones, weights, strategic plays and whatever else Coach Briggs comes up with.

I'll have to take it easy without drawing too much attention, because I've got to keep my spot after walking on to the team. Palmer's existing line-up hates newcomers, even if Briggs has agreed to try me out. I'm determined to show everyone what I'm made of, if it kills me. Hugging the bench is not an option.

"Sirs, the three-minute bell has sounded, Sirs," the callboy's voice booms through the corridor. "Class B uniforms and raincoats, Sirs."

I sigh. Three minutes to get moving. I scan my roommate's bed. Martin Plozett, the same age as me, but in his third year at Palmer, is already gone, undoubtedly spending the maximum amount of time in the shower.

Plozett likes bodybuilding. "My body is my shrine," he always says. With a full shadow of beard and hair covering his chest he looks like a college student, which is ridiculous considering my chin has barely sprouted five hairs. I wonder if he's been part of the attack. Surely he knows about it, even if he snored convincingly when I returned last night.

The corridor buzzes with half-dressed cadets in various states of wakefulness. Ambling to the bathroom, familiar smells hit my nose: soap, linoleum wax, hair oil, deodorant and dirty clothes. My stomach grumbles while I shower and dress. This time it's from hunger.

"ATTEN-TION. Assemble," the officer on duty shouts. I hurry through the door, pulling my belt and jacket straight and buttoning my raincoat. Dressing takes forever with the stupid shirt, tie and a thousand buttons on the jacket. Flinging on my cap, I throw one last anxious glance at my bed which looks perfectly made. My first room inspection begins in an hour.

Taking my place in line, I glance at Tom who nods in return. I watch the other cadets, their faces sleepy concentration. Again, I wonder about last night. Cowards. I'd fight them openly, fairly, one on one.

"ATTEN-TION!" The officer yells. "Forward MARCH! Left, right, left, right…" Heels click on the linoleum in near perfect rhythm, a shuffle and swish like fifty brooms sweeping at once. I stare at the neck in front of me, shaved from collar to the ears. I'll have to remember to go to the barber this week. If my hair grows past fourteen days, I'll be reported. Behind me someone is yelling at a plebe to get in step. As we round the corner, I try a ninety-degree turn, overshoot and find myself facing the wall. I quickly correct, hoping nobody noticed.

Outside, a cool drizzle hits my face. Gaining speed across the lake, wind gusts whack us with invisible arms. Fall is here and I long for bed.

I shiver as my squad of six lines up behind two others. More cadets join at a leisurely pace—oldmen don't have to march to assembly. I'm thankful for standing in back, away from the prying eyes of the regimental officer of the day.

Muller, a sixteen-year old junior, has already risen to officer rank. A hair's width over five feet tall, he stares unblinking as if he were on the battlefield assembling the troops. I suppress a smile. What a farce.

"Fall in. Parade, REST," Muller shouts. His voice, arrogance mixed with Mickey Mouse, annoys me. Like everyone else I spread my feet and place my arms behind my back.

Muller studies a sheet that lists every single cadet in the platoon. Roll call.

Unless you're sick and in the infirmary you better be standing right here. I carefully adjust my position so that I'm nearly hidden behind the front guy.

When I hear my name, I jerk my arms to my side and click my heels, shouting, "Present, Sir." It's taken a week to get the hang of this weird movement and I still have to concentrate to get it right.

After the last name is called, Muller walks past us one last time. The drizzle is turning into a full-blown storm, but he doesn't seem to notice. I think about breakfast and the load of assignments awaiting me. While I remember pretty much everything I read, I'm slow at it and the quantity of stuff we have to learn is staggering.

Finally Muller is satisfied. "Right FACE." I turn a perfect ninety-degree angle, checking distances to my neighbors. "For-ward, MARCH."

Across campus tight formations approach the mess hall. Like puppets we march everywhere—to breakfast, dinner and assemblies. If we aren't marching, we stand at attention, open doors and shout greetings to show respect to upper classmen. *A ridiculous waste of time*, I muse, keeping my eyes on the neck of my front man, constantly judging the distance and adjusting steps.

"MARK TIME," Muller yells when we reach the stairs to mess hall. We begin marching in place though I hardly notice because the air is filled with the tantalizing aroma of fried eggs, bacon, sausages and toast.

"FALL out."

With a sigh I hurry into the dining room. Tom has to be somewhere ahead.

"You better make sure your room is perfect," Tom says after we sit down under the ogling eyes of an oldman. "I heard Muller is pretty tough." Tom's picking through a pile of scrambled eggs, but docsn't seem anxious to finish them.

I eye his plate. "Are you going to eat that? He's an idiot."

"…who has the power to make our lives miserable." Tom shoves his eggs across the table. "My inspection is after yours."

I no longer taste the eggs, silently checking off the items in my room. I've made my bed well and dusted. My shirts and underwear are folded to school regulation width of exactly nine inches.

I breathe easier and arrive in my room with three minutes to spare. Plozett sits slumped over his desk reading the *Count of Monte Cristo*. I envy the ease with which he maneuvers the school's rigidity.

"ATTEN-TION," someone shouts in the corridor. "Officer Muller in attendance."

"You ready?" I ask, trying to calm myself.

With a nod Plozett shoves his book into his desk and straightens. "No sweat."

"Cadets Olson and Plozett ready for inspection," I shout, standing to attention as Muller appears with his second in command. Staring straight ahead, I concentrate on my posture: fingers curled, thumbs pointing down just behind the stripe that lines the side of each pant leg, chest out, shoulders straight, feet at a forty-five degree angle, heels together and hat at a slight angle.

Muller turns to my bed. He hesitates for a moment as if contemplating his next move. Then he rips away blanket and sheets.

"Glove," he says, extending an open palm. I scramble to retrieve one of my white gloves reserved for formal assemblies. Pursing his lips, Muller snatches it from my fingers and wipes underneath the bed frame. "What's this, Cadet Olson?" With horror I stare at the faint speckles of grayish fuzz. Muller's expression is cool, but I can tell he's hiding his glee. "You call this clean? Your space is supposed to be spotless."

I stand frozen at attention, unsure if I'm supposed to answer. Apparently not because Muller heads for my closet. He briefly scans the stack of folded clothes and throws my shirts on the floor. "Isn't nine inches. Refold."

Last he picks up my parade hat, some foot-high contraption, its brass eagle looking indifferent. "Needs shining, so do your shoes." He nods at the pair of black formals that sit below in perfect alignment.

Muller steps closer, his forehead inches from my nose. "Cadet Olson, you call this clean and ready. Inspection failed. Re-inspection scheduled for this evening at 19:30. If you fail again, you'll march. You're a disgrace." Muller grimaces as if I'm a poisonous snake.

He turns to Plozett's closet, scans across and checks the bed—taking all of two seconds. "All in order. Dismissed."

"Yes, Sir," we yell. I catch sight of the clock over the door and suppress a curse. I'll have no chance to redo everything and still make it to English. Thanks to Muller, I'll be in my room, wiping and folding while everyone else can relax for an hour before dinner.

I make it to class with five minutes to spare. Tom slips through the door right before Mr. Brown, the literature professor, closes it with a bang.

"Just in time," I whisper under the cover of chairs sliding and papers shuffling.

"I hate that guy." Tom's cheeks are the color of burgundy.

"Muller?"

Tom nods. "My bed was all torn up. I had it perfect before going to breakfast. Somebody pulled it apart. Muller had a fit. I have to report to him tonight."

"Me, too."

"Cadet Zimmer, who does the title *Taming of the Shrew* refer to?" Brown waves the book of Shakespeare's play as if he's directing traffic.

Tom jumps up. "Sir, to Katherine, the daughter of Baptista Minola, Sir."

"Correct, Zimmer. Sit down. You were paying attention after all." Tom glances at me and I can't suppress a grin. Tom loves Shakespeare and has read all his major works, just for fun.

For the rest of class I keep my head down. Unlike Tom I'll have to wade through English like it's a rotten swamp. My mind drifts as Mr. Brown drones on about the play. I got my first letter from home last night. It rustles in my back pocket, but I can't make myself read it. Not yet. I've got to be alone.

The bell rings and Tom hurries off to intermediate French down the hall. I remain, dreading military history, Mr. Lowell's yawn-inducing lectures on past conflicts, soldiers marching, battle dates and ridiculous political agreements. I've got no memory for years and names.

The door snaps shut. A guy in uniform with a broad chest, short and compact as a tank, marches to the desk. Red splotches and craters left by pockmarks or bad acne cover his face. He scans the room, his gaze a laser. Convinced the man can read minds, I duck behind Plozett.

"Sergeant Russel, your new military history teacher," Russel's voice booms, thundering to the back corners with ease. "Sit."

I stare at the new teacher, whose jacket carries various decorations. This is worse than Lowell.

"You." Russel stabs a finger at a boy in the front row. "What have you been working on?"

The boy jumps up. "Sir, Napoleon's invasion of Russia in 1812, Sir," he shouts, his voice shrill with nerves.

Russel stands without comment, the room quiet except for the suppressed breathing of eighteen sets of lungs. "Sit," he finally says to the boy who dunks into his chair.

He steps to the front wall covered in layers of maps. "Let's change the schedule," he says, rifling through the stack. "What do you know about Vietnam?" He pronounces *nam* as if he's pinched his nose.

We sit frozen in silence and I wonder what the man has seen, what he's done in the war. The news is full of horrific stories of jungle fights, mutilations and explosions. I haven't paid much attention except when some of the older boys in my former high school talked about volunteering.

"Who can tell me about the Vietnam War?" Russel asks into the stillness. I stoop low behind Plozett. I've heard about North and South Vietnam, about Charlie, the Vietcong. But it isn't very clear in my mind. No way I'd volunteer to make a fool of myself. Nobody else does either. We wait.

Russel's expression remains blank while he heaves his bulk into the metal chair on the podium. "We'll get to that." He pauses, his gaze sweeping by just as I look past Plozett's shoulder. "Let's talk about combat. Imagine it's night. Pitch black, rain pouring buckets. You're doing surveillance on a village. Rumor has it Charlie has taken cover among the natives."

Russel's voice lowers itself to a whisper. "Just as you're sneaking up on the outskirts, you see him…A man with a rifle, nearly shapeless among the huts. He's quiet, waiting, listening. Across from him, another Vietcong stands in the shadows. There is only one solution. You must sneak up on them one by one and kill each of them without a sound." We stare in silence, I mean you can clearly understand the voice of Mr. Brown two doors down. I imagine myself in the dark, hear the downpour of rain. "I need a volunteer," Russel says. For the first time, the indication of a smile plays around his lips. "No worries, I'll only demonstrate."

A few indecisive chuckles erupt and disappear like water evaporating in sand. Tony White, the captain of the football team, raises his hand. He's an easy six-foot-two of pure muscle and several inches taller than Russel. Tony throws us a superior smile as if he's waiting for applause.

"Name?" Russel says from his chair.

"Cadet White, Sir, at your service." Tony grins—the same arrogant smirk he shows when telling stories about his conquests with girls. I'm jealous of Tony's experience because all I've done so far is kiss a girl, not even a French kiss. Thanks to the new school, chances of ever making out are non-existent. I'll be an old man by the time I leave here …and still a virgin.

A commotion makes me look up. Russel has left his chair without a sound. In a split second Tony is on the ground, his face pressed into the floorboards, Russel on top. One hand grabs Tony's chin and pulls back his head. The other fist holds an imaginary blade like an ice pick. He stabs at Tony's neck, quick movements, easy as slicing a banana.

"I'd have a knife, of course." Russel straightens while Tony scrambles to his knees. He no longer smiles.

Russel addresses Tony's back. "It's easier to fight the big guys. They're not used to getting attacked and you can catch them by surprise."

Ignoring the uneasy chuckles, Russel returns to his chair. "Let's talk about the politics of the Vietnam War."

I can tell that Tony's face burns pink by the way his ears glow. He's pissed for sure. Military history is going to be better than I expected.

***

After classes and group studies I hurry to football practice. No matter how hard I work, the thought of Muller's inspection keeps nagging. Worse, Coach Briggs ran late, insisting on drilling us on strategic positioning. I manage to reach mess hall before the final bell, legs aching with fatigue, stomach angry with hunger.

Tom sits with Markus whose light-blue eyes remind me of a rabbit trapped in a cage.

"You look beat," Tom says as I slump into a chair next to him.

"And I didn't have time to finish my room this morning," I mumble, attacking the mountain of mashed potatoes, meatloaf and broccoli. I don't care for green vegetables, but I'm famished. I've got to hurry before Muller gets to me. I can't afford to blow the second inspection.

"I'm scared of Muller," Markus says. "He's mean."

Tom leans back, picking brownie crumbs off his plate. "Strange how some people revel in power. I could swear he gets off on tormenting us."

The room around us buzzes with hundreds of voices in various stages of development. The faculty tables are in back and I watch Russel leaving, nodding curtly at his colleagues. I never noticed the limp before.

"My father would probably love it here." Tom's voice is bitter. "In fact, we should trade places. I bet he'd do great."

"My dad loves the Merchant Marines," I say. My stomach feels better, but the anxiety about Muller's inspection returns full strength.

When the buzzer sounds, I jump up. "Better run. Got to finish my room."

"Good luck," Markus calls after me.

I sprint to the barracks thinking about Tom and his dad, how they hate each other. Right now I can't stand my parents either. Obviously they don't care to have me around. And yet they make it sound like they're sacrificing because this place is stinking expensive.

I'm the first back on my floor—fifteen minutes until inspections. I better be ready in case Muller comes to my room first. I remade my bed this morning, but I check it again, wipe the bed frame with a used pair of underwear, every move concentration. The sheets are stretched like a drum, the wool blanket tucked with perfect corners, tight enough to bounce a quarter on top. I check it again with the ruler. The sheet has to overlap the blanket precisely fifteen inches. You've got to ask yourself what these people are *thinking.* Why is a sheet covering fourteen and a half inches grounds for disciplinary action? I'd laugh but my throat is dry with nerves.

I yank open my wardrobe. White undershirts, blue dress shirts, underwear and socks lay helter-skelter. With a sigh I pull everything out to refold. What a bunch of bull.

My heart beats in my neck when I glance at the clock. Two minutes. I shove books and notepaper into a drawer, throwing a longing glance at Plozett's deserted chair. As an oldman Plozett is impervious to inspections. Scanning the top of the empty desk, I wipe down the surface and chair. Done. I throw my gym clothes into the laundry bag at the bottom of the closet, the only item allowed to be unfolded.

Plozett arrives. "You ready?"

I nod. "Think so."

"Muller is two doors down. He'll be here in a minute."

I stiffen when Muller's shadow announces his arrival. "Cadet Olson, room 212, at your service, Sir," I shout, watching with envy as Plozett draws geometric patterns on a piece of scrap paper. Study hour has begun.

Muller walks straight to my bed. He bends lower, his nose an inch from the blanket as if he's searching for fleas. Then he straightens and I breathe easier.

"Closet."

"Yes, Sir." I open the cabinet. Muller examines the folded shirts and underwear, the shoes at the bottom.

He mumbles something.

"Excuse me, Sir?" I say, following Muller's every move. He's controlling my life.

Muller doesn't answer, but turns around to face me. It looks as if he's ready to dismiss, and inwardly I relax, when his eyes pull away to something behind my back.

"What's this?" Quick as a flash Muller steps back to the bed. I turn just as he shoves something with his foot. One of my dirty workout socks is half hidden under Muller's immaculate dress shoe. It must've fallen out when I unpacked my gym clothes.

"Olson, you're just too stupid. I'm filing a report. Two inspections and you're still a pig. Get this thing out of here." With that Muller kicks the sock across the room against the wardrobe where it comes to rest in a damp heap. "Disgusting filth."

"Sir, sorry, Sir," I stumble, but Muller has already turned his back.

"Dismissed."

I swipe up the sock and fling it into the laundry bag. How could I've overlooked something this obvious? I did so well, measuring and folding and then I miss a stinking sock. My cheeks burn with frustration.

***

"You should've seen Tony's face." I'm lounging on Tom's bed, carefully adjusting my right shoulder which got hammered again during practice. After tattoo is called at ten o'clock, we've got thirty minutes of free time. I feel like passing out after the classes, studies, practice and two inspections, but personal time is too precious to waste on sleep. "Sarge Russel is scary."

"Sarge?"

"Yeah, seems like a good name."

"Made a few changes. It's not bad." Tom grins and throws the summary of Shakespeare's *Taming of the Shrew* on the bed, where I catch it with a wince.

"Thanks, man. I got a letter...from my parents."

"And?" Tom rifles through the newest copy of *Motion Picture* magazine. He's a movie buff and watches every new release.

"Haven't read it yet."

"What're you waiting for?" Tom's brown eyes look thoughtful. "At least they write to you. My father forgot I existed the minute he dropped me off."

I pull out the letter, wrinkled from spending too much time in my pocket. "Maybe tomorrow… Your parents divorced?"

Tom sighs and closes the magazine. "I guess technically. My mother got sick when I was little. She… sort of faded. Forgot I was there. One day, I wandered outside where a neighbor found and returned me. My mother hadn't even noticed I was gone. I was three. They fought, my father got angry and then one day, she was gone."

"Is she dead?"

Tom shakes his head. "Hospital. According to my father, it's the best place in the Midwest. I haven't seen her in years."

"But why's your father forgetting—"

"You need to leave." Allen Todd, Tom's roommate, moseys in with a towel stretched tight around an ample waist. His face and torso are covered with moles and everyone calls him Toad. "I got to change," he squeaks in indignation.

"Turn around then," I say, waving him off. We've got five minutes.

"Did you hear about the movie theatre in town?" Tom says. "I guess our school hangs out there on weekends."

"Let's check it tomorrow. I can't believe it's finally Saturday."

"I *must* go to bed now." Clad in a tent-sized plaid pajama, Toad sinks on his mattress which creaks in protest. "I don't want trouble."

I ignore him, but get up. The clock controls my life, besides, I'm ready to crash anyway. "See you in the morning. Any idea what happens after Muller files a report?" I say at the door.

Tom shrugs, but his eyes are filled with gloom.

CHAPTER THREE

When I return from breakfast the next morning, a note is taped to my door next to our sign-in sheet. All rooms list the cadets who live inside and give a day-to-day account of our whereabouts. *Cadet Olson to report to Counselor Barberry at 11:00.*

Muller hasn't wasted any time. Five minutes before eleven I check my uniform. *Shirt tucked, pants straight and clean, shoes shined.* Grabbing the soft cap we wear on weekends I head downstairs. With every step my heart beats faster until I'm breathless.

All barracks have a counselor living in an apartment on the first floor. They're either retired military or regular faculty, and spend nights in the barracks, so they can check up on us.

I knock.

"Come in."

I push open the door and stare. It's like walking into a mineshaft, dark and stuffy, the room's only window covered by blinds and a curtain. A tiny wall lamp glows yellow, doing little to brighten the shadows.

"Sir, Cadet Olson at your service, Sir."

Barberry, we call him Beerbelly because of his plump middle, sits behind his desk. A wave of citrus aftershave hits me, which can be useful because it announces his presence wherever he goes. Though nobody has ever seen him, it's rumored that Beerbelly hides booze in his office and camouflages the smell of alcohol with his cologne.

"Cadet Olson, right." He rifles through a file on his desk. "You failed two room inspections."

"Sir, sorry Sir, I—"

Beerbelly raises a hand to cut me off.

"You're new, a late comer?"

I nod. How can the man see in this dungeon? "Yes, Sir, my junior year."

"You should know better. You're certainly old enough. Respect and cleanliness are a cadet's first objective. Five demerits. Get five more and you'll march extra duty next Saturday."

"Yes, Sir."

"Dismissed."

"Thank you, Sir."

I rush upstairs, equally worried and fuming. Last weekend, half a dozen guys were out there in the drizzle, marching up and down the field. Extra duty lasts three hours. Rain or shine. It's only the middle of September, there's plenty of time to collect demerits now that Muller has it in for me.

***

Tom sticks his head in my door. "Ready to go?" He's attempted to tame his short curls with gel. They refuse to be controlled.

"Give me two," I say, urging my pen to write faster. "Just finishing this stupid summary for Sarge."

Tom sinks on the only available seat at Plozett's desk. Nobody sits on beds during the day—undoing the measured edges provokes surprise inspections.

"Can't believe it's finally the weekend." I close my notebook with a thud. "Muller eyed me this morning like he was waiting for me to trip up."

"He reminds me of a praying mantis," Tom says dryly. "The way he sticks his neck forward. Like he's ready to tear off your face." Tom pushes his head out and holds up his forearms at a ninety degree angle.

I chuckle though I can feel Muller closing in on me. "Yep, that's him all right. Let's go." I straighten, my fingers anxiously patrolling my pocket. Two dollars. One per week since my arrival, allowance sent by my parents and doled out by the bursar. I'll have to find candy somewhere in town. It'll be too expensive in the theatre. Tom doesn't have that problem. His father is wealthy and Tom seems flush with cash. I grimace.

"Something wrong?" Tom asks.

"I just thought how your old man keeps you in the green."

"He doesn't feel it. Whereas your parents are making a sacrifice."

"I wish they weren't."

"I know. Let's try to have a good time anyway."

We head into the corridor, marching perfect steps. Whenever an oldman appears, we jump out of the way and squeeze against the wall saluting. It takes several minutes to leave the building, stopping, standing at attention, shouting the name of the oldman, waiting for the dismissing nod which is always serious and always critical. I breathe deeply as soon as we're outside. At least I haven't been ridiculed for dress infractions.

We take off across the lawns, Tom's legs propelling him as if on stilts, me shorter but fast. I'm giddy and curious—our first escape from campus. According to what I've heard the village is a dump, not worth mentioning, a town of losers and deadbeats. Except for the movie theatre which provides the only entertainment for thirty miles around.

The path, no more than two feet wide, but trampled clean from hundreds of feet in search of distraction, leads us through a forest of pine, oak and beech trees. After the stuffiness of our rooms and Beerbelly's citrus stink, I'm enjoying the smoky and spicy smells of fall. Ahead the trail rises and I make out the silhouettes of Tony White and his best friend, 'Big Mike' Stets.

As the captain of the football team, Tony runs the show on the field and in the locker room, unless Coach Briggs is near. Big Mike, large and square like a wardrobe over tree trunk shaped legs, is the star defensive tackle on Palmer's football team. Most cadets give him a wide berth. He loves using his physical strength to intimidate smaller students as he plows through the school corridors.

Tom nods ahead, "I see meat hook is also going to the movies. Let's slow down a bit. I don't care to see him up close."

"Big Mike is a heck of a football player," I say, feeling resentful that I want to justify Big Mike's actions. "It's like having three guys on the team instead of one."

"I heard he's not too bright, but the school carries him anyway. They don't want to lose games and his father is a big shot in D.C."

"The coach thinks he walks on water."

Tom shrugs. "Bullies, nonetheless. Especially to those that aren't into sports."

I know Tom includes himself in the group. Coach Briggs acts like a bully most of the time. He breaks out in screaming tirades and gets in my face when I slow down during practice, even if it's a hundred-fifty degrees under my helmet. Maybe that's why the coach likes Big Mike and Tony.

"I can't believe you don't enjoy exercise," I say. "You could probably be a speed walker or long distance runner."

"I play chess, run the knight and his queen around the board until they're out of breath. I just don't like sports."

"Because you're good in school and don't have to find other means to get ahead. Like me."

"Except math."

"That's why you have me to help. Enough about school. What're we watching again?"

"*Bandolero* with Jimmy Stewart and Dean Martin. And of course... Raquel Welch." Tom grins. "What a bod, the best tits you've ever seen on a woman. It's a western. Out since June, but they're slow here."

"You think we can buy candy in town?" I pat the bills in my pocket.

"I could do with something sweet."

"Raquel will show you sweet. She's super sexy," Tom chuckles when he stops in his tracks. "What the heck…"

I look up.

The forest opens onto a field of grass, burned from a scorching Indiana summer. Hip-high it falls gently toward the valley, swaying like a reddish sea. And there between the folds of two limestone formations squats the town of Garville.

It's like we're in the twilight zone.

The lone church tower, brick worn and pale, stands at the center, the houses are in need of paint and a handful of stores cluster around the market square. Vintage model trucks sit along the road. A layer of dust extends onto the sidewalks. There is no traffic signal, not even a street light.

As we draw near, the general store's dull windows watch blindly from across the street. An old enamel sign above the door swings in the cool breeze, a reminder of the approaching winter. In front of the tavern two men stare at us from shredded wicker chairs. One spits tobacco into a metal bowl, the *ping* clearly audible in the silence.

"The movie theatre is at the other end," Tom says, watching three youths exit a barber shop. Judging by their torn jeans and shirts they must be townies. Palmer cadets are required to wear class B uniforms—blue pants, white jackets with blue stripes and matching caps. I feel self-conscious about my outfit, the brass buckle on my belt lending too much shine to the afternoon of this town.

"Remember the candy? I'll be right back." I cross the street to the general store and pull on the door so faded it looks colorless. I expect the shop to be closed, but the hinges squeal open and I creep inside. Dust specks float in the sunrays that make it through the door's smudged glass.

The store belongs to a different time, maybe an old frontier town like they show in westerns. Shelves, packed with an assortment of cans, hardware, work shirts and winter hats, cover the walls floor to ceiling. Counters with a collection of glass containers with gumballs, hard candy and licorice line the front while the aisles are crowded with baskets and sacks piled high with onions, apples and potatoes. Pieces of farm equipment clutter the floor, leaving a two-foot space for walking. What a mess.

"You lost?" A man, bald except for a fringe of gray, approaches from the back. "You fancy boys need—"

Just then Tom enters, looking bewildered. Hollers and hoots drift in after him and he quickly closes the door.

"I'd like to buy something," I say, my eyes finally adjusted to the murkiness. I scan the displays in search of my favorite candy bars. Behind the man who impatiently drums his fingers on the counter, I discover the silver-colored wrappers. "Two Zeros, please."

Tom, obviously distracted with the antique quality of this place, walks toward the rear where glass drawers hold bulk tea, coffee, flour and an assortment of spices.

The shopkeeper grumbles and smacks two Zeros on the counter. "Forty-six cents."

"Thanks." I pay and stuff the bars into my pocket. I want to get the heck out of here, but Tom has disappeared.

As I wander toward the back, a girl enters by the side door. Piercing blue eyes, framed by black braids, meet mine, momentarily narrowing into a frown. Her mouth, finely shaped and shimmering, turns down in distaste. It's as if time stands still because I notice her eyebrows that arch above the pools of a Caribbean sea, intense and cool. She wears a denim work shirt, clearly meant for boys, its shoulders too wide and its sleeves rolled up to show tanned forearms. For a moment, I forget to breathe. But the girl has already turned and disappeared behind a shelf stacked with rubber boots.

Tom materializes next to me. "Ready?"

I nod, staring after the apparition. "Let's go."

The Raquel Welsh movie takes me away. The theatre is packed with cadets, the air fogged with cigarette smoke. Tom elbows me several times, chuckling when the actress appears in yet another skintight outfit and deep cleavage. But I keep thinking about the blue eyes narrowed into disapproval. Why does it bother me that the girl acted unfriendly? Why am I surprised? I look pompous in my uniform and the townies obviously have nothing in common with Palmer's fanciness. It's a different world. They don't know I feel just the same underneath—a regular guy.

On the way back, as the sandstone bulk and square towers of assembly hall come into view, I feel the air closing in again.

"What's the matter with you?" Tom says. "She was hot."

"What?"

"Raquel Welsh."

"I guess."

"You guess. Were you asleep in there? Did you see her rack? There is something to be said for tight clothes. That was amazing." Tom shakes his head.

"You want to go again next week?" I hear myself say.

"You kidding? Any time we can get away."

"Let's check out the lounge. It's too early for dinner."

Better known as the 'cave', the lounge is a cavernous room filled with an assortment of worn-out couches and mushy chairs, shelves, scuffed games, books and magazines. It's located in the basement of the classroom building and the only onsite refuge free of ranks and rules.

Cigarette smoke thickenss the air, making it hard to see and breathe. A handful of cadets lounge around the room, playing chess and practicing smoke rings. Plozett sits in the back corner reading Playboy, disguised by the cover page of a farm equipment catalog. It's forbidden to own or read any sexually explicit materials, but they find their way into the school on a regular basis, make the rounds underneath mattresses and inside lockers and disappear in shreds or are confiscated into school offices.

"This is the biggest mess since World War Two," Tom says, sinking into the cushions of a mustard-colored couch that resembles a sponge—yellow and soft, yet comforting like a hug. He shakes his head and nods toward the mute television where U.S. troops march along an airfield, switching to the bodies of demonstrators at a sit-in in front of the White House.

"What?" I sag into the opposite corner, a tattered auto magazine in my hand.

"The Vietnam War. The government makes one stupid decision after another. I'll sure be glad when Johnson leaves. Our troops are paying for screw-ups of the military leadership."

"Sarge says it's been bloody, but necessary. He says we need more troops there to make a difference." I haven't followed any of the news. I know I've got to get my facts straight if I want to argue with Tom.

"I wish they'd stop and get our boys home. It's not going to work anyway."

"Sounds like deserter talk to me." Tony White smacks a hand on the couch between us.

"Let's watch cartoons," says Big Mike and twists the TV knobs. "I can't stand this bullshit. Beat it." He sags between us, filling out the space with ease.

Tom jumps up. "Got to go." He turns to catch my attention, but I only nod and remain seated. Without a word, Tom heads for the door.

"What're you doing with that flake?" Tony says as the sound of Mickey Mouse squeaks across the screen.

"Freaking candyass." Big Mike's eyes are glued to the TV.

"We're just hanging out." I feel like a traitor, but I want to stay on Tony's good side, afraid of him lashing out or teaching me a lesson during practice. I sit rigidly and pretend to watch the show, but somehow I wish I'd gone with Tom. *I'm a wimp.*

"See you later," I finally mumble. The sniggers of Big Mike and Tony follow me into the hallway. I'll hang out with Tom tomorrow, to hell with Tony and Big Mike.

That's when I remember the letter from my parents, buried in my back pocket. The rustle of paper has accompanied me all week. I've been too busy and too emotional to open it. I'll read it tomorrow, once Plozett had gone to breakfast and I'm alone.

Just in case.

CHAPTER FOUR

After sleeping late I listlessly leaf through my English grammar book and realize that I don't remember a single word. Time to go to lunch. Tom is nowhere in sight, not unusual because Sunday is the only day we're allowed to sleep in.

Back in my room I retrieve the letter. It feels like a brick in my hand. I twirl it back and forth before tearing at the envelope with a sigh. Homesickness grips me, a sort of heaviness in my middle that feels like I'm dragging a weight with me. I remember my room with the frayed posters of the Beatles and my idol, quarterback *Bob Griese*, my brothers and sisters at the dinner table munching cookies, going fishing with my dad. My mother's neat handwriting blurs, the thin long letters delicate. I know better. My mother rules the house.

Until a few months ago, I didn't know Palmer existed. But then everything changed when my father casually mentioned military high school. Shortly after, he asked me to remain at the table. It was oddly quiet, my mother watching me. That's when I knew something was wrong, my father's face sort of stony with his jaw muscles working under the skin like miniature golf balls.

Sure, I'd slacked off in school. Each year on the first day of school, teachers smiled as soon as I entered, expecting the same outstanding performance as my older brother Gary, Mr. Perfect Grades. It was not only annoying, it was impossible and I gave up trying. I'd rather play football and though I'm pretty average in size, I've got reflexes that spin my body forward effortlessly. I expected my father to preach about hard work, dole out house arrest or some other punishment, but never this. Never being sent away, cast from the family like a broken toy.

"Dear Andrew,

I hope you're adjusting well to life at school. We're busy as usual. Gary received a scholarship to Indiana University and is making us proud once again. He's such a good student. We took a trip to the Indianapolis museum and walked around downtown. Your grandparents are doing well, always so busy with the farm. We'll visit them again Thanksgiving. It'll be strange not to have you home. I'm sewing Halloween costumes, Mary will be a clown. She even has one of those cute red foam balls to stick on her nose. Dad is quite busy at school, but he still works on the addition of the house every evening. It's coming along well.

We hope you're studying hard and are thrifty. It's such an honor to be a cadet at Palmer. Take good care of your clothes. They're expensive. I better finish, the cookies are almost done and I have to pick up your brother from the library.

Love,

Mom"

I crumple up the letter and hurl it into the corner. Deep down I remember incidences from long ago, dozens of scenes like sharp jabs…fighting with my siblings, teasing them and arguing with my parents. I wanted attention. I know that now. Instead of working things out, they got rid of me, discarded me like an old rag, a cardboard box of used-up newspaper. Thrown out and forgotten.

Sitting in the stuffy dorm room I wonder if they ever considered my feelings. What I wanted? I stare out the window where the occasional cadet saunters along. After a while, I pick up the wad and smooth it out. How I hate everything. I can't figure out why my father is so excited about the military. So what if he was in the Merchant Marines. The news is full of stupid military stories. Somehow I hoped they wanted me back, but there is nothing mentioned in the letter, just *study hard and be thrifty.*

The room shrinks, suffocating in its stillness. No way can I study now. I need air.

Rushing outside I fall into a run, away from the rules, away from the controlling eyes.

Faster…sprinting. It feels good to move, my sweats with the school's white horse emblem on my chest, comfortable. I'm only allowed to wear them during sports and informal times in the barracks. Leaving campus without proper uniform is prohibited. I don't care. Not now.

When I finally slow down, my thighs burn and my breath comes in spurts. I trudge on without looking, my feet hidden in foot high leaves. More fall from above, a rain of earth colors.

A creek appears out of nowhere, gurgling along pebbles like polished glass. I hop across and keep easy balance on the slippery stones. The earth crumbles as I climb the opposite bank. The pungent smell of mushrooms mixes with rotting bark. Squirrels rustle through the oak branches above, a blue jay squawks to announce my arrival. The letter in my pocket crackles.

I jog some more, but not far enough to leave the pain. My thighs ache and I throw myself into a pile of leaves. The September sky hovers above me like a gray cushion, fluffy but airless. It's much cooler today without the sun. I dream of hitchhiking to California, joining one of the communes in San Francisco. They do what they want, smoke weed and drink. Rumors have it there are wild parties with lots of sex.

I grimace. Who am I kidding? I'll do nothing. Not drinking, not smoking and certainly not sex. I overanalyze everything, one thing about having a math mind. What if I run into a serial killer on the way? What if I get pneumonia? Besides, I'm broke. Truth is I've got zero control, I *am* a wimp at the mercy of Muller and company. I angrily swipe an arm across my damp eyes. The world retracts.

I wake with a start. It's dusk. Jumping up I look around, the trees standing silent watch. I love the woods, am comfortable with its smells and sounds. But this forest is unfamiliar and I've got no idea from what direction I came. If I get caught, I'll march extra duty until I'm old and gray. Beerbelly will see to that.

I examine the ground for footprints, some trace I've left. But the leaves have shuffled in the wind and sharpness clings to the air. I shiver, unsure if it's from the cold or the realization that I'm lost. I begin to walk in a circle around the tree I've slept under, searching for something familiar, signs of crushed leaves or twigs. I recognize nothing.

The trees above me whisper, limbs sway against the dull light above. Ever so faint I hear a trickling of water—the creek.

I zigzag between the trees, stop again and again until the sound of running water grows more distinct. Except it's louder, more aggressive than I remember, splattering and spewing like miniature rapids.

Past the next rise I see the water below. It foams, deeper and faster. This is not the area I crossed, maybe not the same stream at all.

The last light reflects off the current that hastens into a shallow waterfall. I look for a place to cross to keep my shoes dry, but it's impossible to see clearly. Sliding down the embankment I lose my balance. Mud grinds into my hands and the sides of my pants.

Shit, I'll be in deep trouble. Maybe they'll send me home for breaking more rules, unfit for the academy. I remember my parents' faces when they announced I had to attend Palmer. Unfit for my family. I really *want* to go home. But then my parents would kill me. I'm screwed.

The water instantly numbs my toes. By the time I reach the other side, I'm soaked up to my calves and the forest has turned into shadows. A half-moon creeps above the horizon and peeks through the leaves. I stretch out my right arm to avoid walking into trees, my drenched feet squishing with every step. I'm cold and hot at the same time, my face feverish and damp, my feet frozen.

Time passes slowly like snails gliding on rotten bark. I have no idea how late it is. Brush scrapes my face and tangles my feet. I stagger across roots and boulders. What if I'm totally lost? The creek is definitely different. Maybe I'm heading into the country of southern Indiana.

I know how to build a bed from leaves, stuff my sweater with dry grasses and crawl under a brush pile—cold yes, but I'll make it through the night. The worst part is that I'm starving, the meal at lunch a distant memory.

The trees thin, then disappear. I'm on some kind of gravel road. In the distance I make out a faint glow, no more than a shimmer like illuminated needle pricks. I keep walking, my eyes firmly set on the lights.

With a sigh I recognize Garville. Except I'm approaching from the other end. The movie theatre's only window shows a faded poster of Raquel Welsh. I've made a huge circle around the town.

I imagine families at dinner—even the townies—spending time together, sharing a Sunday roast and potatoes. An intense feeling of loneliness sweeps through me. I think about Tom whose father doesn't care and whose mother is locked away. Tom has it worse.

The general store hovers to my right. The upstairs lights throw patterns across the dusty street. Pink curtains hang neatly behind the glass and cover the bottom half of each window. I must hurry but something draws me in.

Maybe I'll see *her* again. Jogging across the street, I stop to watch the windows from the shadows of the barber shop. The air feels lifeless as I lean against the wooden siding next to a photo of a man with pomade hair and a waxy mustache. A cigarette would be nice. Not because I smoke but because it'd give me something to do. Behind the pink curtain somebody moves.

The girl. So, she does live here. Her arms rise and fall as if she's shouting. Her hair looks even blacker, loose and flowing without the restraint of braids. I can't see her face or if anyone else is in the room.

The front door of the shop opens with a bang. Something heavy drags across the ground and from the darkness a wheelchair appears and rolls to the edge of the sidewalk. A light flashes. A cough. Someone is starting a smoke. A man with a black mane, barely controlled by a bandana wrapped around his forehead, sits no more than thirty feet away. I move, intending to disappear
between the buildings. But the man in the wheelchair seems to have extraordinary senses.

"Who's there," he yells, at the same time rolling off the curb. To my alarm he's heading straight at me. "Who's there? I'll shoot!" The voice sounds fierce despite the feebleness of the chair.

"Please don't, I…was lost and…had to rest."

"What?"

I step from the shop's alley. The wheelchair stops.

The man's eyes narrow. "What the fuck!" He takes a drag from his cigarette. Something fragrant drifts into my nose. "What're you, a freaking spy? Shouldn't you be with the blue coats?"

"I got lost in the woods…"

"Eric, where are you?" a voice calls from the door. "You know Dad doesn't like it when you smoke that—"

"Over here. Look who's spying on us."

The black-haired girl appears next to the man she calls Eric. To me she seems to float. "What're you doing here?"

I want to bolt. "I'm not—"

"I already asked him," says Eric. "He claims he got lost. And he's not telling us his name, either. Big fucking secret."

"Maybe he's right. Look at his pants and shoes. What a mess." The girl's nose wrinkles in disgust.

I want to sink into the ground.

"What I'd like to know is what he's doing in front of our store," says Eric, sucking on the fumes. "Looks like a fucking peeping Tom to me."

"I needed to stop a minute and this is the only building I know," I stammer. Great, I sound like a numbskull.

"Yeah, right," Eric says.

"Got to go. I'll be punished as it is."

Eric flips a burning stub my way. "Serves you right."

"Why do you always have to be so mean?" the girl says, her eyes still on me. "He's obviously in trouble."

"I tell you, he's checking us out. Reminds me of a spook." Eric lights another smoke and inhales deeply. Leaning back he stares at me as if I were some disgusting hairy spider.

Acrid fumes drift across, tickling my throat. My cheeks blaze. Without comment I break into a run.

"I'll keep my eye on you," the man in the wheelchair shouts, his voice following me to the edge of town.

I duck behind the city sign and look back. The girl is pushing the wheelchair through the door. For a second she turns, her eyes searching, looking right at me. I'm sure that I'm hidden, but I feel as naked as if I stepped from a bathtub.

Remembering school, I sprint uphill. Time to face Beerbelly's music.

Dampness has crept up to my knees and my feet are so cold, I can't feel my toes. Surely, I've been missed by now and there will be hell to pay. Do they throw students into a cell or will they expel me outright?

From a distance, Palmer looks like a wealthy resort—manicured lawns, trimmed hedges and straight-edged flowerbeds as if the school is forcing its military discipline on nature. I long to be inside, warm and… something I've never considered desirable before… behind my desk, studying. Crouching I look for cover, but the bushes are trimmed short and few leaves remain on stubby limbs. I've heard of patrols who circle the grounds like ghosts and I want to postpone punishment as long as possible.

Voices drift near. Unsure where they're coming from, I throw myself on the ground. Somebody approaches on the path above. Mr. Levins, the science teacher, a tiny man with round glasses thick as the base of a bottle, is in an animated discussion with Mr. Brown. When they disappear toward the administrative building I peek across the lawn. Silence. No movement, even in the shadows beyond the barracks.

I force my aching thighs to move and breathe a sigh of relief as Barracks B comes into view. Most of the windows are lit. Cadets at study hour. I scan the second floor, wondering if Tom has looked for me.

Ears on high alert, I slip inside, ignoring the mumbling of voices from some of the downstairs bedrooms, mostly second-year cadets I hardly know. I'm almost there. If I open my books as if I were studying and had just stepped into the john for a minute, I'll have time to sneak into the washroom to get cleaned up.

I catch a glimpse of my shoes and lower legs, a soggy mess. So much for impressing the only girl in a thirty-mile radius. She must think I'm a total moron. Feeling my face grow hot with embarrassment again, I round the last corner and collide with something massive.

"Damn," booms the deep voice of Sarge Russel.

I freeze.

CHAPTER FIVE

"Olson, is that you?" Sarge stares at me as if I were an alien with a green head and antennas. "Why aren't you in your room?"

I nudge my brain to say something smart, but nothing happens. My strategies and prepared arguments have drained away, leaving a vacuum. I grope for words, some explanation. Nothing. Instead, I tremble. I'll be going home tonight, thrown from the school in dishonor. Everyone will stare and shake their heads while I'll wait for my parents. My parents!

"What's the matter with you? Answer!"

I return to present time. "Sir, I got lost. I... the letter." My mind clamps shut.

Sarge remains still. Not even his eyes move as he watches me. Seconds pass—a minute...eternity. In the distance the steam radiators creak. Low voices drift like fog from one of the rooms.

"Sir, I ran out this afternoon. I was mad and...fell asleep in the woods. I couldn't remember the way."

"Olson, look at yourself. Filth and confusion. Is that how you want to be known around here?"

Now it's coming. I lower my head and stop breathing. A puddle of filthy water is forming on the linoleum next to my feet.

Sarge's hand lands on my shoulder. It feels heavy like a sack of potatoes is weighing me down.

"Get yourself cleaned up and to your desk. On the double. Tomorrow, report to me at 19:00."

I stare. Sarge has spoken Chinese, but somehow I translate I won't be thrown out. At least not yet. Maybe Sarge will get the Dean and they'll have an official expulsion procedure. I shiver.

"Olson, did you hear me? Get cleaned up. Now."

"Yes, Sir. Thank you, Sir." I dart down the corridor.

"Tomorrow, 19:00 in my office," Sarge yells after me. "I'll clear it with your counselor."

"Yes, Sir."

In the washroom I catch a glimpse of myself in the mirror. The face staring back at me looks frightful, eyes and hair caked with mud, shirt and pants stained brown. My limbs shake as I tear off my clothes and step into the nearest shower. The hot water feels heavenly.

Within minutes I'm at my desk, thankful that Plozett is absent. He's got to be at the library, the only other place allowed during study hour. I rifle through the books, remembering homework, another English paper—we've moved on to Romeo and Juliet—and the geography exam in the morning. My stomach lurches. Rummaging through the desk drawers I find a piece of licorice and wolf it down.

"Where the heck were you all day?" Tom leans in the doorframe, his forehead wrinkled with a mixture of scorn and concern.

"Got lost in the woods. Sarge caught me."

"Are you serious?" Tom rushes into the room and sags on Plozett's chair. "What happened?"

"I was mad about the letter my mother sent. So I took a walk and fell asleep in the forest. It was getting dark and I couldn't remember the way. I circled around, got dirty and wet, missed dinner. I thought I'd made it safely when I ran into Sarge."

"Beerbelly will have your hide," Tom says, making a face. "You'll have to march until the end of time."

I shake my head, my mood dark again. "Sarge said he'll talk to Beerbelly. I'll have to report to Sarge tomorrow evening. He'll expel me. I know it."

Tom is quiet for a moment. "Naah, doubt it. If he did, you'd be gone tonight or in the morning."

"Maybe Sarge gets the Dean and they'll call my parents. Then tomorrow night…" I can't go on. The face of my father appears like a ghost…angry and twisted with shame about his rotten son.

"You'll march." Tom nods reassuringly, unfolds his legs and straightens. "I better head back—before they catch me."

"Later, man."

"Later, good to have you back."

"You wouldn't happen to have any food?" I call after him. "I can't study from the rumbling in my stomach."

Tom shakes his head. "Sorry, I never get care packets. Ate dinner in the mess hall." Down the corridor, a door slams and Tom hurries off.

The radiator creaks. In my mind blue eyes drift past. The scene on the street keeps repeating itself like a bad movie. Maybe I should tell Tom. Tom who seems to have forgotten about Big Mike's insults—about yesterday. My thoughts return to Sarge and the worry of being thrown out. I'll have to wait an entire day. I hate waiting.

***

The exam in the morning is a miserable failure. I tell myself it doesn't matter, I'll pack my bags after tonight anyway.

The hours drag on endlessly. It's hard to focus, even in math and physics which I usually enjoy. I watch the clock above the classroom door move with excruciating slowness, my stomach a dull ache. I've eaten a huge breakfast, but regret it now. The eggs and bacon blob and dance, refusing to digest.

Now that I'll go home, I ask myself why I've trained to march and memorize countless names of cadet officers I don't care to know. I've wasted time learning to make my bed so that the top sheet covers exactly fifteen inches of the wool blanket. I've trained to wipe down the unlikeliest crevices of furniture so that the glove comes up clean, at least most of the time, and fold shirts so they measure nine inches in width and twelve inches in length after they return from the laundry. None of this is useful in the real world.

Monday's inspection is scheduled for 19:30. Muller again. I'll have to hurry back from Sarge to make it. But then, I probably won't rush back except to pack my bags and be escorted out. I sigh.

"…of minus six? Cadet Olson?" Mr. Levins stares at me.

I shoot from the chair. I haven't heard a word. "Excuse me, Sir?" The room is deathly silent.

"Olson, it's obvious you're not with us today. Are you sure you belong in this class?"

"Yes, Sir."

"I asked what the absolute value of minus six is."

I just read about it last night, but I can't think.

"The absolute value is …" I look straight ahead, feel the eyes of my classmates on me.

"Olson, sit down."

"Plozett, why don't you help him out?"

"Sir," Plozett stands up. "The absolute value of minus six is six."

"Correct."

I want to disappear. I'm ruining my math grade, too. I glance at the clock: 14:00. Five more hours 'till the meeting.

I barely taste the pork roast and mashed potatoes we have for dinner. Tom tries to engage me in conversation, make me laugh, telling a story about his roommate.

Toad squeaked his way through a French poem, his eyes turned upward behind the glasses when he forgot the words, Tom trying to help from the second row, but Toad misunderstanding and altering the poem into a jumble of nonsense. Everyone laughed except Toad and the teacher. Toad threw angry glances at Tom afterwards. Appreciative of Tom's efforts to entertain me, I attempt to smile, but I can't shake the sense of doom that grows stronger with every minute.

My knock on Sarge's office door sounds weak. A firm *enter* comes from the other side. My knees turn to jelly as I straighten to attention in front of the massive oak desk and Sarge's barrel chest behind. Sarge is chewing an unlit cigar and studying a set of maps. He keeps his head low and I notice a bald spot spreading on top amid the salt and pepper stubble. Finally Sarge looks up and pushes his chair back.

For a moment he watches me, not saying anything. I hold my breath until my lungs buck and I gulp air. I take inventory of my pose, but how can you concentrate on standing straight and still like a statue when your nerves demand release.

"Sit down, Olson."

"Yes, Sir."

Sarge continues to stare, his face impenetrable while I try to control a new twitch in my calves that threatens to take over my body. I want it to be over with.

"You look better today," says Sarge. A spark flickers across his eyes but I can't tell what it means. Surely, Sarge will yell any second.

"Thank you, Sir."

"Now tell me what happened yesterday. From the beginning." Sarge leans back in his chair.

I sit up straight and recount reading the letter, the walk in the woods, falling asleep, getting lost in the dark and hiking back through town. I leave out the encounter in front of the store.

"That's it. By the time I got back it was late and I met you."

Sarge remains silent. He squints as the cigar travels between his lips. I try looking him straight in the eyes, but soon lower my gaze. My shoes sparkle in the faint light of the desk's shadow. They seem to belong to someone else.

"Olson, I'm sure you know that you're not to leave campus without permission. This is a serious issue. We can't have cadets traipsing all over the place. Maybe this isn't the right place for you. Palmer carries the responsibility of keeping everyone safe. You understand what being responsible means?"

I nod and grope for enough energy to speak. "Yes, Sir. I—"

"If you were in Nam, you'd be dead." Sarge sucks on his cigar, spitting a piece of tobacco into the wastebasket. "I've been watching you, Olson. Looks like you're a decent athlete, but your grades are lousy. Any idea why?"

I shrug. How can you like studying with a brother like Gary who produces only A's. He barely leaves his room while I want to run around, be active, win. There's no winning at my old school so I gave up long ago.

I struggle for something to say, but Sarge waves a hand as if he's heard my thoughts.

"You know, many boys have issues with their families, some real serious. Have you thought about your future, what you'll do when you're finished here?"

I stiffen. Now it's coming, I'll be sent home. "I guess I'll go back to my former high school. I can be packed in an hour."

"What're you talking about? Oh, I see." Sarge's eyes crinkle into a smile. "You aren't getting away that easy, Olson. I have other things in mind for you. Looks to me like you need a lesson in orienteering."

The weight on my chest eases and I remember to breathe. I'll not be sent home like a failure, crawl back to my parents, my high school and face my father, my siblings and my friends like I can't make it.

"Listen to me, Son. I want you to really think about your life. You can make an outstanding soldier if you want to. The country needs boys like you, strong and fit and adventurous. Even a bit headstrong at times. Or you can continue to mope along and be mediocre. It's your choice. Understand?"

I nod. "Yes, Sir. Thank you, Sir." I jump up and send my chair flying.

"Not so fast. Sit down!" Sarge's voice booms.

I scramble to retrieve my chair and sit on the edge. "Sorry, Sir, I—"

"What're you doing next Saturday? After inspections, of course."

"Nothing, Sir, maybe go to town and watch a movie with Tom…Cadet Zimmer."

"You aren't marching extra duty?"

"No, Sir, at least not yet. I have an inspection in a few minutes, I—"

"Try to stay out of trouble, will you?" Sarge straightens and steps to the bookshelf to retrieve a lighter. "Why don't you stop by, say 13:00? A lesson in orienteering will do you good. In case you find yourself in the woods again." Puffs of cigar smoke begin to swirl around me.

"Thank you, Sir."

"Dismissed."

I hurry out the door.

"Olson, don't forget what I told you. You have a choice."

"Yes, Sir." Leaving the admin building I want to do cartwheels. I'm safe and Sarge wants to teach me something cool. Maybe this is the way to go. I see myself next to Sarge, faces painted green, sneaking on hands and knees across the jungle, running and throwing grenades, rappelling from a helicopter. I imagine myself in uniform, my chest decorated with medals, my father shaking hands with Sarge and inviting family and friends to hear our war stories of bravery.

"What's gotten into you?" Tom lingers in the hallway with a frown on his face. It makes his features look even longer.

"I got away. I mean Sarge didn't… he spared me."

Tom follows me along the corridor. "You mean he let you get away with yesterday's excursion?" He looks impressed. "Not even extra duty? How did you pull that one off? I thought Sarge was a tough cookie but maybe he's got a soft underbelly."

"He isn't soft," I say, suddenly feeling protective. "He's just, well, he was nice. Said, I have potential—that he'll teach me orienteering."

"What for?"

"He said in case I get lost in the woods again."

"Sarge has a sense of humor." Tom chuckles and swats me on the back. "Way to go."

I don't tell Tom about the other thing Sarge mentioned—becoming a soldier. I don't quite know what to think, but I'm pretty sure Tom doesn't approve.

"I better head back," Tom says. "Inspection is in full swing." Just as he says it, Muller appears from the room next to mine.

Muller entered the school as a freshman two years earlier and quickly rose to officer rank. His father is a big shot in the military and works in the Pentagon. I often wonder how some students can walk around with this confidence that the world answers to them. Muller seems to cherish his power. Though he's inches shorter and weighs no more than my sister Mary, he makes up for it with energetic eagerness to teach others a lesson.

"Shit," I mumble and race after Muller. We're supposed to be in our room standing at attention when the inspecting officer enters. I slip inside behind Muller's back and force my body into the rigid pose of attention. Of course, Muller hasn't missed my late entry and has scrunched his face into disapproval like a shriveled apple.

I know my sash is loose and my cap has slid above my left ear while rushing back from Sarge's office. I yank on my belt and adjust my hat as Muller turns to face me.

"Room 212, Cadets Plozett and Olson, all present and accounted for," I shout. From the corner of my eye, I watch Plozett relax.

Without comment Muller begins to check my bed. It looks perfect as he tears away blanket and pillow. I roll my eyes, but remain silent. I'm still relieved from the meeting with Sarge.

"Unacceptable, Cadet Olson," Muller says, his voice still an octave higher than mine. He continues by throwing my shirts and underwear on the floor in a heap. At last, he plants himself in front of me, looking perfect in the officer's outfit. He yanks at my sash and when it won't come off, he grabs my hat and tosses it into the heap.

"Unacceptable," he says again. "Olson, you're a disgrace to this company."

"Yes, Officer Muller, Sir," I shout, trying to keep my face from showing my contempt.

At the door, Muller turns. "Report to me at 22:00. I'm filing a report. At ease."

As Muller turns away, I make a face after him. I'm mad once again. It's obvious Muller is singling me out. Cadets are given demerits for all types of offenses, repeated failed room inspections one of them. Muller can write a complaint and I'll be forced to report to Beerbelly to explain myself which will most certainly result in more demerits. I already have five on the books for September and once I reach ten, I march. Just as long as I don't have to march this coming weekend. I want to make a good impression on Sarge and watch a movie with Tom.

I swear under my breath while I refold my clothes. I'm starting to feel numb and enraged all the time, a robot going through the motions, no control over anything. I don't even have energy to think on my own because every single minute of every day is run by Muller and the school.

Reporting at 22:00 means I don't even have thirty lousy minutes to myself. I'd planned to see Tom and discuss Sarge. Right now I need to finish a chapter in Salinger's *The Catcher in the Rye,* having wasted most of today worrying. We'll have a test in the morning and, being a slow reader, I'm behind once again.

"What happened here?" Tom says, looking at the mess of shirts and underwear on the floor.

"Muller."

"That mean ditz. He doesn't have anything better to do." Tom picks up a shirt and folds.

"You better get back to your room. Muller might catch you."

"He's too busy nagging the cadets in the next room. Poor Markus. He's got it even worse. Muller loves to push the young ones around. He'll still be occupied for a bit. Besides I'm done with prep except math."

"I really need time to read the stupid book," I say. "I don't get it anyway. That guy seems nuts. Going to New York and buying drinks in a bar. Ha, sounds too good to be true."

"He's pretty crazy but you have to admit, he's really getting away," Tom says. "At least for a bit. I wish I could pull off something like that. Join the hippies in California. Haight Ashbury, maybe. Get blitzed and smoke weed and lay around with a bunch of naked women." Tom smiles.

I grin back until I remember the black-haired girl and feel the blood rushing to my head. I bend lower as I keep folding but Tom hasn't noticed.

"My father says the protesters are criminals dodging the war," Tom continues. "As if he'd know. He hasn't been in any fight, except slugging me." Tom's voice turns bitter. "He's good at that."

"Why do you think there are so many demonstrations?" For the tenth time I vow to catch up on the news. The truth is I'd rather watch college football or whatever sports are on TV.

"Cause the war is stupid. Johnson keeps sending more troops. The military leadership waffles back and forth. Meanwhile our men lose limbs and lives in the jungle. I don't expect the next president to do any better."

"Better be careful what you say," Plozett chimes in. I forgot he's there. "The school loves the establishment. Many of the guys have parents and friends in high places."

Tom shrugs. "I better get back to my room. *Heil* Muller." He throws his arm out in Hitler fashion.

"Better keep your friend quiet. He's going to get himself hurt," Plozett says. "You never know who is listening."

I nod while I secretly try to make sense of Tom's comments and what Sarge has said. Plozett is right and I worry about Tom and his outspokenness. On the other hand I admire him for standing up for himself. Even if he isn't popular. I sigh. I have to think about it later. Salinger's book lays waiting and I'll have to waste more time reporting to Muller.

CHAPTER SIX

All week I put off writing my parents, telling myself that once I figure out what to say, I'll do it. Simultaneously, I assure myself that the few hours of leisure are *my* time to enjoy. But the thought of the pending letter nags. It's like a twinge in my side, a tiny thorn that won't go away. Every day clicks by in structured agony. Now it's Friday. And the school's first football game is tonight.

I stare at the sheet of paper sitting on the edge of my desk. Concentrating is impossible. What am I supposed to write anyway? Describe the school's ridiculous rules, Muller's constant nastiness, my aching body that demands way more sleep than I'm able to get? Or the girl with the raven hair who appears in my dreams and flashes her teeth in a brilliant smile?

My mother disapproves of girlfriends. Gary brought home a girl once, someone he took to the senior prom. During dinner the girl smiled shyly while trying to swallow bits of baked potato. She wore glasses, black horn-rimmed ones just like Gary's that made her eyes look big as marbles. I felt sorry for her because my mother asked embarrassing questions, what her father and mother did, what classes she enjoyed, what college she planned to attend. The girl's voice was low and hard to hear. I stared at her breasts which seemed nonexistent under the wool sweater.

Why do some girls have huge tits while others are flat as boys? I'm not sure what I like. Afterwards I overheard my mother talking to Gary. "You should concentrate on your studies," she lectured. "You're much too young." Maybe she considers twenty-nine the perfect dating age.

My mind drifts to the approaching game and I rub my hands, damp from anticipation. At my old school I did well as a star running back. Here I'm struggling to stay on the team. At least I'll be able to forget about life for a few hours.

My gaze returns to the desk and the task at hand of studying physics. And to the edge where the letter is waiting—beckoning, mocking me. I've deliberately chosen a small sheet. Fragments of sentences sneak into my head, distracting me from memorizing Newton's law of motion.

The room is hot and steamy now that the radiators are turned to full blast to combat the approaching winter. I open the window to cool my feverish forehead.

Dreary clouds swoop past, the trees bare, every last leaf picked up by Palmer's yard crew. Frustrated, I fling the physics book into the drawer and yank the paper in front of me. The tip of my pen hits the note, but I can't make it move.

"Dear Mom and Dad, I hate it here. No, wait, I'm working my ass off. I can't stand Muller and the inspections are so unfair, it stinks to the sky. Oh, and let's not forget, I get hammered by Tony and Big Mike on the field and by Mr. Brown in English."

Everything I come up with is unsuitable. I sound like a whiner. They won't understand nor care. Ever since my younger sister and brother were born, nobody had time, nobody listened. I imagine my father's face, all earnest and hypnotic, "Andy, Palmer is an outstanding school. I wish I'd had
the chance to attend. You can make something of yourself, become a good student and have a great life. They'll help you."

Yeah, right.

Still, I miss them, even my younger sisters and their squabbles, the ever-changing alliances between us, my room, my friends and school, my former football coach, running around the neighborhood. I sigh again. The paper wrinkles under my hand, where I've rested the pen too many times.

Outside, Muller is marching along with a guy from the cavalry. The cavalry is Palmer's pride and joy, the cream of the crop, cadets whose parents can afford for their sons to ride horses. Muller has a cousin in the cavalry, something he regularly mentions as if it's a badge of honor.

I lower my pen into position. I've got to finish, warm-ups start in an hour.

"Dear Mom and Dad,

Thanks for your letter. *Lie.* I'm glad you are having a good time and Gary is doing well in school. *Not really.* I'm staying very busy, but the food is good—a lot of meatloaf, soups and potato dishes. *Yes!* I'm reading Shakespeare's Romeo and Juliet right now. I still have to finish a paper by this evening. I also enjoy the lessons from Sergeant Russel. We call him Sarge. He was in Vietnam and tells stories about combat. He's huge and always chews on a dry cigar. *I smoked a stolen cigarette once. My mother hates smoking.* I have a good friend, Tom. He's very tall, even taller than Dad and very smart. I might visit him next summer. It's getting cold now and I'm starting to wear my winter coat. Can you please send two new pairs of white gloves? *Muller uses them to dust.* The laundry here doesn't get them clean. I also need wool socks, black, not too thick. My shoes are getting tight as it is.

Love, Andy"

I sit back with a sigh. It's done. I've bought time and won't write again for a few weeks. Winter break isn't that far off. I find myself wishing for and loathing the arrival of mail. Maybe they will stop, but then my mother always writes a lot of letters. I'm surely on her list. And she'll expect answers.

I jump up and rummage through my closet in search of clean underwear for after the game. We're playing some high school from Evansville. I fight down the nervous flutters that rise from my stomach and clog my throat. During home games the entire school is required to watch—not only that, they have to march to the field and back. At least I won't march since I have to prepare early, warm up and be ready when the game starts. I don't want to make a fool of myself.

"You ready for the big night?" Tom says, sticking his head in the door.

"Come in."

"Only have a few minutes, got to finish math and get ready." Tom leans against the wall. "I can't believe we have to watch every game. I'm only glad you're playing so I've got someone to cheer for."

"If they *let* me play. Briggs may still change his mind."

"He better." Tom grimaces. "With all the training you suffer through."

"At least, I'll stay fit." I pause. "I used to gain a lot of weight when I was younger. My mother would always offer me leftovers. 'Oh, Andy, why don't you eat this, it's only a small heap of mashed potatoes,'" I mimic in a high voice. "'How about these bacon strips?' So I'd eat, wanting to please my mother and get attention. 'Look how much Andy can eat—isn't that amazing.' Since when is it amazing to get fat? I hate them sometimes." I look at Tom whose arms and legs look gangly, his belt notched tight to hold up his pants. "I guess you never had that problem."

"No, always was thin. I kept growing taller, never sideways. I just wish my bed were longer." Tom's forehead scrunches into wrinkles. "It'd be nice to have a bit more muscle though."

"Why don't you try out for cross-country? That'd get you in shape and it'd please the school."

"I don't care about pleasing the school. I like walking but I'm not going to run around in circles."

I grin. "It's cross-country not track. You'd run through the woods and fields. It'd be fun. Maybe you'll change your mind before spring season."

Tom nods toward the envelope on my desk. "I see you finished the letter."

"Worse than English with Mr. Brown."

"I'm not writing. Why should I? The old man never writes. He's probably forgotten I exist. Until Christmas, when I remind him by being home."

"It sucks either way. Either you have to write some bullshit or you live in a vacuum. What difference does it make? What does your father do anyway?"

"He's a big shot in defense," Tom says. "Developed new radio technology they use on battlefields. The Pentagon loves his stuff. He started in the basement, before he met my mom. He invented something that made him a bunch of money. His company grew and grew and my mom and I became less important. He never even noticed that something was wrong with her. That would have required him to be present. He worked all the time, but he got plain tired of being a husband and father."

"That seems to happen a lot with successful people. My dad never made much. He's an assistant professor at IU, my mom teaches elementary school." I get up and stretch. "Better get ready for the game. The coach will be a basket case. Wish me luck."

***

The locker-room buzzes. Benches and floors are littered with shoulder pads, helmets, shoes and socks. Strips of tape curl through them like white snakes. Doors slam and lockers open and close. Wafts of BENGAY mix with the stench of sweat and stress-induced body odor. The rhythmic slapping of naked skin reverberates from the corner massage table where one of the linebackers gets his calves kneaded. I love the smells and sounds of changing rooms, the disorder and excitement. It reminds me of home.

Big Mike, dressed in jockstrap and socks, his vast stomach wobbling, shoves his way through the crowd.

"Out of my way, dickhead," he grumbles. He calls most people dickhead or loser, except when he's near faculty. Only the coach doesn't seem to care or pretends not to hear. In the locker room Big Mike has free reign.

"What the heck, where are my pads?" Big Mike turns toward the bench where I'm fighting my way into long socks. "You seen my pads? They were in my locker earlier."

I shrug, smoothing the socks over my calves which feel knotty and ache from yesterday's practice. I wish I'd signed up for massage.

"Are these mine?" Big Mike's paw grabs hold of my shoulder pads and I feel myself lift into the air.

"These are mine." I shove at the hand which clamps like a vise. It's about as effective as using a tablespoon against a raging bull.

Tony White draws near and glances underneath the bench. "Right here, Mike. You laid them aside earlier. Remember."

"Right. Thanks, man." Big Mike releases his grip and I sag back to earth. The bench shudders under Big Mike's weight, sending helmets and gloves, mouth pieces and shirts flying.

"Watch it," someone yells. I feel the hair on my neck stand up. Everyone is on edge. I wonder how Big Mike can mistake my gear for his, especially since mine is half the size. In fact, his pads remind me of a bleached dinosaur skeleton.

The coach yells to line up outside and everyone scrambles for their remaining stuff. I throw on my jersey to put distance between myself and Big Mike. I want to preserve my anger for the football field.

"Don't mind him," Tony White says to me. "You ready?"

I nod. I'm nervous as heck, much more than I ever was in my old high school's varsity team.

Tony whacks me on the back. "Let's kick some ass."

I straighten and follow Tony out the door. Behind me Big Mike squeezes into uniform pants, reminding me of a sausage being stuffed with too much meat. I shudder, glad Big Mike is on *my* team.

Whistles blow as soon as we hit the field. I shiver from the cool wind, but soon forget about it. We sprint, shove, jog and stretch until I feel warm and pliable.

I'm ready.

Palmer's marching band, its pride and joy, struts around the field in military precision. The stands are filled with uniformed Palmer cadets— class A full dress, nothing less will do—every last student in attendance. They holler in support, the same screams I recognize from my old games.

I wonder where Tom is. In the conformity of blue and white they all look the same. The faculty is also present and mostly seated in the front rows. On the opposite side of the field, Evansville fans, parents and friends watch. The rival team huddles, their backs toward the Palmer side.

I breathe deeply, indifferent to the wind whipping across the lake. I'll do my best to show them. The whistle blows and we take position.

The game seems to whirl by in minutes. I hardly notice the shouts, the announcements on the loudspeaker, or the girls from Harrison High School with their blood-red pompons glittering and yelling encouragement.

When the opposing team sets their defense, my focus is on running, blocking and catching. I attack on every play, fall and get up, ignoring my fatigued muscles, the angry pain in my ankle when I roll my foot, and my shoulder which feels bruised and tender. Several times I carry the ball and advance the play. The Palmer crowd cheers and I feel elated, a reminder of the old life I knew and loved.

"Not bad, Olson," Tony White says after the game. I grin, happy to please Tony. We won by three points, a field goal in the last minute of the game. Though I didn't get a touchdown I gained yardage. The band finishes, the last blast from the sousaphone evaporating in the cold breeze of dusk.

"We did it," Big Mike says as we walk to the lockers. "Dickhead, you did good." A hand slams my shoulder, sending waves of stinging pain through my body.

"Thanks," I say, eyes watering from the ache. "We showed—"

"I'm starving." Big Mike massages the flesh in his middle. "Could eat a whole pig."

One pig for another.

I remember Sarge. Orienteering starts tomorrow. "Got to run," I mumble. I hear no reply. Tony and Big Mike forgot I exist.

CHAPTER SEVEN

Tom sticks his head in the door. It's early Saturday afternoon and we've survived another round of inspections. "Want to catch the matinee at two?"

"Can't." I stare at my desk, trying to figure out what to do with the books and notepapers scattered across. I have to clean up before I leave or collect another demerit for a messy workspace. I got three more demerits from the failed room inspection last Monday. Muller made sure of that. That makes eight. With September almost over, I may scrape by into October. Thankfully the demerit clock starts over every month.

"Got to finish this paper and report to Sarge. Remember the orienteering?"

"Crap," Tom says. "I forgot."

"Don't know how long the lesson will take." I straighten to stack my books into neat rows. "I'll hurry back, though."

"You seem to be excited about meeting Sarge."

"Sure, he's sort of cool."

"Cause he's been in the jungle and knows how to kill people?" Tom taps a forefinger against his temple.

"I can't explain it."

"It's entirely your business," Tom says, his voice sharp with irritation.

"No need to get huffy. I get it, you don't like Sarge."

"Not in particular. You go and have fun." Tom turns to leave the room, his arms swinging in dismissal.

"Tom?" I call after him. Somehow I'm pissed.

"What?"

"Why are you so angry? Is it something I did?"

Tom leans against the doorframe and sighs. "You're such an idiot. I can't believe you're eating it up, Sarge giving you a *private* lesson. Don't you see, they just rope you in and feed you to the Vietcong—one more bite for the big war machine.”

“I’m just doing orienteering.” My neck feels hot. “I didn’t say I’d sign up for duty next week.”

“You’re too young anyway. But they’re brainwashing you just the same.”

“It’s not all bad. My Dad was in the Merchant Marines. He turned out just fine. Even gets a pension.” I don’t say that my father was shot at only once—nothing like the bloody mess boiling in Vietnam.

“What if they draft you?” Tom hisses. “What if they don’t give you a choice?” I stare at Tom. He’s never been this mad. “What if you become one of the thousands of casualties or get your legs cut off? Johnson and his military cronies are sending troops into the jungle. Who are they fighting with and for? The South Vietnamese can’t be trusted. The North keeps pushing. And there seems to be no end in sight.” Tom’s chest heaves like he’s run sprints.

“What if they draft *you*?” I ask because I don’t have a clue what he’s talking about. “You’re almost seventeen now.”

Tom shrugs. He’s calm again. For a moment the room is quiet. “I’ll disappear before that happens.”

“What do you mean?”

“I’ll find a way. I’m not going! Ever! I’ll catch the movie at two. Have fun.” Without a reply he turns on his heels.

“Are you jealous I’m getting attention?” I yell at his back. Why can’t I keep my big mouth shut? Tom is the last person to be jealous about something like that. What I really want to know is how Tom is going to avoid the draft.

“Why the heck would I be jealous? Bullshit!” Tom shouts before stomping off down the hall.

With a sigh I glance at the clock. Five minutes to get to Sarge. Grabbing my jacket I head outside. Why is Tom such an idiot? Sarge is nice and knows a lot. He didn’t send me home when he could’ve made a lot of stink. I rush through the door.

“Cadet Olson, watch where you’re going,” Muller barks.

“Sir, excuse me, Sir.” I raise my arm in salute and click my heels together, waiting to be dismissed. Seconds tick by.

I’m still reeling about Tom and last Monday when Muller had me stand and wait for minutes, playing the power game. The door to Muller’s room had been open, ready to swallow me. Muller sat, back rigid like a fence post, at his desk reading. I wondered at the time whether Muller continually maintained posture or he put up a show. A framed photo of a senior version of Muller, shaking hands with President Johnson, hung on the wall next to some brown-speckled pooch, the only personal items in the room.

"Sir, Cadet Olson, at your service, Sir," I said after knocking on the doorframe. Muller hadn't moved and I was about to knock and repeat when the chair creaked.

Muller's face had been expressionless, he neither moved nor spoke. I stood waiting, eyes staring at the opposite wall, straining my peripheral vision to see what Muller was up to. At last he straightened and walked to face me. He seemed to savor each moment.

"You're a disgrace, Olson. Why don't you do us all a favor? Quit polluting our school and go back to your trailer."

I remained quiet, confused about the statement that didn't sound like a question, but even more so, furious about Muller's arrogance.

"Loser!" Muller's ogle eyes floated into my vision.

Personal attacks are clearly against school policy but I couldn't do a thing to stop it. I'd kept waiting, distracted by my worry about the shrinking free time and my fingers that wanted to curl into fists. Lights had to be out at 22:30—I wanted to punch Muller's lights out.

I wasted twenty minutes before being dismissed by Muller and I'm ready to hit him now, feeling my stomach clench like a tight muscle. It's hard to breathe against the feeling of helpless fury.

Muller's eyes travel down my arm. "Olson, what's that in your hand?"

"My jacket, Sir."

"Why aren't you wearing it? Even *you* should know by now what proper dress looks like."

"Yes, Sir, I was in a hurry, Sir."

"A cadet is always prepared and organized. With that comes allowing enough time to get ready and from point A to point B."

"Yes, Sir. Sorry, Sir."

Muller walks around me to look for other dress issues. My shoes sparkle in lustrous black. In preparing for Sarge, I spent extra time to polish them with spit, the world's cheapest and most effective shoeshine.

"You may go, Olson. Don't run. Cadets march, understood? And put on that jacket."

"Yes, Sir." I force myself to walk while I yank on the coat, fidgeting with the many buttons. As soon as I turn the corner, I jump down the stairs two at a time, because now, thanks to Muller I'm stinking late. I want to smack his prim round face. Land a fist right on his fat nose. I sprint the rest of the way, slowing down at the administrative building where Sarge has his office. I have to concentrate now, forget about Muller, English composition… and Tom.

I don't want to admit it, but I'd much prefer going with Tom. Relax in the dark theatre, maybe see the girl by chance. My eyes feel like sandpaper, raw and tired. I haven't slept well, worrying about grades, my body remembering last night's game. There's never enough time to prepare for the mountains of homework or for the exams that come with military regularity.

"You're late." Sarge stands in front of an overloaded shelf, tracing the book spines with his forefinger. "Where is it?" he mumbles.

"Sorry, Sir, I got held up in the hall, Sir."

"Never mind. Sit down, we'll do a bit of theory first. Here, look at this and tell me what you see."

Sarge hands me a packet.

"Sir?"

"Come on, unfold it. Imagine, you'd be lost in the woods and Charlie is chasing you."

"It's a map, Sir." I spread the paper on the desk. "Except there's a lot of stuff on it."

"That's right. Look close—what do you see? This is a real map of Nam. Used it myself when I was stationed there."

"Lots of lines—these blue ones are water and this looks like a road or a path."

"It's called a topography map. What's this?" Sarge points at a cluster of brown-colored sections.

"Maybe farmland, fields?" I try remembering what I've seen on TV about the terrain. "Rice patties?"

"Which is it?"

"Farmland?"

"Good. Just one answer will suffice. What about the blue lines?"

"Rivers?"

"Yep, what about this blue circle?"

"Mmmh. A pool?"

"Olson, think. Do the Vietnamese have pools in their yards?"

"Probably not. A well, then."

"Correct, Olson."

"What's this green stuff?"

"Jungle."

"Yes, but why are there different types of green?"

"Maybe these are types of trees—brush?" I look up. Sarge has resumed his post behind the desk, a fresh unlit cigar between his lips.

"Yes and no. The denser the woods…the less penetrable, the darker the green on the map. Some of the jungle is nearly impassable. You need a machete to cut through, fight every inch along the way. There are snakes and spiders, poisonous frogs and beautiful birds. Except that you don't care, you just want to live. The woods around here are nothing like this."

Sarge leans forward and continues.

"What about these lines that look like waves?"

I shake my head.

"The diagonal lines show elevation so when they're close together that means it's steep terrain and when they pull apart, like here, the ground is flat." Sarge gives his cigar a whirl. "The numbers are feet above sea level."

"That seems easy enough."

"Except that you're in the jungle and you can't see squat. It's like swimming in cow shit. It surrounds you, chokes off your air. Strange sounds crawl under your skin, make you jumpy. Of course, you see absolutely nothing at night. It's as black as coal. No street lanterns or electric lights. Just impenetrable blackness, like being blind. There's water everywhere— dripping, soaking your clothes. You sink into the mud. Your feet are wet and infected with jungle rot. And no matter how hard you try to be invisible, you leave a trail. Imagine you're in the jungle. Lost. Maybe it's night. What're you going to do?"

Sarge gives his cigar another workout. The gray pockets under his eyes make him look as if he hasn't slept in days. For the first time, I wonder if Sarge is healthy. Why is he at the school instead of the battlefield?

"I don't know, Sir." I look at the jumbled lines in front of me. I can't find my way in the Indiana woods in daylight. How would I find anything in the dark?

"You need a compass."

Sarge pulls open the top drawer of his desk. "This is an orienteering compass. Take a look and tell me what direction you're facing."

When I grab the instrument, the needle quivers. Like my fingers which have a mind of their own.

"Hold it level. Where's north? The compass always points north and you adjust the needle so that the red end is on the north point. These are called cardinal points—east, west, south and north." Sarge leans across the desk. His index finger taps the plastic dome of the compass. Two thirds of the finger is missing. I try concentrating on the compass needle instead of the stump.

There has been much speculation on how Sarge was hurt. It's rumored he was captured by the Vietcong and chewed off his own finger to avoid infection before being freed in a prisoner's exchange. Others say a snake bit him and he cut off the bite to keep the poison from spreading to his heart. Still others say he was in a shooting accident, something about exploding ammunition and a misdirected pistol.

The skin of what's left of the finger looks purplish and shiny, the scar like a piece of plastic stretched too tight. In class Sarge holds his hand behind his back or sticks his fingers in his pocket or behind the lapel of his jacket. It seems that he doesn't want people to stare at the unsightly flesh. I want to ask what happened but don't have the nerve.

"Now move the red needle to North. Keep it steady."

"We're facing southeast."

"Remember, Olson, the red needle and north always need to be in the same spot. Try again."

"Southwest?"

"Good. Now walk around the room. What direction is the bookshelf?"

I turn the compass. This is not what I expected. I looked forward to hiking through the woods. "Northwest."

"Let me see." Sarge hovers next to me like a tower. "That's right."

"Try the desk. Where is it from where you stand?"

Eyes glued to the compass, I walk back to my chair. "South, wait southeast."

Sarge nods. "You got it. Not bad, Olson. Here's your first homework. Make a list of the furniture in your room and write down what direction they are if you face them from the center. I'll check it next Saturday. Your lesson will start in your room at 13:00 sharp."

"Yes, Sir."

"Dismissed."

I open the door, my mind trying to digest what I heard.

"Olson, haven't you forgotten something."

"Sir?"

"You need the compass to get the readings. Get your head out of your ass. Don't lose it and don't let anyone see it."

"Sorry, Sir, yes, Sir."

I close the door and sprint toward Barracks B, one hand in my pocket holding on to the compass. To heck with Muller and not running. I want to catch Tom before he leaves for the movies.

I poke my head in Tom's room, trying to catch my breath. "You still mad at me?"

Tom, fully-dressed, sits at his desk reading. Without looking up he throws down his book.

"Nope, how was the lesson? I thought you'd be gone for hours."

"We stayed in his office and looked at a map—I learned to read a compass. Sarge will check my room next Saturday. I'm supposed to practice directions."

"You ready to go? It's after one-thirty."

"Give me a minute." I rush to the bathroom and stare in the mirror. No pimples this week. Good. My eyes squint back at me. Why would the girl be interested in me? She probably has dibs on all the town boys. I shake my head. I'm an idiot.

***

"I'm going back to the store," I announce when we enter Garfield.

"Better hurry. Frank Sinatra isn't waiting. I'm sure glad, you didn't have to pull extra duty."

"I'll probably march next month. Muller gave me more demerits for my room. I got one for forgetting the name of that senior, you know, the guy from the cavalry who hangs out with Muller."

"I don't understand why you have such trouble with names."

"It's the same as your trouble with algebra," I shoot back. "My brain just doesn't work that way."

"I get it." Tom slaps me on the back. "No need to get touchy."

The worn-out silhouette of the general store comes into view.

"I'm buying more candy. You coming?"

"I'll go ahead and reserve a seat."

I pull open the door, the squeak familiar. My money is nearly gone.

The shopkeeper appears through a door in the back. "You again?"

My heart sinks. "I'd like a Zero, please. I want to look around first, though."

"Suit yourself." The man shrugs and returns to folding a pile of red flannel shirts. The girl is nowhere in sight. I walk between the displays, pick up a book on raising chickens and growing garden crops. Light shines from the back and I casually walk toward it. A door half covered by a curtain stands ajar.

Something is moving on the other side. Struggling to keep my confidence, I peek through the opening. Maybe she's back there and I can pretend I'm lost.

I shake my head. What kind of lame idea is that? But my body keeps moving and I ever so slightly push against the door. It swings a few inches, an achy hinge creaking in complaint. I step back but it's too late.

"What the fuck?" The voice on the other side sounds like a snarl. I turn on my heels and dash out the door, ignoring the stares of the shopkeeper and the shouts from the back that rise into a fever pitch. I shake my head, trying to make the nasty words go away.

"What took you so long?" Tom is pacing in front of the theatre. "The show is about to start. Let's go."

"I thought you wanted to wait inside."

"You wouldn't have found me—it's worse than fog on the River Thames. Where's your candy?"

"I changed my mind." I hope my smoldering cheeks don't give me away as I smack a dollar on the counter. "One, please."

In the darkness of the theatre, I think about the back office. The man looking at me was Eric, the guy in the wheelchair who'd smoked outside and accused me of spying. His piercing blue eyes were hidden behind a mass of black curls and beard except for a gray strand on the top of his head. In the store, Eric brandished his fist at me like he wanted to hit me from ten feet away.

But what I remember the most are his eyes. Laced with hatred he hurled them at me from the seat of his chair and I still feel them burning on the back of my head. The man's legs were shrunken like those of a child.

"You know anything about that store in town?" I ask on the walk back.

"The dust trap?" Tom has a way to get to the truth. "No, why?"

"Never mind." I'm not ready to explain why I opened the office door in the first place.

"All I know is that they don't like us much here. I wish we could visit Evansville or Chicago, real towns. They show all the new releases."

But I'm not really listening. My stomach hitches with a nervous flutter when I think of the girl. I'll go back, no matter what.

CHAPTER EIGHT

Through the fall I work with Sarge on Saturday afternoons. While we stomp around the woods with maps and compass, Sarge tells stories of finding his way back to base, outsmarting the enemy, learning to listen to sounds, and about close encounters with Charlie and the camaraderie in the camps. It's a different world, hard to imagine, but I'm fascinated about the men who fight, suffer and die together. Maybe one day, I'll be there, in a place I'd belong to like a family.

"You're learning, Olson," Sarge says one Saturday afternoon as we hike back to school. "You'll see. If you stick with it, you'll make a fine soldier one day. A leader."

I smile. "Thank you, Sir." I glance at Sarge, still afraid of him despite the hours we spent together. "It's fun. With you…I mean."

"Spit it out, Olson."

"It's hard to explain. I feel good about the work we do, what you teach me. But so many people are against the war now. They look at us funny. In town… they hate us."

"Who's going to defend our country if you and I don't?" Sarge stops to scan the trees as if he's expecting enemy fire. "If we all say we're against it. If we all refuse. Who's going to take care of the people?"

"It's just, it's *this* war."

"It's the principle. Serving the country. It's our responsibility. You do understand responsibility?" Sarge shoots back.

"I do, but—"

"No buts. A country like ours needs to help out the less fortunate. Those who can't help themselves."

It sounds plausible. Sarge seems so sure of his purpose.

"Keep up, Olson."

I hurry after Sarge and want to ask more questions, but nothing I think of seems right.

***

The weather turns icy. Freezing winds blow across the lake and throw themselves against campus buildings, coating lawns and trees like glass. The air howls with snowstorms and hail. Still we march to and from classrooms, to all meals and organized activities.

I try hard to escape Muller's wrath to avoid demerits and the inevitable extra duty. I imagine prison camp in Siberia when I watch the poor souls march, shake and shiver in the bitter air, their eyes teary, their noses red. Every week I hold my breath as Muller ransacks my stuff in search of dust. Some days he finds something, others he lets me go. There seems to be no logic.

I continue wondering about Sarge's finger but Sarge never mentions it. Some days when the weather is too forbidding, we stay in his office, rifling through maps and photos and talking. In classes, I listen closely, my grades a bit improved except in English. I hate writing even worse than reading literature, and I can't spell. Mr. Brown returns my reports with a spider web of red marks.

Tom has stopped asking me to go to the movies, and we never talk about what he does while I'm working with Sarge. We still hang out on Sundays, but I miss the relaxed fun of escaping to the smoke-filled theatre, diving into the stories on the screen that allow me to forget everything. And I miss seeing the girl, even if it's only an idea in my head.

My last lesson with Sarge is short—a summary of what I've learned and a discussion about my plans for winter break. I whistle when I leave. Today is my last chance to visit town because tomorrow, Sunday, we'll go home for Christmas break.

I've got no gifts. Tom has agreed to go to town with me to buy presents and catch the afternoon show.

"What're you getting your family?" I ask as we trudge through the snow toward Garville. I've got my collar raised to cover most of the ears, but my face burns with cold. Though it's early afternoon, the light has been swallowed by leaden clouds above—taking with them all color except for the brownish black of the trees, their limbs like skeletons against the sky. The air is heavy with more snow. I can smell the impending flakes.

"I'll find something at the bookstore when I get home tomorrow," Tom says. "What am I going to buy a guy who has everything?"

"I guess you can help me. I've got six dollars and fifty cents to spend on my family." I leave out the fact that I've saved my allowance by not going with Tom much this past fall.

"Maybe you should buy something for your parents and leave the rest of them out."

I shake my head. Tom is an only child. He doesn't know about sibling expectations. "I'll get some of the hard candy for my brothers and sisters, different colors. Maybe they can wrap them in something nice. That should leave me about five bucks to spend on my parents."

"What're you going to do over break?"

I sigh. "Sleep, eat and play. If they let me. My mother is an early riser. I doubt she'll allow me to sleep in. Maybe I'll go sledding or skating with my old friends. How about you?"

"Don't know. Hopefully my father will be gone on business and leave me alone. I'll probably read a few books, watch TV and try to look up an old buddy of mine."

"Maybe you could come and visit us." I regret it as soon as it's out. Tom wouldn't be comfortable among the noisy Olson kids, our shabby house and cramped rooms. He's used to having the entire place to himself, eating food served by a maid and sleeping in a king-sized bed.

"Don't know if I'd like to meet your mother," Tom smirks.

"Hah, she'd be very impressed."

"Right." Tom's forehead scrunches into a frown. "Maybe you'd like to visit *me* sometime. My father would probably not be there anyway. In case you're worried about meeting him."

"That'd be fun. Maybe during spring or summer break."

We walk on silently. Only our steps squeak in the frozen snow. A few crows screech overhead before landing in a field fifty feet away. I ponder what awaits me at home. The excitement of seeing everyone makes me giddy. I won't make my bed the entire time and run around in my oldest jeans, the ones with the hole in the knee and the shredded cuffs that look like the fabric was mauled by a raccoon. But I can tell that Tom's mood is dark and that he doesn't share my enthusiasm.

Suddenly I feel sad for Tom. Christmas has always been my favorite holiday, filled with whispers and secrets behind closed doors, shiny presents and guesses of what's waiting under the tree, the smells of roasting meat and chocolate chip cookies and candy dishes that appear everywhere. I can't imagine not looking forward to it.

I vow to be Tom's friend. Forever.

Aloud I say, "It'll be okay, right?"

Tom pulls his cap lower over his ears. "Right."

The street is empty and the store looks dark when we approach. I worry they're closed. I'll come home empty-handed and have to ask for a ride to town to get something. But when I push against the frame, the door opens with a jingle. A pine branch, decorated with a droopy velvet bow and a couple of bells, is taped to the glass.

Two bulbs burn in the back though the store is deserted. I shake myself, the heat inside a welcome change, and I remember the first time I came… the girl. Outside when they caught me peeping in their windows. I shudder when I think of the man in the wheelchair, the hateful eyes following me into the night.

"Maybe they forgot to lock the door," Tom whispers into the gloom. "We should go."

Ignoring Tom, I take another step. "Hello?" My voice sounds thin and refuses to carry.

"May I help…" the bald man appears from the back office. "You again," he pauses.

I wonder how well the man remembers me or if I'm the only cadet ever to set foot into the store. I don't doubt that most students stay away from town, their lives—except for the theatre—much too fancy for this place.

"Maddie," the man yells over his shoulder. "Can you take this one?"

Before I can change my mind, the black-haired girl comes bouncing down the stairs. She swiftly walks behind the counter, her feet light as a dancer. "May I help you?"

Her gaze, all business, lodges on me and I try to remember why I'm here. Her name is Maddie. I notice her eyes shine even in the low light—the blue intensity of the southern sea.

"I need gifts to take home," I mumble.

"You sure waited to the last minute. Christmas Eve is Monday." Maddie's cheeks glow pink, but her eyes flash with defiance. She has placed her hands on the counter and is leaning forward. Expectantly. Waiting.

"I, yes, I didn't have time."

"What do you want?"

I remain quiet, my mind doing somersaults. What's the matter with me? I wanted to see the girl, dreamed about her, sometimes imagined meeting her in the woods. Now I stand here like an idiot gaping.

"Candy, right?" Tom suggests. He wandered off and now returns to the counter. "Didn't you say you wanted to get sweets for your siblings?"

I nod. "Can you count out a dollar fifty in candies and divide it into four portions? Maybe put a bow around. I don't have much money."

Maddie points to a square glass jar on the counter. "How about these red and green ones? They're festive for Christmas. A penny each. Or you could add a few sticks like this red licorice. They're five cents." A small smile has crept onto her face.

"Great!" I try a grin which feels strange. I barely laugh anymore except when Tom and I joke about Muller or Tom's roommate, Toad.

"It won't come out even." She remains quiet for a moment, her lips moving to do silent math. "If you give two people two licorice sticks, it'll work."

I nod. I've forgotten how to count. Her lips are pink and shimmer. Maybe she wears lipstick, but I don't think so. Her face is clean and free of makeup. It doesn't go with the worn blue coveralls and the white wool sweater.

Maddie looks at me expectantly. "Is it okay then, the extra two?"

"Um, yes, perfect."

"How about fishing lures for your Dad?" Tom offers. "You said he likes to fish. Maybe they have worms or some miracle bait to catch the big ones."

"My Dad would like that," I say, keeping my eyes on Maddie's hands filling four cellophane bags. Her fingers—long and thin with smooth white skin—move swiftly. Her lips part in concentration, showing the tip of her tongue as she counts each piece. I try to pull away, rack my brain for something savvy to say. My brain refuses.

"Here we go." Maddie lines up four miniature packets on the counter, each with a red paper bow and Santa sticker. "The fishing equipment is over there. I'll show you."

She walks around the counter and heads toward the front window where several shelves hold an assortment of fishing poles, snow removal tools and salt. Barrels with potatoes and onions are stacked in the aisle and she climbs across. We follow.

On the wall, small packets glint with a rainbow of lures.

"Do you know what he likes to fish for?" Her eyes burn clear through the back of my skull. I forget to breathe. "It's late in the season. We have a lot more choices in the spring."

"Mostly bass and bluegill." I watch Maddie's waist and legs as she turns to sort through the display.

"How about these? The brown jelly worms are great with gills and sunfish. They look ugly but I've tried them myself and they work. Each packet is 75 cents."

"Perfect." I feel myself smile. "Great idea. I'll take two."

"Thanks," Tom says dryly.

"You have any ideas for my mother?" I follow Maddie back to the counter. "She likes bright colors but I don't know what I can get for three dollars."

"How about an apron or a Christmas candle? This one here comes with a glass plate."

"Maddie, close the shop when you're done," the bald man calls from the back. "Nobody will be out in this weather. I'm heading upstairs to check on Eric." He throws a last disapproving glance at me before fading into the stairwell.

"Yes, Dad." Maddie turns back to me. "Except you."

"What?"

"I meant nobody is shopping except for you."

"I guess." I peek through the steamed-up window. The light has faded further, extending shadows across the counter. To heck with the weather. I want to stretch out the moment, keep talking to the girl.

"We better scrap the movies and head back." Tom nods toward the front door. "The storm is about to blow."

I'd forgotten about Tom. "I'll take the candle, then."

"Good." Maddie rolls the gift in red tissue paper.

"I'll put it in a sack. Here you go." She moves her lips calculating the total. "Six dollars and twelve cents—with the tax."

I place the dollar bills and coins on the counter. "I guess I'm all set. Thanks." I open my mouth, but forget what else I want to say.

"Here's your change. Merry Christmas," says Maddie.

"Thanks, you too." I grab the bag. When Tom opens the door, a wind gust pushes frigid air into the store. I glance toward the girl, but she's moved behind the door, waiting to lock up. I feel disappointed and elated at the same time.

Tom punches me in the arm. "What the heck was that?" His mouth is curled into a smirk despite the icy gusts hitting us. "She's cute."

I clear my throat, "Yeah, pretty."

"You should ask her out some time," Tom shouts against the wind. The street has disappeared behind a curtain of white. "If you can find your voice by then," he chuckles.

"Very funny." But then I smile, glad Tom knows. Tom is my best friend, no matter he disagrees with Sarge. "I'll do that," I say. "Next year."

CHAPTER NINE

On the way home I stare out the window counting miles. I'm ecstatic, spending the holidays with my family and hanging out with my old buddies. Two weeks of bliss, sleeping in and no homework. Except for the English paper I have to write on *All Quiet on the Western Front*. I'll read a few pages each day, no sweat.

Our home in Fritz Terrace looks smaller than I remember.

"He's home," Robert, my younger brother yells when I open the door.

"Couldn't wait to get here." I push past him to look around. I expect relief and joy, yet it's not happening. The living room feels small as I shove my gifts underneath the tree.

Within an hour I'm antsy. Gary is at the library, Robert way too young to be interesting and my two sisters and assorted girlfriends are giggling downstairs. I have the impression they're talking about me. I shed my uniform, but can't do anything about my shorn head. A dead give-away if you ask me.

"I'm going to see Daniel," I yell to my mother.

"Dinner is at six."

I jog down the street, glad to be outside. Two weeks of freedom lie ahead. I smile.

"Andy?" Daniel's mom looks me up and down. Daniel's father is a doctor. They've got a huge house, even a pool.

"Is Daniel home?"

Daniel's mom shakes her head. "Sorry, he's with Scott and John. They went into the woods looking for sassafras."

"Do you know which woods? Maybe I can find them."

"No idea, why don't you check back after Christmas? I'll tell him you stopped by."

"Sure. Thanks."

I feel deflated. But then why would my old friends expect me? The wind has picked up again and I hug myself. I need to find another coat. One that isn't military.

I hope Daniel will stop by. After all, he's been my friend since grade school.

But he never does. When we finally get together a few days later, I want to know everything—about school, our old teachers, neighbors, our friends and classmates. Daniel never asks about Palmer. What I have to deal with.

"You and your fancy school," Daniel says a few times and makes a face like he's disapproving. As if I have a choice in the matter.

My sisters squabble and whine, getting on my nerves. Nobody seems to care about my life. Just making it through each day without being disciplined is a major feat. Dealing with the Mullers and Tonys, Sarge and Beerbelly.

By the end of break I find myself looking forward to returning to school, especially seeing Tom. The drive to Palmer is silent, my father saying little and I'm saying less.

***

Tom is full of bile. "You should've seen them. I wanted to puke." His eyes burn with frustration and his cheeks glow. "They held hands like they were twenty, that woman hanging on my father's lips as if he were the President. He ate it up. She looks like Barbie and laughs like a hyena. Nauseating."

"Sounds like a trophy wife," Plozett says. "Did you do *anything* fun?"

We're hiding underneath the bleachers in the gym, sharing a bottle of Boone's Farm Strawberry Hill wine Plozett smuggled into the school inside his trumpet case.

"It's all about sex. He better not marry her, though I wouldn't be surprised about anything." Tom takes another swig. The liquid inside the bottle sloshes. "I mostly read and listened to music…stayed in my room."

"It's different to go home. Either they've changed or we have," I say, belching. It's strange how I considered my family home, the place I belonged. Right now I don't belong anywhere… I'm in a permanent state of visitation.

"I noticed it two years ago, the first time I went back. Nothing was the same," Plozett says.

I feel envy rise from my stomach like an ugly snake. Plozett is an oldman. He has it easy. At least he doesn't make us salute in the hall.

"The only bright thing that happened was my father gave me this." Tom tugs a pocket watch and chain from his pants. "Belonged to my mother, actually her father, but it became hers after he…died suddenly."

"Cool. Does it open?" I ask.

Tom nods. The gold is engraved with a swirly pattern of leaves, precision work that has to have taken a goldsmith many weeks. The inside reveals an old-fashioned watch with delicate hands on one face and a photo of a dark-haired woman on the other. I zoom in on her eyes—soft brown and vulnerable—like Tom's. "Your mother?"

"When she was young and well. Before she had me."

"She's pretty," Plozett says. "What happened to your mom's father?"

Tom opens his eyes wide, a sign he's getting emotional, but Plozett doesn't notice. "After my mom got sick, my grandmother took care of me. She told me the story last year—before she died. My grandfather killed himself when my mother was ten. She found him.

"My father insists she never got over it. They met when she was eighteen. She was beautiful then—fragile. That must've appealed to the old man. She probably admired his strength, confidence and success. He loves being admired." Tom pauses, taking another swig. "She tried to please him, but he was barely home. He never noticed she got worse, especially after I was born. Had more important things to do."

"Is she dead, too?" Plozett asks.

I glance at my friend. The pain on Tom's face has spread to his voice. It sounds as if he's choking.

"She's in a home for the insane, a sanatorium—all white and shiny with perfect lawns and flowerbeds, perfect rooms and schedules. Sort of like this place. I hate the smell, like antiseptic mixed with bleach. My father insists it's the best place in the country, but she's locked up just the same. I guess he has us both squared away."

Plozett jerks up and whispers, "Somebody's coming."

I hear footsteps on the other side of the bleachers. Getting to my knees, I glimpse through the space between the bottom seats. Tony White and Big Mike are heading our way. Tony is out of breath. His eyes flash, the same look he has when we're ahead in a game. I stuff the empty wine bottle back in Plozett's case. The sudden movement makes me dizzy.

"Do they know we're here?" Tom asks.

"Doubt it," whispers Plozett.

Tony and Big Mike are crossing the wooden expanse of the gym and stop in front of a metal door in the far corner, painted the same pale beige as the walls and easy to overlook. I hear scraping and metal clinking.

Tom shakes his head, but I get up and walk around the bleachers. I don't even know why.

"What're you guys up to?" I say, surprised they jump at the sound of my voice.

"It's you, Olson," Tony says with a sigh. He scans the empty floor of the gym. "We're checking out the tunnels."

I'd heard about a network of underground pipes that feed the radiators with superheated steam. "What for?"

Tom and Plozett appear at the edge of the bleachers.

"You got an army back there?" Tony sounds irritated and I wonder if he'll throw a fit, like he does on the football field when things don't go his way. He paces back and forth and shouts worse than the coach. Since he's a great quarterback, hard to stop and scoring most of the points, he gets away with it.

I shake my head. "Just the three of us."

"Keep it quiet then," Tony says with a low voice, his attention back on the door. A moment later metal hinges creak. We all jump and scan the gymnasium for signs of life. Nothing moves. "The tunnels connect all the buildings. We want to take a look." Tony hesitates. "You can come but I don't want the others."

"Why?" I ask, my voice sounding strange in my ears. I feel lightheaded. "I vouch for them."

"Don't ask stupid questions," Big Mike says. "Only the team goes."

"Thanks anyway, I've got math to finish." Tom turns away.

"I've got band practice," Plozett says.

Doubt creeps up inside me, a tinny voice of warning. Still I want to be on Tony's good side. I'll look like a wimp pulling out now. "I guess it's just me."

Tony and Big Mike disappear inside the door. "Hurry up, Olson," Tony says.

"If I'm not back by tomorrow, find me," I yell after Tom who's walking off without a word. I'm irritated that Tom didn't even try to join.

A steep metal staircase leads into the void below. We search and find a light switch by the entrance. A bulb springs to life, barely illuminating the steps. Compared to the perfect condition of the school's facilities, the handrail's white paint is covered in rust and black mold. I follow the others downstairs. Behind me the door slams shut.

We stop at the bottom. I see nothing beyond five feet. It's how I imagine a coal mine, black stuffy emptiness. Tony fumbles for another light switch. Fluorescents crackle above, illuminating a low-ceilinged brick tunnel leading in two directions. Every thirty feet, a single bulb creates a pattern of light and shadow. Beyond, complete blackness. Three sets of pipes run along one side and the ceiling, the largest one hissing like an angry snake. Hot steamy air wraps around us, reminding me of Indiana in August.

I hesitate. Tight spaces give me the creeps.

"How did you get the keys?" I say to distract myself.

"Found 'em hanging in the door to the study room when we got back today," Tony says. "The janitor must've forgotten them. He'll be in deep trouble." He lets out a holler of glee. "This way." Tony's voice continues in an echo of whispers.

"You think they hear us?" Big Mike says.

"Nobody will hear us," Tony says, shouting louder, the sound ricocheting off the walls. "Let's find the faculty building and drop in on our teachers. Heard they're keeping a bunch of liquor—for parties and stuff."

Big Mike laughs and punches Tony in the shoulder, but I feel woozy from the wine and heat. Uneasiness spreads through my stomach which has turned into a queasy sponge filled with acid. My sweater sticks to my back. It has to be a hundred degrees down here. I wonder what Tony means to do when we arrive below the teacher's dorm. Cadets aren't allowed inside. If we're caught demerits will be the least of our problems. But then Big Mike gets away with lots of things and so does Tony. Palmer wants to win football games.

"What if there isn't a door?" I ask.

"Has to be," Big Mike says.

"All buildings have access," Tony says. "We'll sneak in, grab a bottle and leave. This is the best time, when they all go to dinner. We'll catch the second dinner shift. Easy as pie."

I wonder how Tony knows, but more so, I want to return to my room. "I'll head back."

"Come on, Olson, you're one of us." Tony stops and stares down at me. "No skipping out." Though he isn't much older, he's half a foot taller and looks like a grown man. Like Plozett's, Tony's jaw is dark with stubble. "What's with you anyway? You're turning into a sissy like Tom."

"Leave Tom out of it. It's just my stomach." I'm taking deep breaths though the dizziness is spreading to my skull. Tony is an idiot, but fighting him is no option. "I must've eaten something bad," I stammer.

"Bullshit. You're turning into a wimp. Better straighten out if you want to remain on the team."

"He's been boozing," Big Mike says as if I'm not there. "Smell the stench a mile away. You could've shared," he says, turning to me.

"I thought you were one of us. A *team* player," Tony says.

I shake my head, which has begun to pound in rhythm with my heart. "The wine wasn't mine. Besides... I might throw up."

"Sissy," Big Mike says.

"Knock yourself out." Tony shrugs. "Come on, let's go. First dinner starts any time." They walk on. I follow. Too much effort to argue or make a decision. My stomach churns as I burp sour strawberries.

We come to an intersection, dark beyond the cross path. Tony finds the light switch high on the wall.

"Man, these pipes are freaking hot," he says. "You almost boil, standing near them. I'd say the faculty dorms are this way."

Big Mike nods. I don't care because I'm focused on keeping my stomach from erupting.

"Come on, Olson. Keep up."

We continue down the path. The thick air, our hollow footsteps and the tunnel leading into blackness make it impossible to know how much time passes or how far we've come. At least the ground is even. I keep my eyes wide open to catch every last beam from the dim shine overhead.

"I hope you know how to get back," Big Mike says. A pinch of doubt has crept into his voice.

"Sure thing, we just go back the way we came and turn right once," Tony says. "What's that over there?"

Gray light filters from above. We stop below a grate—the sky above sliced into perfect squares. Outside, dusk is setting.

"I bet we're in front of the admin building. The ground always steams. I bet it's from this hole." Tony sounds confident.

I lift my face to catch a whiff of fresh air. The space down here is too damp and thick, too wet to breathe. Sweat beads roll down my temples. Tony's face glows. Big Mike looks as if he's been in a downpour. We continue until another intersection appears out of nowhere.

"Which way?" Big Mike scrapes his paw-shaped hand across the walls in search of a light switch. "Ouch, that's fucking hot."

Tony stares into the shadows as if he can see beyond. "We should be underneath the admin building now. I say, we go straight. In a few feet we should reach the teacher's dorm."

I'm not saying anything. The darkness and heat are closing in like ghosts. I wonder if anyone ever died down here. I can only see about thirty feet at a time. Everything in front and behind us turns black, a murkiness that swallows sound and light, sucks it away like a black hole in space. Even the echo of our steps sounds alien.

Big Mike stops abruptly and I bump into him.

"Watch it."

"Let's go back," I say.

"Almost there," Tony says as if he knows where he's going.

Above our heads a pipe vibrates. With every step, the whistling hum grows louder, the air thicker. I think about Sarge's description of the jungle. What did he say? *Impenetrable blackness and humidity like boiled fog.* We slow down as the whistling turns into a scream. At the next intersection we peek around the corner. Twenty feet ahead, steam explodes into the corridor. Pipes rattle and the air groans like a choir of ghosts.

"Damn. What's going on?" Big Mike sounds pissed. "Looks like a leak."

"We have to tell someone," I say. "It might blow."

"You nuts? Let's go," Tony says. I'm relieved except the fog seems to follow us. The pipes above creak and rattle from the pressure and I worry they'll burst and scald us alive.

Big Mike breaks into a run. "This is crap." Tony follows. But I have trouble keeping up, my eyes filled with vapor.

"Hurry up, Olson," Tony yells over his shoulder. "This way."

We turn right. The lights have gone out and Tony finds another switch. They must be on timers.

"The stairs should be on the right. Keep an eye out," Tony says. I search, but everything is drenched in shadow and I barely make out the wall. The noise behind us has turned into a low hiss. We slow down. Another intersection appears, only noticeable by the black void that seems more dense than the stone walls.

"Where is it?" Tony says. For the first time, he sounds uncertain. "You don't suppose we passed it?"

Big Mike shrugs. We walk on but the walls look the same, then another junction.

"Shit," Tony yells. "I don't remember this. Olson, do you remember this?"

I shake my head and picture smacking Tony's big mouth into the pipe. But my legs are like molasses, muscles replaced by gooey softness. My temples pound against my eye sockets, making it hard to concentrate. I want to be in bed…wake up from this nightmare.

"We should've passed the grate," Big Mike says. "Did you see a grate?"

"Can't remember," Tony says. "Shit!" He suddenly stops. "We must've missed it. I say we keep going in one direction. There has to be a damn door somewhere."

"Good idea," Big Mike says. Hard to say if he means it.

I think about my joke that Tom should look for me tomorrow. It doesn't seem funny now. Palmer's campus spans a hundred acres and the distances between buildings are huge—we can go on for miles and never find a way out. My lungs are heavy, refusing to breathe.

We rush on, only stopping to turn on the next flight of lights. Some of the bulbs are burned out, the space beyond in shadows.

"I see light," Big Mike says. We run forward as the glow becomes stronger. The ceiling grows bright—almost like a spotlight. We stop underneath and stare into a streetlamp. "Hello," Big Mike shouts. "Anybody there?"

"Are you crazy?" Tony says through his teeth. "What if the faculty hears us?"

"You want to stay down here?" Big Mike grumbles. "I'm starving. I'd rather get a few demerits than rot in this hellhole." It's well-known that Big Mike isn't afraid of collecting demerits. Somehow they always disappear before it's time for extra duty.

"I have an idea," I say. "Give me a lift, I'll push against the grate. Maybe it opens and we can climb out."

"Ha, great idea, Olson," Tony says. "You mean you'll leave and we're stuck down here. No way, Big Mike is too heavy."

"The boathouse has a ladder," I say. For a moment it's quiet as we stand below in the tunneled prison, trying to come up with other options.

"Fine," Tony says, folding his hands. "I'll lift you. Step on Mike's shoulder and try to reach the grate." It sounds as if the rescue is his idea. I find myself swinging high.

For a split-second I admire Tony's strength. Big Mike's shoulders seem impossibly high. I struggle to keep my balance and raise my fingertips toward the iron bars. They feel rough and very cold as I press against them. The metal doesn't budge.

"Push harder," Tony yells from below. I try again but nothing happens. Despite the street lantern I can't see much. The glare is blinding, shadows join above and below. My hands are ice. I slide a forefinger along one of the iron bars to the end. There's a bulge.

"Walk to the right a bit," I croak. My feet pull away underneath. "The other right." I straighten and grope along the rim of the grid. There's another bump. "It's hinged—like a trapdoor," I say. "To the left now, slowly. Maybe there's a latch."

Big Mike moves below me while I hold on to the grate. In position, I move my hand along the opposite side. Nothing. I push and feel the cover move. I press harder imagining the hitting exercises on the football field when we thrust our shoulders against the heavy blocking sled. The cover lifts with a screech. I stand too low to push it up all the way and it falls back, nearly pinching my fingers.

"Damn. I'm not tall enough," I whisper into the shadows. "Can you lift me higher?"

"Stand on my head," Big Mike says. His voice sounds compressed underneath my hundred and seventy two pounds.

"You sure?" I ask.

"Hurry up. Tony is too heavy. You'll have to do it."

I place my right foot on Big Mike's head, hoping I can balance, at the same time thrusting an arm upward. The grid lifts and crashes back down with a sharp clank. I slide off Big Mike's head. Flailing I hook two fingers into the grate. For a moment I dangle in midair. My hands are sliding when I feel Big Mike's shoulders under my feet.

"Steady," he pants. "Again."

Tony is quiet for once. I keep my eyes on the unlocked side of the grate and step on Big Mike's head once more. Taking a deep breath I swing an arm upward. The cover becomes airborne and falls away to smash against stone or pavement beyond, leaving an opening of two by three feet.

I pull myself up, commanding my biceps to do the chin-up of my life. Lifting my chest through the hole, I sink forward to rest on the ground. I know I've got to hurry or risk being discovered. The thought of a dozen teachers staring at me from multiple windows makes my skin crawl. As I raise my eyes, I begin to tremble. I'm in the worst possible spot on the entire campus.

Not fifty feet away stands the Dean's villa, a two-story whitewash with Greek columns lifting the entrance into grandeur. I'm practically in his front yard.

"Damn." I scoot on my belly to pull out my legs. The street lantern above throws a spotlight on my back. I'm in plain sight of a dozen windows.

"We're near the Dean's house," I whisper into the hole. "I'll get the ladder." Without waiting for a reply, I race off mumbling "pompous ass" toward the villa. The boathouse is two-hundred yards to my right. Thankful for the darkness and that it hasn't snowed yet, I sprint across the lawn. *What if I flee and hide in my room? Not an option.*

The grounds are silent, paths empty. Everyone is eating dinner. Cadets never miss a meal, and I'm out here like an idiot.

After the hot steamy air in the tunnel, I soon freeze. I don't have a jacket and the air is icy crystals. After a few minutes I'm questioning whether I should've collected my coat. The air grows more frigid by the second.

Ahead looms the boathouse, closed up for winter. A long narrow shed sits along the back wall. A padlock is latched into place. *Damn.*

I consider getting a couple of jump ropes from the gym, but Big Mike would never be able to pull himself up. Even if Tony helps we wouldn't be able to lift Big Mike, especially not in front of the Dean's watchful windows. I must get the ladder which is locked inside the shed. For a moment I stare at the canoes mounted on racks like the rib bones of a whale.

A rowboat, turned upside down, rests near me on the ground. I pace nervously, aware of time ticking away and the ever-increasing chance of being discovered. My fingers are like icicles. I can't think straight.

To my left something sparkles on the ground. I rush to investigate and drop to my knees. An anchor is tucked beneath the boat. I yank and the anchor appears, followed by a length of rope. I grab the freezing iron, the rope uncoiling as I pull it toward the shed.

Ramming the anchor against the wood, I hook the tip below the latch. I throw my weight against the curved iron until the board gives with a sharp crack, safety lock and latch catapulting into the grass beyond. I heave a sigh. The Dean will have me for lunch if he finds out. No time to think about that now.

I drop the anchor and open the door. Lifting the twelve-foot ladder across my shoulders I rush toward the road, the weight digging into my biceps. I decide to take the shortest route back. This time I feel thankful for the darkness.

Ahead, the Dean's villa sits prominently along a looped driveway. I remain on the lawns, my eyes glued to the street light and the hole below. Forty yards to go.

Suddenly the road turns bright. Three pairs of brilliant headlights follow a curve and are about to hit me. I crash to the ground, the ladder clattering next to me. If they see me I'll be finished—a careless remark about a cadet doing a maintenance job on the Dean's lawn will be all it takes. What if the approaching cars blow a tire on the grate or get stuck in the hole I've created? It'll be all over.

I watch the cars creep toward the gap, colder than I've ever been in my life, even more terrified to be caught or letting my teammates down. Tony and Big Mike are certainly not my friends, but I don't want either of them to face the Dean, even if Tony started the whole damn mess.

The cars approach… and pass. I sigh.

Doors slam and the Dean's voice drones across the gravel driveway. He and his wife, a mousy thing with tiny heart-shaped lips and a permanent squint attached to her fake eyelashes, stands under the Greek columns to welcome their guests. Piano music plinks in the background and I smell the rich aroma of roast beef. The wine has finally worn off and I'm unbearably hungry. My last meal was a peanut butter and jelly sandwich my mother packed for the journey down here. It seems like a week ago.

Exclamations of delight and sugary greetings drift across as the Dean and his guests disappear inside the house. At last, the door closes and I grab the ladder, forcing my frozen legs into action. Behind the villa's picture windows not fifty feet away, people mingle, fixing drinks and munching on nuts and fancy appetizers.

Ignoring my clenched stomach, I guide the ladder into the hole, hoping it'll be long enough. I sigh again. Three inches protrude into the street.

"Hurry," I call into the void. "The Dean has guests. There may be more cars coming."

Tony's face appears above the hole. He looks pale, his hair drenched, his chest as wet as after practice. He climbs out quickly and drops to the ground.

"Your turn," he whispers into the hole. Big Mike squeezes through the opening, his breath labored and fast. "What took you so long?" he grunts.

I push the anger about not getting the slightest thank you to the back of my mind and nervously watch the brightly lit windows.

The streetlamp above blazes, showing our every move. To my frustration, Big Mike acts like a beached whale, large, slow and very visible.

"Faster," I whisper. "Help me pull out the ladder."

We yank and the grate smashes into place. I don't dare stop to check for eyes behind the windows. "This way."

Nobody speaks as we reattach the ladder and close the door of the shed. It's past eight when I return to my room. Dinner is over and I search for the cookies my mother sent along earlier.

None of us spoke on the way back and I can't believe they didn't even thank me. I'm mad about my day, angry about Tony and his foolishness, but even more furious about my own weakness in following along, ignoring my gut.

"What happened to you?" Tom stands in my door.

I don't feel like talking right now," I say while I yank off my shirt to inspect the five-inch tear in the elbow and the mixture of grime and blood ground into the fabric. "Damn, it's ruined."

"Fine. Maybe tomorrow." Tom shrugs. "Let me know if you want to do something."

Ignoring him, I hurl my clothes to the floor. I could've been comfortable in my room like Tom, taken a nap and enjoyed a nice dinner.

Instead, I shredded my clothes, risked my neck and went hungry. I don't want to admit it, but I'm jealous of Tom, jealous of his ability to be himself and not care what anyone says. I want to punch him for that.

CHAPTER TEN

Too hungry to sleep in, I get up early. On Sundays, the school serves breakfast after nine and I'm forced to wait. Plozett sounds like a chainsaw, a lump of stubbly black hair and an arm clad in blue and white checkered pajamas peak from the wool blanket.

With a sigh I plunk down at my desk. The new semester starts tomorrow and I already feel behind. Over break I was supposed to complete a paper on *All Quiet on the Western Front*, Remarque's World War One classic. Of course, I put it off.

I pick up the paperback and stare at the tattered cover, the pencil marks in the margins. The bookmark is missing and I try remembering how far I read. Why didn't I study at home when I had time, instead of lounging in front of the TV feeling bored? I'm sure Mr. Brown will test us first thing tomorrow, just the foul thing he'd do after a nice break. I'll have to waste most of today to finish.

My stomach gurgles. It's no good. I can't concentrate until I eat. Maybe I can run into town this afternoon and check on Maddie. I'll stop in to buy candy with my Christmas money, saved just for this occasion. Now that the cookies are gone, I'll need something to munch on next time I miss a meal. Hopefully Tom will go along. It'll look more natural if I don't go alone.

Rifling through my desk drawer, I come across Sarge's compass. The needle quivers north. I can't remember what Sarge said about returning it. What if he believes I kept it on purpose? I glance at the wall clock—plenty of time before breakfast to drop it off. Maybe Sarge will suggest more lessons. The sessions have been sort of special and I find myself looking forward to seeing the man. He's probably sitting behind his desk chewing on a cigar.

When I slip out, the hallway is quiet, cadets enjoying their last free

Sunday and loading up on precious sleep before the semester takes off in earnest. I jump down the stairs and leave the building.

Why haven't I written a note in case Sarge isn't at his office and I leave the compass at his door? But then…unlikely the faculty steals. And Sarge would know who left it.

I slow down. The lawns have turned brownish yellow and a cold wind whips across, carrying light rain that coats my face and makes the ground soggy. I shiver, contemplating if I should get my coat.

"Olson, where're you headed," Muller shouts from behind.

I sigh and turn around. Here is the one guy I don't care to see and he pops up everywhere. Even on Sunday—when everyone else sleeps. I know I can't keep my face from showing disgust. Muller's sweats look ironed.

"Sir, I'm going to see Sarge, Sir," I bark.

Muller shakes his head. "Sergeant Russel isn't at school."

"What do you mean?" I stumble, forgetting the formal address.

"He didn't return after the break." Muller's eyes looks smug. I can't tell if he really knows something or is just playing Mr. Important.

"Where is he?"

Muller shrugs. "Probably in Vietnam."

I stand, my purpose for the morning evaporated, the wind nipping at my bare hands.

"What's that?" Muller stares at my fingers.

I remember the compass I'm still holding. "Nothing."

"That's *something*. I'd like to inspect it." Muller's voice sounds forceful. Inspections of plebes are permitted at all times and include the cadet's room and dress.

I slowly raise my arm and open my fingers to reveal the compass.

Muller grabs it without comment. "It's a real military compass. Don't tell me it's yours." I ask myself how Muller knows these things, but then his father is in the Pentagon, so he probably sees all sorts of tools and secret weapons.

"It's not."

"You stole it."

"No. It's on loan." I don't feel like explaining my Sarge lessons to pompous Muller.

"Is that what you call it?" Muller mocks. "In that case I'll keep it and report it to the counselor." Sarge's compass disappears in Muller's pocket and he turns.

To my own surprise I hear myself shout at Muller's back. "It isn't yours to take. You're stealing it from me."

Muller swivels on his heels at a surprising speed while managing to look indignant. "What did you say? Watch your mouth." I notice Muller's hand slipping inside his pocket to pat the compass.

Before I can stop myself I swing at him, my fist making contact with Muller's chin. Unprepared, Muller hurdles backwards and drops into the privet bush next to the path. I jump on top and thump Muller in the nose, releasing an explosion of bloody snot. Muller gurgles and scrambles out of the bush to leap on me. Despite his shortness, he's strong and sinewy and we fall on the sidewalk in a fighting embrace. I struggle to get my arms free to throw another punch while worrying about the compass. Sarge will be furious if it breaks.

"You ass," I hiss. "I've had enough of you. Give me my compass." I grope for Muller's pant pocket, but his hand clamps down on my forearm like a vise.

"I'll report you, Olson…an unwarranted attack, total disrespect," Muller grunts, landing a blow on my cheek. Pain sears through my skull as I feel my head jerk back. I punch blindly and hit something soft. Muller's lip. I feel him cringe, his hand flying to inspect his mouth. Blood is everywhere.

I suck air and position for another swing. "You're a thief, Muller. A pathetic hypocrite."

"Damn you, Olson. You shouldn't be allowed—"

"Cadets Olson and Muller, what're you doing?" someone yells. I feel my arms yanked backwards, unleashing fiery pain in my shoulders. I'm covered in slimy red and still trying to land another blow, but the grip behind me holds. "Stop it, Olson. Turn around. Slowly."

As I turn I recognize the barracks counselor, Beerbelly. "This is no way to behave. You're keeping me from my service and I resent it." A devout catholic, Beerbelly never misses Sunday mass at the campus chapel.

"He attacked me." Muller straightens himself, adopting a tone of superiority. "He should be thrown from the school."

"He took my compass." I grit my teeth, my fury barely contained.

"Stop! Right now!" Beerbelly shouts. "Return to your rooms, both of you. Clean up. Then you come and see me. Muller, you in ten minutes. Olson, in twenty. You're wasting my time."

"Yes, Sir," I yell, throwing a murderous glance at Muller. I still don't have my compass and stomp off without looking back. Upstairs, I enter the washroom. The face in the mirror looks like someone else. Blood covers my cheek—Muller's slime. My eyes shine as if I have a fever. Quickly turning away from the mirror, my attention moves to my throbbing knuckles.

I splash water on my skin and keep my hands in the cold stream until they're numb. Worry spreads across my stomach and into my throat. I cough, but the pressure remains. I've recklessly ignored rank—the rule of rules. My punishment will be harsh. Fresh anger roils: at myself, my lack of control, at Muller. I remember the clock—even the washroom has one— and hurry downstairs.

Beerbelly's door is closed, the corridor silent. I sigh, remembering my previous visits. Coming here always means trouble. I knock. When nothing happens and I prepare to knock again, the door swings open. Muller passes me without a glance. Though he has changed, his nose is swollen and looks like a bulbous onion tinged blue, his lower lip the size of a walnut.

I shuffle into the counselor's office. At least I didn't bleed like Muller—the pig. Even if my knee is bruised from crashing onto the concrete and my shoulders burn like I dipped them in hot coals.

I'm still wearing my gory sweats, rust-colored splotches drying on my shirt. After ruining one set yesterday I have no other pair. Laundry won't be picked up until tomorrow and uniforms are prohibited on Sundays unless we have a special event, like this evening when the Dean gives his customary welcome speech, requiring class A uniforms. Just the thought of seeing the man makes me cringe.

"Hurry up, Olson." Beerbelly waves at me impatiently. "Looks like we've got a problem, but I want to hear your side of the story." He squints and leans back in his easy chair, a fifties vintage of brown plaid, doing double duty as a desk chair, the same place he always sits when I report about demerits. "Why didn't you change? You're filthy."

"Sir, I'm out of clothes."

"Already? You just got here.

I shrug.

"Then you need to get replacements. I can write to your parents, if—"

"No, Sir, excuse me," I hurry. "I'll write to them. It's just that I got my other set dirty yesterday." I think of the torn sleeve and the grass stains from lying on the Dean's front lawn.

Beerbelly shakes his head. "Didn't you just *return* yesterday?"

"Yes Sir, but I had an accident."

Beerbelly looks at his watch. "Never mind that now. I better catch the end of mass. Quick, tell me what happened."

"Cadet Muller took my compass. I mean it's not mine, what I mean is…"

"Spit it out, Olson. You're interrupting my Sunday."

"Yes, Sir, sorry. Sarge gave me the compass to carry and practice-use for orienteering. I was going to return it to him today, but—"

"You decided to beat up Muller instead."

"No Sir, Muller requested to inspect the compass and I gave it to him, but then he accused me of stealing and kept it. I got mad."

"Cadet Muller is your superior officer and you are supposed to follow orders."

"I did until he took …"

Beerbelly shakes his head. I can tell it's not going well. "You've been here four months and you still don't know how to act. You're a plebe and must obey orders. Control yourself. Ten demerits for losing your temper and… a report to your parents. Cadet Muller was supposed to return the compass to you. He received five demerits. I'll hand the compass to Sergeant Russel myself when he returns."

I stare in disbelief. The ass Muller stole and got away and I have to march. Ten demerits means automatic Extra Duty and next Saturday, my first weekend back, will be shot. Not to mention that marching for three hours in subzero temperatures feels like frozen hell. I haven't even been here twenty-four hours. I'm really making progress.

Just last week, my father preached about getting ahead in school and making them proud, about having opportunities he never had. I can just imagine the letter my mother will send—full of scolding remarks and disappointment. I stand steaming and don't listen to the rest of Beerbelly's sermon. At least I'll see Maddie this afternoon. Hopefully she's around to sell me candy. If not, I'll find an excuse to hang around for a while.

"One more thing," Beerbelly says as if he's heard my thoughts. "You're confined to campus for the rest of today." And after a look at my chest. "Not that you'd *want* to run around looking like that. Dismissed."

"Yes, Sir," I shout and turn on my heels. I'm ready to vanish from earth and wish I'd never set foot in this place. I remember Maddie, her face ghostly, her features shifting like clouds. Only her eyes blaze.

Thanks to stupid Beerbelly I won't see her today. Next week is shot, too. And where in the heck is Sarge?

CHAPTER ELEVEN

I spend the afternoon in my room finishing the paper, but my mind keeps wandering. My cheek aches from Muller's blow—the sniveling guy is stronger than expected. My knuckles throb from making contact with Muller's skull.

And where is Sarge? I feel let down, a disappointment I can't explain. *Did I expect Sarge to tell me about his plans?* Maybe I should've asked more questions. I go over our last encounter before Christmas break. Nothing stands out. We talked about general army stuff and orienteering. What if Sarge doesn't come back?

Tom materializes next to my desk. "What happened?"

I manage a grin. "Muller took Sarge's compass from me and I lost control."

"You had a fight," Tom says dryly.

"He looks worse."

"Way to go." Admiration has crept into Tom's voice. He settles in Plozett's chair.

"Except I scored ten demerits. You know what that means."

"You got caught."

"Beerbelly was on his way to chapel."

"If you march next Saturday," says Tom, "maybe we can catch a show on Sunday. We'll just have to mingle with the townies."

I think about the girl. "I don't mind, time to stock up on candy."

Tom grins. "I bet."

I feel my cheeks grow hot. "What's so funny?"

"You're a terrible liar. She's pretty cute, I must admit. Though I still like Raquel's tits. That woman has curves, mmmh," Tom sighs. "Unattainable, though. You need help with your paper?"

I shrug. "Only twenty more pages, though I can barely remember the beginning."

"You know Brown. He'll do an exam."

"Shit. How can you memorize these characters? This is too depressing."

Tom chuckles. "Speaking of characters. Don't forget the Dean's speech. Assembly hall at 17:30."

"Yuck." I check the clock. It takes at least ten minutes to change into formal dress. I step to the closet to inspect my uniform. All in order. Blue shirt, tie, pants, jacket, hat, white gloves. Belt buckle shined to brilliance without a speck of tarnish.

"See you in a few," Tom says, heading for the door.

"You wouldn't know where Sarge went?" I say over my shoulder. Somehow I don't want Tom to know how important it is.

"He isn't here?"

"No."

"Not a clue."

***

A steady stream of companies—artillery, infantry and cavalry, all easily recognizable by the insignia on their chests—march toward the largest building on campus, platoons filling every path.

Except for six giant chandeliers that sparkle above and remind me of a ballroom, assembly hall looks like a mixture between an oversized gym and a church with polished ash floors and ten-foot tall stained-glass windows clad in navy colored velvet. Hundreds of chairs sit in perfectly aligned rows, enough to house the entire student body.

"Wonder what he'll talk about this time," Tom says as we file into an aisle in the back.

"I'd rather go to the dentist," I mumble.

"Root canal," Tom says.

Plozett chuckles behind us. "I want ether."

I grunt to suppress a laugh when I catch a glimpse of Beerbelly patrolling the aisles, raised brows above squinting eyes. How can you make your face go in different directions? I slump into my seat, resigned to wait things out.

The whispers and murmurs evaporate into hushed silence as the Dean, shoulders hunched, walks to the podium.

"Welcome back," he begins. He glances at the rows of metal chairs packed with every last cadet. He looks plain in a dark suit except for the eyes magnified by black horn-rimmed glasses. Nobody ever forgets the eyes once they've met the Dean, metallic gray like galvanized nails that bore into your soul and don't match the soft-spoken voice.

I still shiver, remembering the first day of school when the Dean took possession of my mother's arm in a familiar gesture like a long lost uncle.

My mother practically ate from his hand. My dad nodded and smiled. They ignored me though I stood right there watching the spectacle, too numb to feel anything but my heart beating staccato.

"Let me assure you," the Dean took on a familiar tone and patted my mother's arm, "we have an excellent reputation raising boys and molding them into responsible adults." His lips curled into a smile. "We'll take good care of him," he drooled in his southern accent. "Andrew will do just fine."

Right! Even now I feel my throat constrict, something anger always does. No doubt the Dean is as cold as a frozen fish, a shrewd business man, calculating how he can maximize profits.

As I sit squeezed between Tom and Plozett, my neck itches from the new shirt my mother bought in an after-Christmas sale. The cummerbund squeezes my belly. I tied the knot standing, forgetting to anticipate that stomachs expand in a sitting position. I stretch my legs under the front seat and lean back to relieve the pressure.

"…challenging year ahead," the Dean drones. "Let us reflect on Palmer's achievements which are of course *your* achievements." He pauses, his eyes scanning the room.

I hold my breath. Surely, the Dean can't see me in the crowd. I lower my eyelids just a bit to scan the rows in front of me. I should've picked a seat behind Big Mike who towers to my left and whose bulky shoulders offer a perfect shield. Neither Tony nor Big Mike have uttered a word about the tunnels.

The Dean moves on, "… as a first-class academy, Palmer prepares you for college…and life through sacrifice, hard work and discipline. Maintaining your individuality is our goal, but not," here he points a forefinger to the ceiling, "at the cost of conformity, unity of the school and what it stands for…a tradition more than a hundred fifty years old. I want to inspire you to search deep within yourselves to find the meaning of education, what it means for each one of you, how it prepares you for your goals. We must place most of the burden on our first-classmen to lead the school's activities, teach the younger generations of lower classmen to be future leaders."

What's the guy talking about? I zone out again and scan the crowd.

Most cadets look comatose. I discover Muller three rows ahead to the right, his neck stretched long, doubtlessly catching every syllable the Dean utters. The thought of Saturday's drill inspection makes me cringe. Muller has the power of making my life miserable for one more semester. Then I'll finally become an oldman. *If* I make it 'till then. I sigh. Almost five months to go.

As the Dean continues I suppress a yawn. The air is hot, most of the oxygen consumed. Hard to believe I've only been back from winter break for a day. I've already destroyed two outfits, gotten lost and been in a fight.

I must be mad. On the drive down here, I made up my mind to do well. That is obviously not going to happen. I'm on my way to a disastrous semester. I sigh again.

"What's the matter?" Tom whispers. "You groan like a freight train."

"Just thinking it's a lousy year already."

Plozett cuffs my other side. "Shhh."

He's right. Better to shut up and wait, not be made an example of in front of the school. What time is it? For once I look for a clock but don't see one. My mind wanders to Maddie. I'll go next Sunday, unless something else happens.

I've never seen eyes so intensely blue…a mouth that curls up on one side to mock me. I'll invite her to the movies or something. What do other guys do to interest a girl?

My middle begins to tighten. I abruptly arrange my jacket, which is thankfully long, and fold my hands on my lap. A boner during the Dean's speech is the last thing I need. Rumor has it that our food is spiked with saltpeter to curb the sex drive of eight hundred adolescents. I wonder if it's true. *Saltpeter is surely no match for Maddie.* I grin to myself.

"… and let's remember that tradition and a commitment to excellence should guide every one of our steps, every day. Good night."

The room erupts in applause from 1,600 hands, plus the assorted faculty. Around me chairs screech and feet shuffle.

"Let's hurry. I'm starving," I yell over the swelling noise of cadet chatter. "I don't want to stand in line for hours."

We successfully wiggle around several cadets before coming to a halt by the exit doors. By the time we reach the mess hall, dozens of cadets, trays in hand, stand waiting.

"Too slow," I say. "Did you catch anything the Dean said?"

"Not really." Tom yanks off his gloves and loosens his collar. "I'll be glad when I can get out of these clothes. The stupid collar has a mind of its own and tries to choke me."

We fall silent as the Dean passes by on his way to the faculty dining area. I hear applause when he approaches.

"He gives me the creeps," Tom says. "He'd make a great assassin."

"I heard he has ties to the CIA," says Plozett.

Tom stops fixing his belt. "Doesn't surprise me. I bet the CIA is busy in Vietnam."

"Doing what?" I ask.

"Black ops, intelligence stuff. Who knows?"

Plozett fishes three trays from the buffet line. "Why don't you ask Sarge? Isn't he your buddy?"

"He never said anything. Besides, isn't that classified?" I scan the food offerings ahead: creamed corn, roast beef, fried potatoes, mixed salad and chocolate pudding. At least we can always count on eating well.

"Wonder what happened," says Tom. "When he'll be back?"

"He's gone?" Plozett asks.

"Nobody's seen him, right?" Tom asks me while I'm trying to fit a second helping of potatoes on my plate.

"That's what I heard."

"Bummer," Plozett says. "At least his class was entertaining. Maybe he'll arrive late."

What if he doesn't? I remain quiet, surprised to feel sad at the prospect of never seeing Sarge again.

"Let's eat."

CHAPTER TWELVE

I stare out the window. Campus has disappeared under a blanket of white—even the air is milky with frost. The lake has turned into an expanse of ice that blends with a whitewashed horizon, making the school feel like an island amid a frozen world. When the ice is thick enough, we use our spiked running shoes to visit the ice fishermen who settle in a patchwork of huts. It's forbidden to go onto the ice, but considered *harmless* fun by the faculty.

I've been extra careful, prepping for room inspections to avoid demerits and marching extra duty in this weather. Strangely, Muller seems less inclined to find fault with my room.

Every few days I pass by Sarge's office, always hoping to see him lumber across the hall, a fat cigar in his mouth. But the door remains stubbornly closed.

I've taken up chess with Tom and occasionally with Plozett who annoys me with his obsession for body building. On Sunday evenings, Plozett produces a measuring tape and wraps it around his biceps and thighs. One time, I asked him if he was training for Mr. Universe. After all, Plozett showed me a poster of *Arnold Schwarzenegger* he's hidden in his desk. He even keeps detailed charts of workout routines, weights and measurements. Anyway, Plozett got all red in the face. I could swear Plozett shaves his legs like a girl.

I haven't been to town except for one brief visit a few Sundays ago when the weather warmed enough to make the air breathable. Maddie was in the store, but seemed distracted and returned to stacking gloves and wool hats after selling me licorice.

In my dreams, she always smiles. Sometimes her face is close, but I always wake before she kisses me. Still I'm turned on, aching for relief as soon as Plozett leaves the room. Pathetic that I don't even know her last name or really anything about her.

School goes on in never-ending routines, classes from eight to four, sports and evening study. Each morning we start again until my days become mindless routines of marching and studying—a thousand structured activities.

I want to scream with boredom, yet I feel drained as if the school is sucking away my energy. I'm not thinking much of home these days nor do I care that my mother's letters arrive less frequently. I'm not even sure I like being home anymore. I'm not sure of anything.

On Saturday evenings, when I hang out with Tom at the cave, we watch the news about Vietnam—soldiers marching and rappelling from helicopters, the peace protests, thousands of people demonstrating together, shouting discontent.

My parents would never openly complain about anything, definitely not march and shout or sit silently among a forest of handmade signs. I secretly chuckle, imagining my dad next to the longhaired hippies singing and smoking weed. I admire them the most, living without rules and doing what they want. My family neither smokes nor swears. They don't even have beer in the house. Ever.

I wonder what Sarge is doing and if he'll show up on TV among the grave men talking politics. He remains missing and nobody seems to know where he is or if he'll return. Not even Tony who is usually well informed about what goes on in the faculty building.

Tom sits next to me as we listen to the casualty reports and the growing disapproval ratings of President Nixon. He shakes his head and mumbles but never says anything. It's the one subject we avoid.

By April the football team moves outside to practice sprints and short games until we're drenched and coated with muck.

"We'll see who wins," Tony White shouts in the locker room. The air is thick with the stench of sweaty uniforms. "It's a tradition. Every year, the sophomores and juniors compete in a canoe race. We're all going."

"But I don't know how to paddle," one of the sophomores says. "My family has a sailboat."

"Pussy," Big Mike hollers. Roars of laughter erupt around me. "Loser," Big Mike adds, feeling emboldened by his buddies. More whistles. Next to dickhead, pussy has got to be Big Mike's favorite word.

"Learn from the others and find a partner," Tony says. "We better come in first. The race is Saturday. Remember, we stick together. The football team must win!" The room echoes with more hollering and whistling.

I glance around. Despite training and playing with the team for months, I don't feel particularly excited about canoeing with any of them. I want to go with Tom, even if Tom hasn't seen a canoe in his life. I'll be good enough for the both of us. Besides, Tom is smart and will learn quickly.

"Olson, who are you going with?" Tony yells above the chatter.

I shrug. Somehow I don't want Tony to know that I'm an expert canoeist who's spent countless hours on scout outings. I won lots of races during the annual summer camps.

Tony materializes next to me and shoves me in the shoulder. "What're you waiting for?" He points at Peter Linnehan, one of the defensive players who mostly warms the bench. *"He* needs a partner. Go with him."

Tony looks irritated but then he always gets bent out of shape over nothing. I slowly nod.

***

Race day starts with overcast skies that threaten rain. A cool wind blows across the lawns as our busses roll from the parking lot. We're heading for Blue River, a tributary of the Ohio. Trailers loaded with canoes follow our busses which wind through the narrow roads of southern Indiana.

I stare out the window, ignoring my canoe mate, Peter, who participated in the race last year. I imagine arriving first and enjoying the picnic lunch the school dishes up at the park. I've heard they do all sorts of delicacies like brownies and fried chicken, potato salad and apple pie. My mouth waters. I want to win, beat Tony and Big Mike. Badly. They'll be mad, but probably secretly admire me.

"We have a good chance," Peter whispers. He's bragged about his experience from last year.

I grin. "Big Mike will load down their canoe with his fat ass."

"I told Tony you are an expert," Peter says proudly. "We'll be eating dessert by the time the others get there."

I swallow a nasty comment. Peter is an idiot. As we scramble from the bus, Tony is yelling commands and ordering people to unload the canoes. My irritation grows. The sooner we leave, the better our chances.

"Move," Big Mike bellows. "Pick it up, dickhead." He towers next to Tony instead of helping. A canoe lands on somebody's foot, followed by cries and curses.

Tony shouts over the din. "Over there, drop the damn boats along the shore."

More buses arrive, but I don't pay attention. They'll be behind us on the water and they surely won't catch us.

Tony studies a clip board and assigns canoes. Each has a number painted in navy blue.

"Linnehan, Olson, 65."

I shove Peter in the side. "Let's go. Hurry."

The first dozen canoes have already taken off. Some are struggling to get away from the muddy banks and the limestone overhangs near the starting point. A couple of teams are moving in circles as neither of them knows how to steer.

I smile. We'll be gone in no time.

"I'll take the back," I yell at Peter. The water flows dark and fast, a remainder of last winter's heavy snows and not at all blue like its name. I grab the paddle and guide us away from shore to put distance between us and the later groups. The shouting quiets as our canoe channels into faster water.

"Don't slack off," I yell. Peter's movements are entirely too slow.

"I want to conserve energy. It's a long race. At least two hours."

"Maybe it wouldn't take so long if you'd paddle faster." I eye the water inside the canoe. Can't remember if we tracked it in when we started. It sloshes back and forth, licking at the rubber soles of my shoes. I dip the oar hard, ignoring the low throbbing in my shoulder. I'll ice it when we get back. For now I'll enjoy myself and show the others how it's done.

Within three minutes I know something is wrong. The water level inside the canoe has risen to an inch. Big Mike and Tony pass us.

"Tired already," Big Mike yells.

I silently swear. This isn't at all what I envisioned—we're falling behind.

"We must have a leak," I shout against the wind. "Let's stop at the next sandbar. I've got to find out what's wrong."

"Do we have anything to bail with?" Peter asks.

Of course, we've got nothing.

A gravelly spit appears to our left. "Over there, hurry." The water inside splashes as I jump out. "Let's turn it over." I run my forefinger along the seam underneath the canoe which is covered with a strip of aluminum. "Shit. See this?"

Peter bends low to inspect the bottom. "Looks like a cut."

"No kidding."

A tear like a knife wound—black against the gray metal—is partially hidden underneath the flashing that runs along the underside of the canoe. I push against the strip, trying to force it down. It doesn't budge. I pick up a rock and pound. Nothing. I need glue or something to seal the damn leak— at least chewing gum which, of course, is forbidden in school. I remember the gum balls in the general store. We might as well be on another planet.

"Let's go," I say. "We'll paddle as fast as possible."

Water seeps inside as soon as we take off.

"I'm freezing," Peter says.

I feel my heart beat in my neck. "It's going to get a lot colder if you don't move faster. You remind me of my grandfather."

"My hands are getting sore."

I swallow another insult. I'm beginning to sound like Tony. With every minute the water level rises and pushes the canoe lower. Paddling becomes harder, like moving a submerged log against the current. Sweat drips from my forehead. My toes are submerged. I can't feel them.

I point at the sandbank to our right. "Let's dump the water over there." My legs are ice by the time we climb back in. "Turn around," I order. "You'll have to paddle backwards. Put your foot on the hole and push down. I can't reach it from my seat."

A dozen canoes pass us, hollering with glee. Peter struggles with the paddle, while shoving his foot against the flashing. The water keeps coming.

"It's not working."

I feel fresh anger rising. Peter barely helps moving the canoe. "Turn around. I'll have to come up with something else." My cheeks burn despite the cold wind.

Water seeps in steadily now as if someone opened a hose. I try to think of ways to stop the leak. Anything to reduce the flow.

"Look for trash," I say.

"Trash?"

"Something to stuff in the hole."

We stop again, empty the boat and take off. The sides of the creek grow wilder. Poison ivy covered limestone formations tower on both sides, forcing the water to run faster through the narrowed riverbed. The river gurgles and spews, oblivious to our struggles. I aim for the strongest current to take advantage of the speeding water. Though we travel more rapidly now, the water level inside the canoe continues to rise. More canoes pass us accompanied by victorious shouts.

I anxiously scan the steep limestone. "Faster!" No place to stop, no sandbanks either. The canoe sags lower, its weight dragging us down.

"Over there, in the branches." Peter points at a pile of debris, pieces of logs, sticks and something fluttering in the breeze.

"I see it." I push hard to make the canoe move sideways, but it's like moving a raft with a soup ladle.

"We're going under," Peter shouts. I stare in horror at my submerged feet.

We'll never make it.

Whether one of us moves too much or the weight is too great, the canoe gives way and disappears, icy water sloshing over my head. For a split second I hear the sand grinding below, the swish of water rushing between rocks and the splashes from Peter.

The river is much deeper than I expected and I kick hard to get to the surface. Forcing my eyes to remain open against the freezing burn, I come up sputtering. The icy water takes my breath, crawls inside my shirt and underneath my skin. I gasp and suck air, aware of every fiber of my body. Our canoe is nearly submerged.

"Shit." Peter thrashes near me. I look up just as Peter's paddle slips past him and out of reach, gaining speed.

"Idiot!" I gasp to force air into my lungs. "Grab the canoe and pull it up, then tilt."

I fight to stay calm, but my body is rigid with fear. It's as if each cell has turned to slush and moves me closer to hypothermia.

Treading in place, we manage to lift and tilt the boat, slowly releasing the water. I pull myself up and climb inside. The wind whips my wet hair and I shiver so hard that I can barely grip the paddle. I want nothing more than to give up right now. Go home and take a nap in my warm bed. It isn't going to happen.

"Keep looking for stuff," I shout instead. "Take off your shirt and sop up the water."

"But I'll be even colder."

"Hardly possible. Why didn't you wear a sweater?" When a gravelly island appears in the middle, we stop and unload. I take off my sweatshirt, squeeze out the water and throw it at Peter. "Use that."

"You don't have to yell. Can't we just wait here until they get us?" Peter's lips are bluish and tremble.

I scan the deserted banks downstream. "They can't reach us here." I want to explode. "No roads, lots of undergrowth and no place to get in or out. We must reach the park."

I run back the way we came and climb through undergrowth and vines. Leaning across a stack of logs, I grab hold of a plastic sack.

Back on the riverbank, we turn the canoe on its side.

"I'll stick the end through and you grab it from the other side." I crush the material together. The plastic is rotten and tears, refusing to slide through the gash. "Shit. It's probably been here ten years. Let's find something better. I wish we could walk and carry the damn thing."

The overgrowth has a greenish tint. Honey suckle and poison ivy wind around tulip and sassafras trees. Blackberry, spice and black elderberry bushes form a brownish wall. Even if we were able to climb the rocks, there is no way to carry a boat through the thicket.

I feel frozen to the bone. Shivers run in waves through my limbs and no matter how hard I try, the trembling never stops. I squeeze the paddle, afraid to lose my grip, lose the one tool we need to move forward.

I wonder if I made the right decision to go on. Palmer might send a search party, but it'll be hours away even if we wait. The sky looks gray with rain, the clouds menacing, bulky and thick with water. We'll sit here and freeze to death.

"Let's go," I say. Being still is worse than paddling. "How much farther?"

"Don't remember," Peter says. "Look, my paddle." He points downstream.

"You guys need help?" Tom and his partner are gaining on us fast. Tom looks awkward with his knees high on the seat, but he seems to do well enough steering through the rapids. "We got the hang of it. We're the last ones," he shouts.

"Go on," I say, "tell the others we have a leak. We'll be there soon."

"Maybe you should join us," Tom says, attempting to make a stop on the gravel.

"Then we'll all sink. You can't take two more."

"You want us to wait with you?" Tom says.

I shake my head. "No need to make you late. We'll finish somehow."

Tom looks doubtful. "You'll freeze."

"Tell me about it. You wouldn't happen to have any gum or a bottle of superglue?"

Tom shakes his head.

"Go on," I say when Tom hesitates. "We have to go too or we'll get even colder.

"All right then." Tom pushes off. "I'll tell them."

For the fiftieth time I feel thankful for my canoeing experience with the Scouts. Pushing hard against the current, I force the sluggish craft toward Peter's paddle, stuck in an assemblage of branches along the bank.

"Keep looking for a can or a cup or something to bail with," I shout. The canoe continues to fill and I worry about capsizing again.

"For once there's no trash," Peter says as he retrieves the paddle. The riverbank is clean except for piles of driftwood and last year's fallen leaves.

"I wonder what time it is." I look at the sky, trying to gauge the sun's position, but the gray above is only slightly lighter than the murkiness below. I can't go on much longer. My body is fighting back, the muscles in my arms and legs like cordwood, hard and rigid. My feet no longer belong to me.

Every time we round a bend, my hope rises. The park is supposed to be on the left, but nothing appears except empty forest and brush. Normally I love the woods, the quiet of the trees, the occasional chatter of birds and squirrels. Now it's torture. I wonder why our canoe is leaking when all the others are fine. Something nags at the back of my mind, but I've got to concentrate my last shred of energy on paddling.

I worry about finding enough sandbars and low banks. I can't handle another bath. Several times, the water climbs to our ankles. Every inch of my skin screams for attention. My hair is glued to my skull and every move reminds me that my legs and arms are wet, rubbing against the sopping cloth of my pants and shirt. The skin under my arms burns from chafing.

I try imagining something warm, like the bonfire my grandfather lights every fall on the farm and the hot chocolate my mother makes for Christmas, topped with marshmallows, sweetness melting in your mouth.

Instantly I'm back on the river, my body demanding to be relieved of the torture.

"I can't go on." Peter sits down and empties his shoes. We've stopped for the hundredth time, a drizzle adding dampness from above. "They can get us if they want or we can just walk on and leave the damn boat. I'll never canoe again in my life."

"It'd take hours for someone to find us. They'd have to go to the beginning and paddle the entire way. You have any idea how long that'll take? We'll freeze." I scrutinize the vegetation above. "We'll be quicker on the water."

I want nothing more than to give up and forget about this nightmare. Still I can't sit here and wait. "Come on, let's go. It can't be much farther."

"Maybe they'll leave without us." Peter looks downstream as if he can see the buses pulling out.

"Nonsense. They'll do a count and notice we're missing. Besides Tom will tell them."

Time turns into oblivion. Nothing matters but the movement of paddling, the sloshing of water inside the boat, the gurgling of the river around us. By the time I hear shouts, my shoulders have turned into fiery lumps, my legs stiff as if my veins are filled with ice.

"Olson, you're a disgrace. What happened to you?" Tony sneers. "You know what time it is? The other buses left, but we had to wait 'cause you were on *our* bus. The football team was supposed to win."

I want to smack Tony, but I want to be warm even more. Besides, I've got no strength left. Shivers crawl up my spine and I drag myself up the hill. While a couple of cadets take our canoe, I scan the picnic tables: nothing except bare wood.

"Sorry, too late," Tony says. "It's 13:30. We finished everything hours ago."

I only stare. Despite his insults, Tony looks pleased, shoving Big Mike in the side and play-tackling some of the other teammates. A dull ache of suspicion begins to grow in my mind. Has Tony sabotaged our canoe? We've all been assigned one from a list Tony kept. What if…

"Into the bus, quick," the driver says. "Cadet White, stop wasting time and round up the others."

"Yes, Sir," Tony says, immediately shouting orders.

The return trip on the bus seems to take longer still, exhaustion creeping into my body, making me heavy. I long to sleep, but the wet fabric hangs on me like sticky sand and keeps me awake. Peter seems even worse. He's slumped into his seat, his face pale as milk.

The hot shower water burns as I rub my skin back to life. My ears and toes tingle. Scenes of the race, of Tony and Big Mike float into my mind. Now that I'm beginning to feel human again, I think of the canoe, the strange slit. I can't be sure. Why would Tony do that when he says he wants the football team to win? I rub my head to make the thought go away, but the feeling of doubt remains. I watch the watery steam that hangs in wafts around the white-tiled washroom when I see movement. Markus, the shy freshman from next door, is waving at me.

I stick my head away from the gushing water. "What?"

"Sergeant Russel wants to see you."

I manage a nod. Sarge is back. Where in the world has he been and why? I grin. Despite this having been one of the lousiest in a string of lousy days, I feel a surge of excitement.

CHAPTER THIRTEEN

Sarge's door is closed. Made of dark oak, it reminds me of a fortress. I wonder what Sarge wants, if he'll suggest new lessons. Maybe he'll thank me for the compass. With a sigh I knock.

"Ah, Olson, come in." Sarge stands by the window. "I heard you took a cold bath today," he grumbles. "You're tough. Great preparation for the jungle. Except it's putrid water, warm as piss."

"Yes, Sir," I manage, covering my surprise. How can the man already know about my rotten day? Sarge is pale, the pockets under his eyes puffy shadows. Except for the reddened eyelids, he stares with the same fierceness.

Sagging into his chair he waves a hand. "Sit."

I plunk down.

"You got into a fight with Muller. What's the matter with you?"

I'm equally pleased and shocked: pleased that Sarge is still interested in me, shocked that he already seems to know about my every move. I wonder who's told and if there's some thick file about me. Has he talked to Beerbelly? I have a hard time believing Sarge likes guys like Muller. Even if Muller is Mr. Perfect.

"I'm listening," Sarge barks.

"Sir, I'm sorry, Sir. Muller took my...your compass—it made me mad."

Sarge sighs and leans back. "You're a plebe. He's *your* superior officer."

"He was going to keep it. I worried he'd not give it back. He..." In hindsight it seems ludicrous. Of course, Muller would've returned the compass. He'd never risk being accused of stealing.

"Without self-control you've got no chance. What if we all flipped out when we didn't like something or someone?"

Sarge stares at me. He's never lectured like this. I open and close my mouth. Somehow I know it isn't a good idea to explain further.

"Instead of fighting the enemy we'd knock each other out. Unacceptable!" he thunders.

I want to look away but can't. I just sit and wait, feeling smaller by the second. The room turns quiet. I've really done it now, made Sarge stinking mad. I didn't expect this. Not after the ordeal this morning. Surely, Sarge knows what a jerk Muller is.

"We learn to live with people we don't like. Respect them," Sarge says as if he's heard my thoughts. "At a minimum we respect their rank. It better not happen again." He smacks a hand on top of the desk. "Enough said."

I nod and get up.

"Sit, Olson. I'm not finished."

I lower myself. The knot in my throat is tightening. I can't take anymore. Not from Sarge.

Sarge leans forward and raises a forefinger. "Leadership is one of the most important traits of a good soldier." He pauses. I can't tell if it's for effect or from exhaustion. "If you want to get ahead, become an officer, you've got to learn how to take charge. Next Saturday, you're going to be one of the trip leaders—for your bus. You show me what you're made of."

"Trip leaders?" Somehow my brain isn't working right. I still reel from being chewed out. The hollow in my stomach churns.

"We're going on an excursion. You'll get details later."

"Of course, Sir, thank you, Sir," I stammer as new excitement floods in.

"Dismissed."

I jump up to leave.

"And Olson, get your act together. No more screw-ups."

"Yes, Sir."

Back in the hall, I sigh. I'll have another chance to work with Sarge. Get on his good side. Except I forgot to ask where we're going. And Sarge hasn't said where he's been, either. I scold myself for being tongue-tied once again. Why didn't I ask why he looked so tired, how long he's been back? I haven't learned a thing.

Walking back I stare at the clock—15:35.

"Shit!" I mutter, breaking into a jog. Tom will be mad. We wanted to leave at three to catch the second afternoon show. Tom has been planning the trip to town all week to catch the latest movie. It isn't new because the theatre only shows one movie at a time and changes its program every other week at most.

Who cares? We'll get away from Palmer. And maybe…see Maddie.

Tom sits fully dressed at his desk, rifling through Look magazine with John Lennon and Yoko Ono on the cover. His long legs are propped on the bottom frame of the bed.

"Sorry, man," I say, ignoring Toad who's reading some spy novel, his nose about two inches from the page. He looks soft as a pale peach. "Had to report to Sarge."

"He's back?" Tom puts down his book.

"Yeah, I just ran late with the stupid race and cleaning up."

"Where's he been?" Tom unfolds his legs and grabs his coat.

I shrug. "He looks terrible. Like he caught some disease."

"Quite possible. Vietnam is full of critters and Agent Orange, courtesy of the U.S. Armed Forces. Maybe he's stressed out. Lots of guys go nuts. When they return, they just flip, don't fit into the neat classes of society anymore."

I nod, wondering if that's why Sarge acted so mad. My shoulders ache and I still feel cold, but I'm thinking of Maddie.

"I'm ready—we better run."

"You should ask him," Tom says as we hurry across campus.

"Who?"

"Sarge. Ask him what he's been up to?"

"Maybe I will." But I know I'll never muster the nerve unless… What if I do really well leading the fieldtrip with Sarge? We'll hang out together and afterwards…

I see myself in Sarge's office chewing a cigar, listening to his war stories. I'd make smart comments and then casually ask where Sarge has been and if he's okay. I smile. Life is getting better after all. The trees are turning green. The air smells of promises of spring, full of unknowns that make me giddy. I'm thankful for the dry warmth covering my skin.

"What happened this morning?" Tom asks. "I thought you were supposed to be really good."

"The canoe leaked and Linnehan was slow as a snail."

Tom listens as I recount my ordeal. "You don't suppose somebody cut your boat?"

"Why would somebody do that?" I say, not mentioning that I had the same idea.

"So you wouldn't win, of course. Quit being so gullible." Tom sounds angry.

I consider Tony's snide comments, the clip board. How he runs the show. He obviously had the opportunity.

We approach the store and I get distracted. "Give me a minute. I need to buy something to hold me over 'till dinner."

"I'll reserve seats. Hurry."

I have already opened the door. The store looks the same, dusty and silent. I move to the counter where chocolate bars are stacked in a crisscross pattern like miniature logs. Nothing moves. I grab three bars and amble toward the back.

"Hello?"

Somebody is moving behind the curtain. Maybe it's Maddie. So what if I miss the first few minutes of the movie?

A shadowy figure emerges. It's the old man, Maddie's dad.

"Need more Zero bars?"

"Yes, Sir."

The man squints at me. "Sixty-nine cents. Don't they feed you anything in that fancy school of yours?"

"I missed lunch," I say.

The man keeps staring.

I fiddle with my wallet. "Here." Including Christmas money, my stash has built to more than fifteen dollars.

"One penny's your change."

I glance toward the back, still hoping to see Maddie. But the store feels like a tomb and I'm suddenly glad to leave. "Bye."

Slamming shut the door I dart down the street, throwing one last look at the apartment above. New red and white checkered curtains cover the glass in lifeless pleats.

My timing was lousy once again.

CHAPTER FOURTEEN

All week I wait to find out about the excursion, but Sarge rushes past in the hall several times as if he doesn't even see me. After class he leaves in a hurry. With every day passing, I get more nervous. Maybe Sarge has changed his mind.

"Fieldtrip tomorrow," Sarge announces Friday afternoon. "This class and two of Mr. Brown's will travel to Evansville. I expect every man on his best behavior. Class B uniform, assembly at 08:00. We leave at 08:30 sharp."

A low buzz of mumbles spreads across the classroom.

"Sir, what're we going to do?" somebody asks.

"We'll visit the Evansville Museum. You boys need some culture, a taste of history and art. Olson, here, will keep an eye on the younger boys. Talk to him, if you need something or have a question."

I feel eyes on me and my cheeks grow hot. Nice of Sarge to put me on the spot without warning.

"Sucker," somebody mumbles close to me.

"Dismissed," Sarge thunders upfront. I duck beneath my desk for my bag. "Olson, a word."

"Yes, Sir." I'm glad the classroom empties quickly.

"Just watch the young guys. Understand. Tell them if they get out of line, too loud, roughhousing, you know what I mean. Find me if you run into trouble. I'm counting on your help."

"Sure."

"See you in the morning."

"Yes, Sir."

***

After evening study, I rush to find Tom. How could I've been excited about being a trip leader? Tony and Big Mike will laugh and ignore me, Muller will make sniveling remarks. They'll embarrass me in front of the group. In

89

front of Sarge. Why haven't I come up with an excuse why I can't do it? With a grimace I wipe my damp forehead.

"What if they ask me stuff I don't know?" I say aloud. "They won't listen to me. You know how some of them act."

"You'll have to put your foot down," Tom says. "Look on the bright side. You don't have to worry about me. I'll be the model of a Palmer cadet."

"Very funny."

"Seriously, I'll watch with you. Surely they have a bunch of faculty going."

***

When reveille sounds at 06:30, I wake from a deep sleep. I race to shower before the horde of cadets descends on the washrooms. Nervous anticipation makes my movements jerky. In my room, the uniform hangs waiting in perfection. I've prepared all week, brushed my jacket, polished brass buttons and the eagle on my hat. My gloves and shirt are new and my shoes gleam. Not even Muller can find fault in my outfit today.

The drive to Evansville is much shorter than I expected. I sit up front, watching and listening to the first rows, but it's mostly quiet except for a few low voices mixing with the sound of the diesel engine. Most are sleepy after the week's stringent routine.

We park near the art museum. I review the paired rows of cadets lining up in front of the bus, looking at Sarge who nods approval. After signaling Mr. Brown we march to the entrance. Once inside, we're allowed to mingle and study the art exhibits, sculptures and natural history section. I keep glancing at Sarge who ignores me and walks off with Mr. Brown.

Tony and Big Mike are giggling in front of a nude painting. After scanning the room for faculty, Big Mike moves his hips forward and back, making moaning sounds. The woman in the painting looks old and fat. Maddie's face emerges in my vision and I smile.

Tony hollers and slaps me on the shoulder. "Olson, what's so funny. What're you doing with Sarge, anyway? You his new pet?"

"Suck-ass," Big Mike says.

"Just helping out," I say. I want to tell them to shut their mouths, but I'm liable to get destroyed during next practice.

Muller's prim face appears in the distance, followed by his cousin from the cavalry and more guys from the football team. Muller will get a kick out of me for failing to supervise Tony and Big Mike. Time to go. No need to give him satisfaction.

"Keep it down," I say before rushing off.

I hurry past a bunch of weird paintings, abstract scribbles, created by crazy foreigners and stop at the exhibits and artifacts from the pioneer days of early U.S. history. American Indians, faces painted white and red, stand in front of a teepee, the fake camp fire glowing orange. An overstuffed bison towers nearby, his glass eyes coated with dust. Life-sized posters of a herd cover the wall behind.

Most cadets stroll around in groups of two and three. Tempered giggles, a few scuffs. Mr. Brown lurks nearby and I sigh with relief. This is easier than I thought. I'll hang with Tom this afternoon, maybe still make it to Garville. I'll stop by the store. Not that it does any good. It's easier to win the lottery than to run into the girl.

"You have an hour to visit the town," Mr. Helms announces as we reassemble in the lobby. He's accompanied us along with Sarge and Mr. Brown. "Keep your purchases to a minimum. The busses are crowded as it is. Stay in groups of two. It's 11:00 now. We'll meet in front of this building at 12:00 sharp and walk to the park for our picnic lunch. Pay attention where you're going so you can find your way back here."

"Let's look for a bakery. I could use something sweet," Tom says.

"Sounds good." I automatically fall in step next to Tom. It's no longer hard to walk in formation. The late April sun feels warm on my face as we head downtown. Ornamental cherry trees line the sidewalks with puffs of blossoms, their petals creating a carpet of pink underfoot. We follow the first group of students, Tony and Big Mike who rush ahead and a handful of brownnosers who circle Mr. Helms and Mr. Brown. Nobody wants to hang out with Sarge who looks right through them and waves away students like buzzing mosquitoes.

As we round the corner to Main Street, a swell of voices hits us.

Instead of cars, hundreds of men and women crowd the road. They hold signs and banners, spill onto sidewalks and into shop entrances, walk between parked vehicles and benches, slowed by the people in front and pushed forward by the masses behind.

"Stop the fighting," they yell in chorus. "No more war." They surge against us, threatening to pull us along. The air vibrates with fury and passion. The noise swells and falls in waves as the men and women shout. They walk slowly, a leisurely stroll of thousands.

I remember the protests on TV, but this is way more intense. I can almost taste the rage—feel the energy of the crowd.

A loudspeaker crackles. "Leave Vietnam," the voice says. "Stop killing." The crowd responds, turning into deafening shouts, *leave Vietnam, stop killing."*

For a moment I worry about our safety. What if these people charge us? The government makes them look like savages. Yet, these protesters look intelligent, some like college kids and housewives, others with long hair and beards—and not much older than us.

I remember Tom and find him squeezed against the window of a shoe store, eyes twinkling with fascination. I push through the crowd to join him.

"Weed," Tom says dryly, nodding at a guy near us lighting up. I breathe deeply and hope for a buzz. All I know is that it makes you relaxed and happy. I can use a mega dose of both.

Sarge's words resound in my head. "You're a leader." But all I can think of is the crowd swaying in front of us. How can I watch my classmates, when I can't *see* them?

I wait. Crossing the street is impossible. The mob blocks everything. Banners sway in a cloud of dust. Handmade signs dance.

"Make peace, not war," a man shouts a few feet away. Driven closer by the crowd, he stares at me. His long hair tangles with the reddish-brown beard that covers most of a rainbow-colored t-shirt. His jeans have holes and a large tear across the knee. He looks tanned and wears sandals as if he's been on the beach.

"Look at these guys," the bearded man hollers. A few demonstrators stop and gape at us.

"You know what you're doing?" a woman yells, her voice shrill against the hum of the crowd. Her red bandana has slipped low over her forehead, the charcoal peace symbol painted like a target between her eyebrows.

I don't know whether to ignore them or say something. I look at Tom who grins and seems curiously relaxed.

Shouts erupt nearby. Tony and Big Mike appear for a moment, and then vanish behind a wall of signs waving and hitting the overhanging roofs. I can hear them yell something, but their voices are drowned out by the racket.

I've got to stop them. I'll be blamed if anything happens. Behind us, Sarge barrels his way through the pack. Whistles sound from across the street. A group of police with helmets and sticks push toward a group of protesters sitting on the sidewalk. More shouts.

"Peace."

"Love."

A few farmers stand watching in front of a farm supply store, their faces weathered reddish leather from decades spent outdoors.

"Cadets, walk. Move!" Sarge bellows from behind. "Straight ahead. Don't stop." I notice Mr. Helms waving from down the street before he disappears from view behind a banner carried by two women. It reads, "*No More Killing! Save the troops.*"

I feel somebody shove me in the back, but it's Peter Linnehan who looks frightened and wiggles past without a word. The mob grows thicker, spilling around us.

"March," Sarge thunders again from the back.

I watch for an opening. "Stay with me," I yell to Tom. I'm ready to use fists and elbows.

"Maybe we should go inside the store and wait there," Tom says, his eyes bright and fixed on the mayhem.

I shake my head. "I've got to find the other cadets."

I look back, but Sarge has stopped moving. He's surrounded by a group of demonstrators.

"Peace, man, take it easy," they shout. "Let's talk about the war."

"Got to go." Sarge shakes his head and pushes away the arms that want to engage him. "Another time." His face looks frozen, his eyes a mix of contempt and anger.

"Relax. What's the rush?" the red-bearded man shouts. Two police officers are weaving across the street and closing in. I stand bolted to the spot. Sarge stares at the hippies, eyes squinting with rage. I wonder why the demonstrators aren't afraid. I'd have taken off ages ago.

A policeman materializes next to Sarge and waves a baton above the bearded man's head. "Get moving!"

Sarge pushes to find an opening, but three of the demonstrators lock arms in front of him. "Let me through," he yells.

"Peace, man," the red-bearded hippie says.

Another officer makes it to the group. "What's going on?"

Sarge opens his mouth, when one of the demonstrators raises his arm to wave his sign. "END THE VIOLENCE," it says. In the narrow space, the sign makes contact with Sarge's shoulder. He swipes at it, its corner smacking the officer with the baton.

In reflex the policeman strikes the red-bearded hippie's face. The man's nose bursts into a bloody spray, his arm flailing as he grabs for Sarge to steady himself. The second officer jumps in. He smacks the hippie's hand from Sarge's arm like a nasty fly, sending the protester to the ground.

The other demonstrators plop down next to the red-bearded man who's raised his arms to ward off more strikes. His nose is dripping red on his jeans and the bare spot on his knee.

Their shouts, "no violence, stop the war," are muffled behind the wall of bodies.

I keep watching the red-bearded hippie as more demonstrators press closer, their chorus getting louder. I can't decide whether to feel sorry or angry with the man. The hippie continues to duck, his arms raised as if he were praying. Surely he has to be scared.

Whistles sound. The sitting demonstrators remain still while the officers hover above them with raised batons. Sarge grumbles something and steps across them, making eye contact with me.

"What're you waiting for?" he growls and hurries past.

"Let's go," I shout at Tom who's still next to me. I rush to follow Sarge who moves through the people like an army tank on rocket fuel. Now I'm behind Sarge, my classmates missing somewhere in front. I've totally screwed up.

"I wish we didn't have to wear these." Tom looks down the front of his jacket. "It's like waving a red flag in front of a herd of bulls."

"Nicely put. You think they'd beat us up?"

"Doubt it," Tom says. "All I've seen is the police starting fights when the protesters hold up the traffic. Or they arrest them for disturbing the peace and smoking weed."

I don't answer because I'm too worked up about catching Sarge. I want to tear off my uniform and melt into the background, get one of the coveralls the farmers wear year-round.

Where are the others? I search for the shaved heads or caps of my classmates and think I see Tony.

The mass finally thins enough that the sidewalk becomes free. A group of invalids follows behind the protesters. Some hobble on crutches, some sit in wheelchairs, their faces pale against bandages and patches, their mouths pinched. Two who look normal to me carry a sign *Vietnam Veterans Against the War*.

I notice one of the men, his eyes hidden under a mass of black curls and beard. I stop when the man looks up and meets my gaze. It's Eric from the store in Garville, Maddie's brother. He shakes his head and throws up an arm in what seems like a mix of threat and greeting. He then looks away, continuing to roll down the middle of Main Street like it's the most normal thing to do.

"What're *you* doing here?"

I wheel around. Maddie stares at me in disbelief. I gape back. She has changed. Her hair is shorter, shoulder-length, and caresses her cheeks. She wears a hint of eye shadow, creating a sea of blue I want to dive into.

I search for something interesting to say, but "Hi," is all that comes out.

Maddie's eyes squint with disapproval as if I've got no right to be here. For the first time, I notice how much she looks like her brother.

"We, our class went to the muse—"

Shouts and whistles explode behind us. Several officers are wrestling with a protester who is lying flat on the ground, his face pressed into the dirt.

"You shouldn't be here," Maddie says. She shields her eyes against the sun, her mouth turned down in scorn. Without the store counter between us, I'm a foot taller.

"I wish I wasn't," I say. "Not like this…" I point at my jacket with the million brass buttons and the cap I've stuck under my arm. "We didn't know about the protest."

Maddie's eyes rove across my uniform. "Obviously. I have to go—my brother…" Maddie points her chin down the street.

"He looked okay." I pause. *What am I saying? I don't know anything about her brother. Say something smart, something witty. Tell her a compliment.*

"I like your hair. It looks nice shorter," I blurt.

I detect a shimmer of a smile fly across her face but I'm not sure.

"We better run," Tom says. "Remember Sarge?"

"See you around." Maddie jumps off the sidewalk to follow the procession.

I kick myself for the empty space that takes over my brain every time we meet. I watch her back, the small waist and the too short jeans that show a pair of scuffed boots.

As if she's felt my gaze she turns. "We've got new ice cream…for the summer—caramel and raspberry."

"Great, yes… I love…ice cream," I shout. But Maddie disappears behind a group of shoppers loaded with paper sacks. I wonder if she heard me.

"I thought you were going to ask her out," Tom says.

"If you hadn't interrupted…"

"Who's her brother?"

"That guy in the wheelchair. With the wild black hair and the stripe of gray."

"Her brother is a vet?" Tom shakes his head. "How ironic. Wonder what happened to him."

"He isn't too friendly. Yelled at me a couple times."

"When was that?"

I remain silent, thinking about Eric pumping his fist at me and smoking weed in the street. I sure don't like the guy. Then I smile. Maddie told me about the ice cream. Maybe she wants me to visit her store.

"Earth to Andy." Tom's voice reaches through the fog. "Let's go. The others are way down there."

"Damn. Better run," I say, but I can't wipe the grin off my face.

"What's so amusing, Olson?" Sarge looks intense, his eyes still blazing. Our classes have assembled around the corner of Main Street. "You were supposed to lead, not follow."

"Sorry, Sir, we ran into someone I knew," I stammer. To my frustration I feel my face burn.

"Let's get to the bus. Tell everyone no shopping today—we'll head back on one of the side streets and eat on the way home."

Everybody talks except me. I try to recover by helping organize the cadets in rows of two.

"That was exciting," Tom says as he folds his legs into the aisle seat next to me. "I can't believe we saw a *real* peace march. Better than any movie. Speaking of movies, we could visit Garville this afternoon and catch a show."

I keep turning my head to watch my classmates, mumbling under my breath, "I wonder if she'll be back." I've failed miserably as a leader and keep remembering Sarge's angry face.

"Only one way to find out."

"You're going with me, right?"

Tom chuckles. "You afraid of eating ice cream?"

"No, you idiot, but I want *you* to go with me. Besides, there's plenty of time to catch the second show."

"That's more like it. I'm always up for ice cream before a movie."

In front of us Big Mike shouts, "Isn't it clear? These losers are afraid of the draft. They're trying to dodge their responsibility to help us win. I mean did you see how they looked and dressed. Dirty, long hair, having nothing better to do than to march around the country, protesting."

"Lazy animals," Muller says.

"Yeah!" Tony throws up an arm with several others following suit. "Lazy animals," they yell.

"What about the vets?" Tom says. He's intended it for my ears, but the bus stops at an intersection and Tom's voice reaches to the very back. "Many left parts of their body in Vietnam."

"What about them?" Big Mike yells. Despite his bulk he's quick and now towers above Tom. "They were stupid and slept on the job so they got themselves shot."

"Unlikely," Tom says to no one in particular. I know Tom considers Big Mike stupid. The bus is silent as everyone strains to listen.

"What would you know about it? Pussy. You're such a patsy, you can't even hold a rifle, not to mention figure out how to shoot," Big Mike yells.

"Wimp," some of Big Mike's friends holler from the back. It's true that Tom is a lousy shot, but I'm pretty sure Tom doesn't *care* to try and he'd be a great shot if he wanted to be.

"Cadet Stets, refrain from this language and sit down this instant," Sarge's voice growls through the bus noise.

"I, for one, have a brain," Tom says as calmly as if he were commenting on the weather.

Big Mike hears it. "You're just like them. Loser," he hisses. "Somebody ought to teach you a lesson." He looks back from his seat and glares at Tom.

"What's gotten into you?" I whisper. "You know he has a mean temper."

"I'm tired of stupid gorillas and this whole drama." Tom looks mad, something I've only seen a couple of times.

"That was quite a demonstration," I whisper to distract him. "These guys weren't afraid of the police or anyone. Not even Sarge."

Tom nods. "They stand up for their beliefs. I bet the faculty is furious that they didn't know the protests were going on. They would've canceled the trip. They wouldn't have wanted us to see that."

"Especially Sarge".

"All of them. The Dean will make them eat dirt."

The Dean and his metallic eyes. Sarge will be chewed out like he chewed me out. I wonder what Sarge thinks of the protesters. He looked like he despised them.

"That was exciting. I loved seeing those guys," Tom says. "When school ends I won't cut my hair for a year."

I grin. "I bet you'll look great." I lower my voice. "I want to try weed sometime."

"Maybe I can get some this summer. I'll smuggle it back to school."

"They'll throw you out, if you get caught."

Tom smiles. "I wouldn't be the least bit sorry."

"But I'd have to make it through school alone."

"You'll have Maddie."

"Ha, very funny."

"By the way, have you seen my watch? I can't find it anywhere. Thought I'd left it in my desk, but it's not there anymore."

"The gold one with your mom's photo?"

"Yep."

I shake my head. "I'll ask around." The bus is slowing down, assembly hall looms ahead. "I better stay behind and make sure the bus is clean or Sarge..."

Tom smirks as he files into the shoving line of cadets. I watch him leave. His head bent, Tom is taller than most. Then I remember Sarge. I've completely messed up.

I try breathing normally, but my heart hammers with worry.

CHAPTER FIFTEEN

I jog across the deserted paths to my barracks. Tom is waiting…maybe Maddie… and I've got to dream up something to impress Sarge.

I blink to make the image of Sarge's disapproving eyes go away. It doesn't work.

He summoned me to his office right after we returned on the bus. I'd made sure all was clean and the cadets left in an orderly fashion. Didn't work. Sarge was upset though it was hard to tell what made him more mad, my lack of organization or the protests. He was chewing his cigar to shreds and kept spitting bits of tobacco into the wastebasket. Otherwise calm, he sat behind his desk watching, didn't raise his voice or anything. Yet with every word he said I shrank… until I wanted to disappear. It was the second time in a week.

In my room I pull off my uniform and hang it with care. I can't afford to replace anything. My mother was clear. I've got to be more careful. The school is expensive, blah, blah, blah. They could've saved all that money.

"You ready?" I say, sticking my head into Tom's room. My neck burns where the new shirt from this morning left a ring of raw skin.

"You're late again." Tom paces like a caged animal—three steps one way, three steps back.

Toad is draped across his chair. He stares at his novel, eyes black raisins behind the bottle-thick lenses. "Where're you heading?" he asks.

Ignoring Toad I say, "Had to report to Sarge." I'm not in the mood to broadcast my miserable failure. "Let's go."

Tom nods toward the general vicinity of Toad's corner and grabs his coat. "To town.

"And?" he says as we march down the hall.

"Sarge called it debriefing. He says, I screwed up, forgot my responsibility." I shudder. "That I should've run ahead. Corralled the guys and led them to a quiet spot. He was so mad, I thought he'd swallow his cigar."

"He was pissed about the antiwar protests. He walked into it and didn't want us to see the demonstration. He's taking it out on you. Is probably worried about the Dean chewing *him* out." Tom yanks on his coat and jumps down the stairs two at a time. "I'm glad people are doing something. It was the coolest thing I've ever seen. Way better than what they show on TV. Wish I could've joined them."

"Ha, the Dean would have your head on a platter."

"For dinner. Next year when we're finished, I'll go to DC and hang out in front of the White House. I might join the peace movement in California. They're protesting on all the campuses now." Tom's voice is dreamy. And then more matter of fact. "You think I'd be good in politics?"

I shrug. "You'd be better than those jokers on TV."

"Maybe a congressman," Tom smirks.

"I could've done better," I say, running to keep up. Sarge's dismissal is still on my mind. "It wasn't exactly a typical excursion. Slow down. Something wrong?"

Tom is already at the barrack's door. "Let's go." He glances back at me, his eyebrows scrunched into a frown.

"You want to tell me what's eating you?"

Tom shakes his head as we step outside. "I guess you're distracted…thinking about the girl." He throws a side glance at me. "I'm just curious how you can feel so calm about the protests. You're more worried what Sarge thought than about the reasons for the demonstrations. Why don't you see the larger picture? Did you notice how they looked at us? Like we were disgusting slimy rats. I can't stop thinking about it. And I can't wait to get out of these clothes."

I shrug but Tom keeps going. "Here you get lessons from Sarge and you consider it the greatest thing since we flew to the moon. Did you notice how Sarge looked at them?"

"He wasn't too happy."

"Are you kidding? He was ready to slit their throats."

I remember Sarge's eyes, how they were filled with disgust. It surprised me. Still, Sarge took time to teach me. "Are you jealous about my lessons?" I stare at Tom. "I haven't had *any* since December. You know he was gone for months."

"Hogwash! And beside the point." Tom stops suddenly, his voice loud in my ears. "Don't you see? They're roping you in just like the rest of the cadets. Idiots like Tony, Muller and Big Mike. And then they send you out to be slaughtered. You could be drafted before the next year is up. Yes, Sir, fine

Sir. Sign me up, take my legs. Better, take my head. That way I don't have to think for myself."

I look at Tom whose face is the shade of an Indiana tomato. "You compare *me* with Tony and Big Mike? I'm not one of them. Sarge has been helping me. Besides, somebody has to fight this war. Why not us? We're learning all the military stuff, how to shoot and do ambushes, strategies. We'd be officers."

"That's what they *want* you to believe. You'd be used and thrown away. Just like the thousands already dead or like that guy…Maddie's brother. Have you ever considered that the school, that Sarge might be wrong? Do you even know why we went to Vietnam in the first place? Why we're still there?"

I say nothing because I have no idea. Tom is a jerk.

Tom goes on as if he's heard my thoughts. "Cause I sure don't get it. We still have half a million guys down there and more are being drafted every day—only to be slaughtered. Nobody can be trusted. It's a bloody mess, a money-making machine for a chosen few. My father being one of them." Tom's voice is bitter. "I don't want to have anything to do with this." He throws up his arms as if he could dismiss Palmer, the military and the entire war.

"My parents want me to enlist because of the free college," I say. "I don't have a clue what they think about the war." Maybe they want to get rid of me. Send me to war like they sent me to Palmer.

"What if you're ordered straight to the jungle? They'll promise you anything to get you enlisted."

"I can't afford school otherwise." Easy for Tom to say. His father can pay for any college in the country.

"You'd find a way. Make up your mind and do it for the right reasons. You're smart."

"You could be drafted just the same," I say.

"Ha, I'll leave first."

"You'd desert?"

"I'd go to Canada. Never come back."

I struggle for something to say, but nothing comes to mind. I don't care about the war. Somehow I need to figure this out once and for all.

Our steps sound dreary on the forest path and the silence between us grows. As if the trees are listening.

"I've been chewed out once already today," I finally say.

Tom shrugs and tries a smile. "Sorry, man. This is an important day for you. Let's try some ice cream."

"No sweat. I guess I'm pretty confused." I push away the thoughts of Vietnam, my family and arguing with Tom. Maybe Maddie hasn't returned yet. I worry she'll find me too eager, stopping by only hours after she's told me about the ice cream. I said next week. I wipe my hands damp with anticipation on my sleeves.

We reach the hilltop, Garville scattering below like random puzzle pieces. My heart beats faster when we reach Main Street. I clear my throat. The giddiness remains.

The store looks deserted as usual except for two clay pots with pink and yellow primroses framing the door. As we step inside, sun streams across the glass in layers of brilliance, illuminating a cloud of dust motes hovering in midair. I squint into the darkness that seems to grow toward the back. Something moves in the office door.

"You again," a voice says. Eric watches us across the counter.

"Yeah," I say. "I… we're here to try your new ice cream. Maddie told me…"

"Maddie?" Eric's eyes, blue flames burning on high, remain focused on me. Abruptly he wheels toward the steps. "Maddie," he yells, "You have company."

I notice how melodic Eric's voice sounds, like a perfectly-tuned bass instrument. He must've been considered the best catch around before his injury. I hear steps above. Light and bouncy they make their way downstairs.

"Who is it?" Maddie says as she appears next to Eric. "Oh, hi."

"We're here to sample your ice cream." I try a smile and hope my face cooperates.

"That was quick."

"Yeah, right," Eric says, turning his wheelchair toward the office.

"You got a minute?" Tom says. To my surprise, he follows Eric. Maddie walks up the aisle, dodging a display of gardening tools. "Better sit down." She nods toward the three faded vinyl barstools in front of the counter, I never noticed before.

Maddie floats toward the back and ties a tiny red apron around her middle. It accentuates her waist and reminds me of a bib. I try tearing away my eyes and work out what to say. I've heard horror stories, some of the cadets being too obvious about a girl's features and getting the boot. Concentrate, I order myself.

Maddie picks up a glass bowl and scoop that look huge in her hands. "What flavor would you like?" She watches me, her expression all business like she's selling tablecloths to a housewife.

"What do you have?"

"Vanilla and chocolate, we have them all the time—and now caramel and raspberry."

"I'll try the chocolate and raspberry. That is if you join me—my treat." I hold my breath.

Maddie looks up from the bowl, her eyes sapphire in the afternoon light. She smiles and two dimples appear on her cheeks. I want to jump across and touch them.

"That'd be nice." Maddie bends low into the cooler to fill the bowl. "Here, enjoy." She slides the ice cream across the counter. I watch her hand slipping away as I reach out.

"Thanks." My palms are clammy when I grab the spoon and sink it into the velvety red. "Very good. Get anything you want."

Maddie hesitates. The tip of her tongue appears between her lips. Then she bends down and slides a dollop of raspberry into her bowl. I remind myself to swallow the ice cream that has melted inside my mouth. I've got to get a grip.

"Come and sit with me," I say, patting the stool next to me. Maddie nods and walks around the counter. She reaches across and pulls the ice cream in front of her.

For a moment it's quiet except for the low hum of voices from the backroom. Spoons scrape across glass as I ache for something smart to say. A whiff of sweetness like honey reaches my nose. I throw a sideward glance at her hair. It has to be her shampoo. Get with the program, I scold. She'll think you're an idiot.

"You still in school?" I blurt.

"Eleventh grade."

"Me, too. What will you do when you graduate?" I'm immediately angry at myself for asking. I don't know what I want to do. Why would she know? Maybe she finds my question prying.

"Probably work here and help my dad," Maddie says. "It's not what I *want* to do but what I have to do."

"You work here all the time, don't you?"

Maddie nods. "What're *you* going to do after school?"

I put down my spoon. Here it is. The dreaded question I don't know how to answer. "My parents want me to join the military. They can't pay for college. My grades aren't…They want me to get a degree while enlisted. But…"

"But?"

"I don't know if I like it enough. There's this teacher, Sarge, he's really into it. He's been nice and I feel…" I shake my head. "I'm not making any sense. Sorry, it's confusing with all the war stuff and people hating it—us." I look down at my uniform.

"Most locals don't like the cadets," Maddie says. "We find them arrogant and they think we're all stupid."

"I don't think you're stupid."

"I suppose not." Maddie licks her lips, turning them red and shiny as if she's using lipstick. I feel momentarily distracted, fighting the urge to grab and kiss her. I only hear "different" as I watch her face.

Pull yourself together. "Sorry, what did you say?"

"I said you aren't the typical cadet."

"Really?"

Maddie shakes her head. A tinge of pink has crept into her cheeks.

I take a deep breath—now or never. "You want to go to the movies sometime?"

Maddie looks up. Our eyes meet and I feel like I've been hit in the stomach. "Sure. But I have to ask first. My dad..."

I nod. "Next weekend?"

"I'll try." Maddie pushes away her bowl. "I better clean this up. Oh," she hesitates. "It's ninety-six cents for the ice-cream. Together." She's barely touched hers and though my bowl is empty I can't remember what I've eaten except for the sweet flavor of chocolate in my mouth.

I pull out a dollar bill. "Of course, here." I remember Tom and look around the room, but Tom is nowhere to be seen. "I thought Tom, my friend, wanted to try the ice cream."

"He's with Eric. They disappeared into the office. You want me to get him?"

"Yeah, we're going to watch a show. It's almost four."

Maddie nods and walks toward the back. Muted voices drift through the door. I follow and stop in the office entrance, not trusting my eyes.

Tom sits across from Eric, his body resting comfortably in an old easy chair that has faded into pale gray, its armrests worn to reveal foam stuffing beneath. They're deeply engrossed in conversation as if they've known each other for years. Eric's eyes sparkle. His cheeks glow underneath the mass of curls. He looks young suddenly, a college student ready to experience the world, not an invalid.

"We'll be late," I say, trying to hide my surprise.

"That's what I told them," Maddie says. "They just ignore me." The dimples appear and I somehow know she's pleased.

Tom looks up as if emerging from another world. "Shucks, I forgot." He straightens and pats Eric on the shoulder. "Sorry, man, I'd love to chat some more."

"Later," Eric says, his eyes crinkling into a grin. It's the first time I've seen him smile, a complete transformation into the most handsome face I've ever seen. "Come and see me again."

"Sure thing," Tom says as our eyes meet. "Probably next weekend."

"Hey," Maddie calls after us.

I spin around. She's still standing in the office door.

"You didn't tell me your name."

I stare. How could I have forgotten? I've known her name for months. "Andrew...Andy Olson. This is Tom Zimmer."

"See you next week, Andy Olson." A smile plays around her eyes as she turns her back.

We rush down the street and I'm fighting down a giggle that threatens to erupt in the back of my throat. I want to shout and sing. She'll see me again. Scenes of our conversation repeat in my head. She smiled at me.

A few cadets mingle in the theatre lobby. Saturday afternoons townies stay away and leave the space to the noisy and smoky crowd of prep school students who hoot and holler with abandon.

I glance at Tom who hasn't said a word since we left the store.

"You okay?" I ask.

"Great."

"I thought you wanted ice cream."

"Forgot. Besides…," he chuckles, "three would've been a crowd."

"Very funny." Of course Tom is right. Being alone with Maddie was perfect. I smile again. "What's up with the guy?"

"Who?"

"Eric."

"He's fun."

"Really?"

"Talk to him. He's very smart."

I shrug. I'd never consider Eric fun. Scary is more like it. Muted sounds of Simon and Garfunkel trickle into the lobby. "We better hurry."

"It's about time they're showing this," Tom whispers through the gloom as we settle in the back. *The Graduate* came out last year. I saw it over break, it's really cool."

The noise inside the theatre swells into whistles and nervous chuckles as Mrs. Robinson takes off her blouse. I remain quiet, feeling self-conscious. I love the story and the music, but I don't need any reminders that I'm a virgin. I wonder if I'll have to wait until I'm out of college like *Dustin Hoffman* in the movie. There're about zero chances to get laid in an all-boys school. Except Maddie, but that's jumping to a lot of conclusions.

Some of the older cadets boast about sexual encounters with girls, sounding like expert lovers. Especially Tony brags about doing *it* on the golf course, in elevators and his parents' bedroom. He describes details as if he's reciting from a porn film. I turn red just thinking about it. I usually listen, too curious to leave and too embarrassed to speak.

Other than getting my hands on some *Playboys*, tattered and missing pages where the model centerfolds have been, I haven't even seen a naked woman. My family is a bunch of prudes. The only girl I kissed was freshman year—a shy blonde who lives a few houses down. We walked to school together and sometimes held hands.

"You two hit it off," I say when we leave the theatre. I'm baffled about the way Tom seems to enjoy Eric and can't let it go. "Looked like you were old friends."

"He's nice and it's fun to discuss war politics with someone who knows. Someone who has been there. He's going to let me borrow some of his books and newspapers. What about you two?"

"We're going to the movies. If her dad lets her. What did you talk about?"

Tom scuffs me in the arm. "Way to go. Better take her to a Sunday show. You'll never live it down if you go Saturday with the rest of us."

"Good point." But secretly I feel a twinge of envy about the easy friendship Tom has developed with Eric.

As the store comes into view, I run ahead. "I better tell her now."

CHAPTER SIXTEEN

The week stretches into oblivion as we march and study. I try forcing my brain into the concentration needed to pass finals. Hard to believe the year is almost over. Despite the stress of cramming every last bit of math, physics and German, the fact that I'm on the brink of a D in English, I often catch myself with a smile creeping onto my face as I think about the upcoming Sunday—followed by anxiety about the prospect of things not working out.

Maybe her father will forbid her from going with one of the snotty cadets from the fancy school. Maybe Eric has told her I'm an idiot. Maybe she's changed her mind about me after eating ice cream, finding me too boring, too childish or too ugly.

I think I look pretty good. My hair is atrocious, of course, way short, never allowed to grow past fourteen days. Still it's a nice color of brown. I've got a tan from spending afternoon practices outside and my skin is clear except for an occasional pimple on my jaw. I like my chin, square and strong, and definitely needed to balance the long nose—a *gift* from my father. I wish I were more experienced with girls, came from a wealthy family or had an important father. Something to feel confident about.

"I'll visit Eric while you're with Maddie," Tom announces Saturday evening. "Stop by the store on the way back and get me." We're lounging in Tom's room, munching a bag of potato chips, Tom has saved as backup for unannounced hunger pangs. It's been the longest day. I haven't been able to study for more than ten minutes at a time, my thoughts returning to those blue eyes... Without the distraction of classes, football and other school programs, I wandered around the grounds, thinking about Maddie and willing the clock to move faster.

"Sure thing." I feel the same twinge of jealousy. It's stupid. After all, I'm the one who's been pushing to go, who is nuts over the girl. What's wrong with Tom seeing Eric? Nothing, I tell myself. Still why haven't I figured out a way to talk to him? On the other hand I'm glad Tom has found a buddy. "What're you going to do?"

"Chat. Eric is stuck so we'll stay put. I may push him down the street a bit if the weather is nice."

"I wonder what happened to him."

"Don't know but I'm not going to pry. He's in enough pain as it is."

Kind of like you, just a different kind of pain or maybe not. I wonder if I can ever understand the emotions swirling through Tom's mind. I've considered myself a close friend, but sometimes I'm clueless around Tom. But then can we ever truly know what somebody else goes through? I'm clueless about my own feelings half the time.

"Right," I say. "By the way, did you ever find your watch?"

"Nope. Somebody must've stolen it. I looked everywhere, even the lost-and-found. Nothing."

"Why would somebody do that? It's not like they could use it here, where anyone might recognize it."

Tom shrugs. "Maybe they needed a gift for their girlfriend. The thing is, it's not the value of the gold... it's because of my mom."

"I know." I pat Tom on the shoulder. "I'm sorry we have a thieving prick among us."

"I shouldn't have brought it to school. I just wanted it here with me."

I nod. "I can't believe classes are almost over."

"My father will force me to spend time with him and that bimbo," Tom says. "I can't stand it. I wish we'd graduate so I could start college somewhere far away. Like California—Berkeley or Stanford."

Or Canada. Aloud I say, "I'll finish my Eagle Scout and go swimming the rest of the time. I don't expect my family will go on vacation." I can only remember two trips. My parents are always pinching pennies. "Maybe you can visit your mom." It's out before I realize what I've said.

Tom's mother left him unattended when he was little, just walked off and forgot he existed. She'd been wandering the neighborhood when Tom's father returned home, finding Tom sitting in front of the TV amid open boxes of cereal and cookies, the family dog beside him licking milk from the carpet. Despite my anger for my own family, I can't imagine how it feels to be forgotten by your own mother.

"You know, maybe I *will* visit her," Tom says, his eyes a shade too bright. "She probably won't know me but still."

"Listen, Tom, I'm sorry," I say. I'm such an idiot. Why don't I think *before* I speak?

The call boy announces five minutes to bedtime. Toad shuffles into the room, towel across his plump backside, looking like the Pillsbury Doughboy.

"Taps," he announces, his voice high with a whistle sound. He claims to be asthmatic and is excused from physical activity except marching and rowing. It'd do him good to move more and work off some of the bulge. Toad is always first in line for meals except when he's shoved aside by the football jocks.

I yawn and head for the door. "On my way."

"Leaving at 12:30 tomorrow," Tom calls after me. "Don't oversleep."

"Fat chance," I yell over my shoulder, grinning. Rushing to my room, I pull off my clothes just in time before lights out. Though I'm exhausted, a feeling I've become used to over the year, sleep doesn't come.

I think about Sarge and how unhealthy he looks these days ever since he's returned from who knows where. I've wanted to ask him where he's been and what's going on, but I haven't had any more lessons and opportunities for private conversation never happen. Nor has Sarge asked for me. Somehow, I'm disappointed.

It sure seems ludicrous to stop by Sarge's office for a chat. He's not one for leisurely gossip. *Hey, Sarge, how's it hanging? Been to the jungle lately?* I shake my head. Sounds of Plozett's even breathing, interrupted by occasional snorts, drift across. I turn on my back and stare into the dark.

Then there is Tom with his problems and Eric stuck in the wheelchair. Compared to them I've got a great life. Well, not exactly. Clearly, my parents got rid of me. I'm like a poisoned barb in our neat family—rebellious, interested in sports instead of books, fighting with my siblings.

Still I miss them. I know I should feel thankful and happy, but except for the excitement about Maddie I feel anxious. At least I'll be done with plebe year. No more jumping to attention for the oldmen. Hard to believe I'll be one myself. I doze off.

***

Maddie looks good enough to eat, wearing a striped sweater in shades of blue that match her eyes, plain jeans and white sandals. Her toenails shimmer pink. Tom and I arrived early, but she smiled when she saw me enter the store.

I sigh in relief. "Looks like you're getting time off with the stupid cadet?"

Maddie chuckles. "Dad is visiting my uncle. I told him I was hanging out with a friend. Hey," she nods at Tom. "Eric is waiting in the back."

Tom heads to the office. "Have fun."

We walk down the street and I'm trying to adjust my steps to hers. The top of her head reaches my shoulders. It makes me feel powerful. She wears her hair open today—a mass of black curls that sparkle in the sun. But where her brother's face disappears underneath his hair, hers is framed by perfect waves.

"How are you?" I ask.

"Fine. How was your week?"

"We had finals—

"I worked," we say at the same time.

She chuckles nervously. "Sorry, I haven't been out in a while."

"I thought you'd go out all the time," I say. "I mean, the way you look…"

"I know what you mean. I don't have much time and I don't like most of the local boys."

"Really? What's wrong with them?"

"They work on their family farms. That's not all bad, but they have these ideas. All they want is to get into my pants. They whistle and make dumb remarks and anyway, they're not worth talking about." She shakes her head and the honey scent hits my nose. I want to lean over and bury my face in her hair and the soft curve of her neck.

"It's still early. You want to walk a while longer?" I say. Maddie nods. "By the way what's your real name? Surely it's not Maddie."

"Madeline Elizabeth Hurley."

"Wow, that's a mouthful," I chuckle, "Mine is worse, though."

"That's what *you* say," she laughs. "What is it?"

"I shouldn't, you'll change your mind about me."

Maddie laughs. "Come on, try me."

"Andrew Balthazar Olson."

Maddie bends over in a giggle.

"I'm glad I can add to your entertainment for the day," I say with a grin. "My grandfather's name was Balthazar so my parents wanted to honor him. Of course, all my siblings have normal names. Like Gary and Mary."

"Poor guy." She laughs again and I can't help smiling. "Andy is nice," she adds.

"Is it?"

She nods, her eyes serious again.

Encouraged I go on. "I don't tell anyone. Actually you're the first. Usually I'm Andy B. Olson. It's nice to hear you laugh. You always look way too serious when you're in the store."

"Do I?"

"Yep."

We've rounded a few corners and are heading back toward the theatre. An occasional couple passes us but I hardly notice. I could be in the middle of a football game and ignore everyone except this girl next to me.

"I heard good things about this show," I say. "Tom is a movie buff. He's already seen it twice. He visits the big theatre in Evansville."

"I love the movies, too, except I don't go very often. We're always short." Maddie's cheeks glow pink. "I don't mean to burden you with our business."

"It's no burden. Besides, it's my treat. I asked you." I pull out my wallet to emphasize the point. A caged *Charlton Heston*, surrounded by a group of chimpanzee-looking creatures, watches from the poster above.

"I heard it's scary," Maddie whispers as we enter the darkness beyond.

"I'll protect you," I say. For a second I put my arm around her shoulder. Electric currents shoot through me, pain from my football injury combining with something wonderful.

The theatre is empty compared to the Saturday shows I attend with the cadets. I'm glad I've followed Tom's advice to avoid my classmates. As I lead Maddie towards the back row, I imagine Tony and Big Mike pouncing on me with lascivious remarks, ruining my chances forever.

Planet of the Apes pulls us in, but I feel as if a part of my body is extended and melts into Maddie's. I feel her every move. Leaning over, I place an arm around her shoulder. During a scary scene when the music swells dramatically and Heston is pursued by a throng of angry apes, she grabs my hand and snuggles into my embrace. I squeeze her shoulder, a feeling of strength and protection flooding me. I want to pull her close and kiss her, but remember her comments about the local boys. I'll take my time even if it kills me.

"That was great," Maddie says as we leave. Red spots burn on her cheeks and her eyes flash with excitement. "Can you believe, he returned to earth and all his family and fellow humans were long gone? I can't imagine being all alone like that." She shudders.

"It's a great story," I say, thinking of myself at the school and the intense loneliness I often feel. "I'd be fine if I had my girl with me." Somehow that slipped out and I worry about saying too much.

"Would you?" she says, suddenly smiling. "I don't know, though. What if something happened to your girl or your partner and you'd be all alone." Her voice sounds small.

I pat her back. "You won't be alone as long as I'm here. I'll take care of you."

"Right. You'll be gone next week on summer break and in a year you'll move anyway."

"Maybe I won't. Maybe I'll stay right here and help you stock shelves."

Maddie laughs but it sounds forced. "Not a chance. Why go through all that education to end up in a hole like Garville?" She pauses. "Let's walk a bit more. It's only three-thirty. Look at these shirts." She pulls me in front of the only clothing store in town. "They're so colorful." The lone mannequin looks faded against the mini skirt with orange and green circles and spheres like floating bubbles. The white top is plastered with flowers of the same color. A banner above announces *spring fashion*.

"I bet you'd look great in that skirt." My eyes wander down Maddie's jeans, hinting at shapely legs, but I catch myself and return to her face.

"I'd be laughed out of town. Besides, Dad would never let me wear it and we don't have the money. We barely make it from year-to-year and Eric needs extra things. He has to take medication now to keep his blood flowing. And he gets depressed. We always thought he'd go far…help support the family but he…"

"What happened to him? You don't have to tell me unless you want to."

"It's okay." Maddie looks into the distance as if to gather strength. "A grenade got him. Eric never told us what happened, not exactly. But we heard from his buddy who sent a letter when Eric was in the hospital." She sighs. "His friend was killed shortly afterwards. Eric took it really hard …harder than his own injury."

I squeeze her hand. I imagine bloody limbs and explosions. Sarge never talks about our men getting hurt.

"Anyway, it happened when he'd been separated during one of these terrible fights. He'd crawled around all night, trying to locate his platoon. Finally he found them all huddled up." Maddie's voice turns into a whisper. "He'd made sounds to announce himself, but one of the guys. He…"

I bend lower, my ear nearly at her lips. "What?"

"One of the privates… he'd been a nervous wreck for months, and they'd tried to send him home. But their commander had refused. Anyway, the guy always jerked and screamed in his dreams. Like he was losing it. When he heard movement that morning, he flung a grenade, thinking it was Charlie sneaking up on them. It didn't hit Eric directly, but the shrapnel…" Maddie, pale as the mannequin behind the glass, is speaking faster. "Eric tried to get up, even though his legs no longer worked. His spine was hit, but he didn't know and he tried to...

"They dragged him to camp and by the time it was safe and they got a helicopter to extract him, quite a bit of time had passed. Too late for his legs."

At a loss for words I keep rubbing her hand.

"He's so angry now. The friendly fire made the whole thing even worse."

"But how could somebody be so sloppy? And why don't they send people like that crazy private home?" Would Sarge have done the same and forced the guy to stay?

"It happens all the time, people are nervous and scared. Many of them shouldn't even be there. Helicopters and planes drop bombs and Napalm on their own soldiers. It's just a messy part of war and the military leaders don't like to talk about it. They murder good people…they almost killed Eric. He'd been so happy and excited. He's changed into a totally different person." Her voice is filled with sadness.

"Sarge says war is messy."

"Sarge?"

"Yeah, he's a teacher who went to Vietnam. He tells stories about combat. He taught me orienteering last fall." Maddie glances at me, her face a mix of pain and attention. How I love her looking at me. I hurry on, "I'd be furious, too. I can't imagine sitting in a stupid chair all day. I get antsy just studying for a few hours… and when we don't have football practice."

The lone church tower tolls four times.

Maddie looks up. "I better get home. I want to make sure my dad will allow me to go again. He'll be home soon."

"So you'll see me next week?" I don't want to release her hand.

Maddie nods. "It was fun. I feel I can really talk to you." Her eyes meet mine, serious like the first time I saw her. I pull her close.

"Are you going to slap me if I kiss you?" I whisper.

She shakes her head and closes her eyes. Her mouth feels soft and opens slightly. Our embrace tightens and I forget everything, but the sweetness on my lips and the blood rushing through my body like a storm flood.

Maddie draws away. "I have to go," she breathes. "Somebody may see us."

I want to stay, ignore the idiots in town who wag their tongues like dogs' tails, ignore the clock and Maddie's curfew. Instead, I force my body into submission, taking her hand. "Let's go."

Since the front door is locked, we enter the store through the side. "I'm back," Maddie calls into the void.

Tom and Eric sit like last time, Tom in the easy chair, his feet resting on a shelf and a bottle of *Jack Daniels* on the desk beside Eric's wheelchair.

"Tom is quite the comedian," Eric says. "You should hear him impersonate his teacher. It's a riot." His eyes are glassy, but his voice sounds steady enough.

Tom climbs from his chair. "Time to go. See you next week?"

"Sure, man," Eric says.

Maddie leans across him and pushes the bottle against the wall and out of reach. "You're drinking again?"

The smell of whiskey hangs in the air.

"You sound like Mom," Eric says.

Maddie's face drains white and she turns away. "I'm going upstairs."

"Sorry, I'm sorry," Eric calls over his shoulder.

Without a word, I follow Maddie. I'm furious at Eric for upsetting her.

"I'll wait outside," Tom says, heading for the door. "Take your time."

Maddie stops at the staircase. "See you next Sunday? Or visit Saturday for ice cream. I have to work, though."

"Maddie?" Her old man appears on the stairs. He's wearing an old-fashioned suit with wide lapels and a shirt with a frayed collar.

"Hi Dad," Maddie says. "This is Andy Olson."

I bow slightly, remembering my obnoxious uniform. "Nice to meet you."

"Didn't I tell you to stay away from the academy?" Her father glares at me. "Come upstairs."

"In a sec," Maddie says while her father keeps watching us from above. "Please?"

"I've got to go anyway," I say.

"Good," Maddie's father says.

I turn toward the side door when I hear Maddie run after me.

"He's upset about Eric," she whispers. "I'll be finished at five on Saturday."

"Maddie!" her father thunders. "Go upstairs."

"I'll be here Saturday at four and wait for you," I hurry. "Maybe we can eat at that diner."

"We could go Sunday before the movie. They have Sunday brunch specials."

"I'm leaving Sunday. Summer break, my parents—"

"Right, I forgot." Maddie sounds miserable. She turns and yells toward the back. "I'll be there in a second."

I squeeze her arm and she turns back toward me. I want to kiss her, but feel the eyes of her old man from the gloom of the staircase. Maybe he'll come down to kick me out.

"Please, don't be sad," I whisper. "I'll be here Saturday and I'll write to you every week while I'm away." She nods slowly then, her eyes shiny with suppressed tears. I want to hold her, shout at her father. And her brother—take away what he's said. The jerk.

"I better go," she says. "See you Saturday." She places a quick kiss on my cheek and runs off.

I watch her disappear. Suddenly I'm furious at myself. I could've had all spring with Maddie, taking her out, if I hadn't been such a chicken. Just being next to her is like medicine, letting me forget everything about school, about home. Now I have to wait all summer, endless months of boredom with my squabbling sisters and nagging mother.

I sigh. There is nothing I can do. I'm utterly in love.

CHAPTER SEVENTEEN

I stare out the window, but ignore the landscape that dissolves into a whoosh of brown and yellow, cornfields with dry stalks eight feet high, the barren earth of late August, cracked and dusty, modest farmhouses and pockmarked limestone formations. The air sizzles, bringing no relief no matter how far the windows are open. My pants stick to the vinyl seat of the car, the orange soda my mother packed, syrupy in my mouth.

To my amazement I don't mind returning to Palmer. All summer I felt like a guest in my own home. No, worse, more like an appendage, a third arm not really belonging. My siblings went about their ways as if I didn't exist. They had their friends, went to camp and the city pool. My older brother acted all sophisticated and hid in his room *studying*.

Nobody ever asked *him* to do chores. Gary is working, my mother repeated daily. Why don't you make yourself useful and mow the lawn? So I helped like a chump. My old friends were busy.

Daniel was attached to his girlfriend and if he'd seemed disinterested before, he had absolutely no time for me now.

If I were honest with myself, I hadn't had such a boring summer in my life. I'd wanted to hide in my room and sleep away the time. Of course, that was out of the question. My mother made me get up by eight every day. Even on Sundays—especially on Sundays—when we all went to church. Sometimes I ran off and hid in the woods to be left alone and daydream.

I lean forward to catch the breeze. Paper rustles inside my jacket—my favorite letter from Maddie. I smooth the tattered pieces. She wrote at the beginning of summer when I felt blue and missed her so much, it was as if the memory of her face had implanted itself on every girl I saw. I sniff, trying to imagine the scent of her hair. *I'm going mad.*

"Dear Andy,

You've only been gone a week, but it feels much longer. The store is a bit busier right now which makes Dad happy. Sometimes, tourists get lost and find their way to us. I'm spending most of the day counting out candy and selling fishing gear.

I'm always glad when school is out, but this year it seems more boring. I wish I could go away to college next year instead of working in the store. Some of the boys come around and hang out, but I'd rather wait for you. I wish we'd had more time together before you left.

Eric is doing okay, though he drinks too much. He always liked whiskey, but now he drinks it like water. He's always moody and sometimes he gets so mean. It makes me sad.

I wonder what you're doing. I wish I could be there with you. It'd be much more fun, maybe go fishing or swimming. I look forward to the school year and seeing you again. We'll be seniors. I better finish. I want this letter to go out and the postman will be here soon.

Miss you!

Maddie

P.S. Come back soon!"

I love that last part.

Then there is Tom. I haven't heard a word except for one lousy letter. A short one at that. All summer I worried and wondered what happened since our arrangements never materialized. To my surprise my parents were open to the idea of Tom visiting, but Tom wrote shortly after break started. No, he couldn't make it. His father had other plans and he was forced to go along if he wanted to see college next year. The letter explained nothing. I wrote back immediately, even raced my bike to the post office to drop off my response, but the mailbox remained empty.

When the familiar limestone correctness of Palmer's campus appears, I perk up.

"I sure hope you're going to finish strong," my father says. "Make it count."

I nod. "Yes, Dad." I'm far away.

My father grimaces. "I better head back, another three hours of driving."

And whose fault is that, I want to say. Instead I hug my father. "Bye."

We were close for a time. Years ago when life was simpler we fished, just the two of us, sometimes we hiked and looked for morels in the spring. As our family grew busier and my brothers and sisters demanded his time I quit asking.

My father gives me a quick squeeze and climbs into our Rambler Cross Country station wagon. It's got to be the shabbiest car in the parking lot. "See you at Christmas."

I grab my suitcase. The place drowns under cars and good-byes of worried parents and their anxious sons. It's easy to tell who is new by the way they look, their mouths pinched, eyes wide with fear. They stumble along with papers in hand and bags dragging behind, trying desperately to find their bearings. I remember well and stop several times to help a new cadet locate his barracks. I want to find Tom who isn't in his room, though the familiar duffel with the initials TZ is on his bed.

It's Saturday afternoon and all cadets soon assemble for the first dinner of the semester. I head for the cave, our only escape from ranks and rules. Parents never see it, so not even the Dean cares. Talking about the Dean, tomorrow I'll have to force myself to listen to another welcome speech. Yuck.

The cave has to be the most worn-out space in the school. Only juniors and seniors are allowed, a privilege each cadet has to work up to. The smoke from cigarettes and the occasional cigar some cadet smuggles in from his father's fancy humidor, makes it hard to see more than a few feet.

The old couches have faded to indefinable beige and gray tones, worn cushions and easy chairs sit in a pattern of chaos. Games are stacked on a few rickety shelves along with books, their covers dog-eared and rubbed blank from thousands of hands in need of escape from military order. The black and white TV blares as cadets' voices mix into the excited buzz that always seems to accompany a first day.

Tony White and Big Mike are surrounded by a throng of football players and third-years.

"She was sweet, her skin soft as peaches. Man, she was something," Tony brags. His voice is even deeper than last year, I note with a twinge of envy.

"Did you do it?" Bloom asks. From the same town as Tony, Bloom's real name is William Bloomfield. A star tennis player, he's won a bunch of medals for the school. Bloom always looks tanned, spending countless hours on the tennis court. Though he isn't as pushy as Tony, I never talk to Bloom who only hangs with the men from the cavalry and a few choice friends of equal wealth.

"What do you think?" Tony says. "She purred like Marilyn Monroe in *Some Like it Hot*. She couldn't get enough of me."

"Out of sight," Bloom says. "What happened?"

"Yeah, details," another guy says. Several boys whistle.

Tony nods. "My parents were gone…I got her loaded on screwdrivers, lots of vodka. She was all wobbly so I put her on the couch." Tony pauses for effect. "And gave it to her good."

I move on, having heard it all before. How the girls fall for Tony as soon as they lay eyes on him. I don't really care, not anymore. And if I ever do it, I'll be discrete. Maddie's face appears in my mind and my stomach lurches.

I pass by a side table. Muller is sitting across from an even pudgier Toad who melts into the cushions, one soft mass meeting another.

"Father took me to the Pentagon," Muller just says. "I got to walk the same halls as the President. We saw the White House and Lincoln's monument." He straightens though it doesn't help much. He's just as short as last May. "Father says I'll join the government after college. He says I'll be groomed to be a general one day. I'll teach these grunts to do a better job in Vietnam. And these hippie assholes and peace demonstrators, lazy and smoking marijuana all day and causing the president a bunch of problems were hanging out in front of the White House. They should all be arrested."

Toad nods. "Yeah," he squeaks. "What's the country coming to?"

A familiar voice chimes in from the corner. "What would *you* know about fighting in Vietnam?" Tom, partially hidden behind the headrests of an old armchair, puts down his book and stares at Muller. "I bet you and your father have never even talked to a soldier, someone who's actually been there, crawling through the morass to fight your dirty war. Imagine, always waiting for a bullet or grenade to find you, getting all sorts of conflicting orders, wasting men on trying to capture three feet of jungle. For what?"

"From what I can see you're a traitor just like these hippies," Muller says, his voice rising, "I watched you when we went to Evansville. How entertained you were. It's all a game for you. Why don't you join them if they're so great?"

"I'd love to," Tom says dryly. "Then you can arrest me. That should give you tons of satisfaction." He pauses. "*You* got it all wrong. It's really a game for *you*. Moving men around as if they have no hearts—no souls. These are people with real lives and bodies, with real families and futures."

Muller opens his mouth in search for an answer. The room has gone completely silent, but Tom isn't finished.

"Let me ask you something. What will you do when it's your turn and you're drafted?" He turns to face Bloom, Tony and his friends. "All of you?" Nobody says a word and I'm just standing there watching.

I've got no clue what I'd do, but I know I wouldn't have the guts to go to Canada like Tom. I'll be eighteen next June. It's sort of a scary thought with all the soldiers returning with injuries, or not at all.

"I bet you'll ask your rich fathers to get you out of it," Tom says. He's smiling though his eyes are serious. "Let the grunts fight it out for you." He slumps back down.

Everyone stares—waits—to see if there'll be a fight, free entertainment to usher in the new semester. Muller jumps up, barely taller than Tom sitting down. "You aren't fit for this academy. I should report you." His voice is shrill. "Better yet, somebody should teach you a lesson.

Traitor!"

"Do what you must." Tom disappears behind his book, ignoring Muller's labored breathing that rattles the air. The mumble of voices resumes. Muller returns to his seat, but still glares at Tom.

I feel uneasy, but the familiar urge to punch him is stronger. "Mind your own business, brown noser," I say aloud. Muller pretends not to hear and grabs a magazine from the side table. Weird, but ever since our fight when I turned his nose to mush he's ignored me. I passed just about all the inspections he did last semester. Even that time when I'd forgotten to clean up my desk.

I stop in front of Tom's chair and play-punch him in the shoulder. "Feisty as ever. Good to see you. Why didn't you write back? I worried."

Tom looks up, a tiny smile spreading across his face. He hasn't been to the barber yet and his dark curls stand in all directions.

"Things didn't go as planned. My father made sure of that."

"Tell me."

"How about dinner?"

"Let's go."

Tom climbs out of the chair and glances at Muller. "At least he can't order us around any longer. How have you been?"

"Your letter was rather mysterious. You never explained…"

Tom bolts into the hallway without answering.

I rush after him. "What's the hurry? Are you worried they'll run out of food? I thought you'd be in touch, visit, you—"

Tom stops abruptly. "I had the summer from hell. My father was a total ass. I'd planned to stay home. You know, see a bunch of movies, read… visit you for a bit."

"What happened?"

"Remember the bimbo?"

"Your dad's girlfriend?"

"The one and only. We had a huge fight. My father told me she wanted to visit her family in Massachusetts. I asked what I'd possibly have to do with his mistress. I mean I was nice, could've called her a lot worse. You should've seen him. He turned all red. I thought he'd punch me. 'She's my *girlfriend*,' he yelled, 'and you're going to act like a gentleman.'"

Tom stops to catch his breath. "He had business in D.C. He forced me to go with them. Said I wouldn't go to college unless I *cooperated*. Ha! Somehow he believes I'll follow in his footsteps. And then to top it off, we went on a *family* vacation in Florida." Tom makes a gagging noise, sticking his forefinger in his mouth.

"Sounds like torture. At least you must've seen something interesting along the way. I spent three months stuck in Bloomington, waiting for letters from you and Maddie. Of course, you never sent any after the first one. Other than a week of Scout camp I felt about as useful as a worn-out shoe. Daniel, my old friend since grade school, couldn't bother to hang out. He was kissy-facing his girl. He didn't really care what I was doing. The other guys were working summer jobs. I just don't belong."

Tom sighs and we resume walking. "I guess I shouldn't be so thankless. At least I get to travel while you're stuck with your family."

"I helped my father finish the garage. Why do they need another family room anyway? Of course, nobody else helped. My sisters went swimming with their girlfriends. Speaking of girlfriends…"

Tom throws up his arms. "You should've seen her fake boobs. She was sprawling in the sand, her tiny swimsuit sort of losing everything…my father ogling and drooling. She reminds me of one of those blow-up dolls, the ones you get in a sex shop: pouty lips and pumped-up tits. At night they drank wine and whispered. Brrrh!"

"Maybe she wanted to seduce you, too," I chuckle.

"Hah, she's so dumb. All she talks about is shopping. Get this. I had to clean the kitchen every day since she'd had her nails done. I don't understand what he sees in her."

"Did you—"

"You should've heard her moan." Tom is on a roll. We're on the main path to mess hall, crowded with students, heading in the same direction. The smells of roasted meat and something buttery grow stronger. "It was embarrassing. The windows were open and she carried on like a cat in heat." Tom pauses as if becoming aware of his surroundings again. We enter the dining room where a line of cadets inches toward the buffet.

I scan the offerings loaded with chipped beef and white gravy, toast, green beans and stewed tomatoes. "Looks like we'll have bird shit on shingles." Dinner rolls are stacked like wooden blocks, apples ooze in caramel next to piles of perfectly square brownies.

Tom shrugs. "Sorry man, I didn't mean to whine."

"No worries. I just thought something was seriously wrong. I mean it was like you'd disappeared into thin air. I couldn't understand why you didn't write."

"I should've."

I grin. "At least postcards. Did you fight a lot?"

Tom shakes his head. "After we left, he calmed down. It's the only good thing about her. He's probably too exhausted from all the fucking." The cadet in front of us, by the size and scared look on his face, a freshman plebe, turns his head. His cheeks glow, but he's smiling.

"Did you hear about Woodstock?" Tom asks after we sit down.

My mouth is stuffed with beef so I shake my head.

"They had this giant rock festival in New York. Expected a few thousand. Guess how many came."

I shrug.

"*400,000.*" Tom's eyes look dreamy. "I wish I'd been there. All peaceful and the best music in the world."

"Like what?"

"Janis Joplin with the Kozmic Blues Band, the Who, Jefferson Airplane, even Jimi Hendrix."

"Why didn't we hear about it?" I say, trying to imagine 400,000 people rocking out.

Tom shrugs. "Cause we live in a vacuum."

Tom is right. The school is isolated, but so are my parents. I might as well live on the moon, I'm so out of touch. "I'm heading to town tomorrow," I say aloud. "Can't wait to see Maddie. Are you coming?"

"Sure, I want to see Eric. He's probably mad at me too for not writing."

"I'm not going 'till later. She's visiting her uncle. We could've had all afternoon, but no. I bet her father made her go so she'd have less time for me. He probably hates me."

"Us," Tom says.

"But you're *Eric's* friend."

"You'll just have to be nice and turn him around. He'll see that you're just a cool guy."

I frown. "Who wants to date his daughter." I think of Maddie's father whose eyes are full of suspicion. "I wonder what he thought of Eric joining the military."

"He was all for it," Tom says, slugging through the second brownie. "Until Eric returned with dead legs. Eric believes his father is blaming himself. That the guilt is eating him up. Especially after their mom died, he'd been happy to have Eric taken care of by the Army."

Why haven't *I* thought of asking about Maddie's mother?

"She had cancer," Tom says as if he's heard my thoughts. "Eric said his father got really strange after that. Yelled a lot. Eric was glad to join the military, get away."

"When did she die?"

"Shortly before Eric left. And then Eric came back in a wheelchair. No wonder the man is livid."

I nod. Everywhere I look people are angry. Of course, Eric has a lot more reason to be upset. But then, what *is* a good enough reason. I just want to be left alone and happy with Maddie. Somehow get through school. Then what?

Maddie is stuck in Garville and I've got to figure out what to do.

CHAPTER EIGHTEEN

The next afternoon I jog to Garville. It's early. Maddie won't be back for another hour. I don't care. I'd rather hang out in town all day than do time in my room. I'll study the window displays and the newest movie posters until she returns.

Like always the streets are quiet. Except today they remind me of a graveyard in the middle of winter. In the distance an old farm truck revs its engine and takes off in a cloud of fumes. I stroll along the storefronts, the lone pub with its regulars sipping weak beer. The church tower clock moves in slow motion. As usual I'm self-conscious about my uniform, always sticking out like an over-polished stone in a field of mud.

Now that I'm here I wonder why I left early. I look like an idiot, wandering around in the open. I round the corner, moseying up the backstreet which is even shabbier than the main road. I should've stayed and studied. Mr. Brown's smug face dances across my vision, the way he squints with his right eye just before he announces another English exam. Then there is German vocab. These long words are impossible to memorize. My evening is shot for sure.

The church clock tolls: three-fifteen. Maybe Maddie is already home. I can at least check. *Why does she have to visit her uncle on the first day I'm back and we have a chance to meet?* I turn toward Main Street.

As usual the side door to the store is unlocked. The gloominess inside always hits me like I've stepped back in time into one of those old westerns. I half expect a man in an apron, cowboy hat and boots stomping up to me. It smells of dust, spices and something like molasses mixed with rubber. I should talk to Maddie about modernizing the place. A hint of light comes from the backroom and I wonder if Eric is back there.

I don't particularly care to see him. Eric mostly ignores me, but not without first flashing his blue eyes. I feel like shouting an insult, but one look at Maddie's pained face and the shriveled legs in the chair hold me back. I can't figure out why Tom gets along with him so well.

"Maddie? Are you back? It's Andy," I shout, walking past the staircase that leads to the second-floor apartment. No sound comes from above. I stop, unsure if I should check the backroom and potentially face Eric alone. Maybe it's better to leave and watch the townies outside. *Don't be such a baby*, the voice in my head sniggers. Tom gets along great, always talking politics and the war. But Tom has mouthed off to Beerbelly this morning and is not allowed to leave campus all day.

I worry how Tom will get through the rest of the school year. We've only been back a day and he's already pissed off half the school. Most of the faculty tolerates him because he's smart and produces excellent grades. His father is probably donating large sums to the Dean's coffers. I don't get why he can't wait out things quietly. As if we don't have enough to deal with. The stupid war continues whether he likes it or not.

"Eric? Anyone here?"

The building seems eerily empty. Maybe Eric has gone with Maddie and her father and she forgot to mention it. I'll just turn off the light and wait for them outside. When I push against the door, searching for the switch, I see legs.

They're still and on the floor. I rush inside, eyes glued to the shape on the ground. Eric lies on his back with his eyes closed. Blood trickles from a cut on his forehead onto the wooden planks where it has grown into a puddle. His wheelchair is on its side, pushed against the wall.

"Eric!" I kneel next to him. Eric's face is completely white as if all blood has drained from his head. His mane is matted with red stickiness. But the spot on the floor, much darker than what I imagine blood to look like, is small.

I lean close like I've seen on TV to listen for breathing. The thick smell of whiskey hits my nose along with a faint gurgling sound. Definitely alive. I wonder whether I should pull him up. I remember from first aid in Scouts not to move an injured person.

What if Eric has broken his skull or hurt his back? I inspect his legs. They're thin but straight—not like broken bones. I hesitate. Should I call an ambulance? One probably doesn't even exist here in the middle of nowhere. I have no idea where the nearest hospital is. Somehow it seems wrong to call an ambulance when they probably can't afford it. Maddie will be angry if I waste money. But then….

I look down again. Eric hasn't moved. His breath seems shallow. What if he's seriously hurt and dies? It'd be my fault. I remember Maddie telling me about Eric being rescued far too late. Too late for his legs.

I've got to do something. "Wait here. I'll get help," I shout into the stillness. Sprinting out the door, my heart beats in my neck as if I were running the football down the field. I've never been to the town doctor—the school has their own medical team, a physician and two nurses—but I remember seeing a sign for a Dr. Smittley on one of my walks with Maddie. The street is sleepy as I race down the sidewalk, searching for the right house.

The two-story building looks empty and I wonder if anyone is in the office. If the doctor lives somewhere else, I'll have to enter the tavern to ask for directions. Pounding a fist on the door, I yell, "Help. We need a doctor. Open up."

Nothing moves as the seconds tick by. I keep banging. Maybe I should've called the police or the fire station. I'm about to run around back when an old woman opens the door. Her hair is pulled into a bun and she wears a long gray skirt with a matching apron.

She squints through a pair of round glasses. "What's all this shouting about?"

"I need a doctor. Eric, you know, the guy from the general store. He's hurt. Where's the doctor?" I try looking past the woman but there is no need. A man in a brown flannel jacket with patched elbows appears with a leather bag in hand. "I'm Dr. Smittley. Tell me on the way."

I explain what I saw, my throat dry with anxiety. The doctor seems ancient, but in good shape. He has no trouble keeping up as we run back to the store. Eric lies unchanged, his eyes closed, eyelids tinged purple. Smittley bends over him, taking his pulse and listening to his chest with a stethoscope. He feels along his back, checks his limbs.

I notice how Eric's legs look like those of a child… and shriveled.

"He has a nasty cut but he's okay. Just passed out," Dr. Smittley says. "Probably too much drink. I'm going to sew him up and then you can help me put him to bed."

"Sure, whatever you need."

I slump into the chair, suddenly exhausted. On the desk a box of ammunition sits open, bullets scattered around a nearly empty Jim Beam bottle. I quickly collect the shells and stick the box in my pocket.

Remembering Maddie's comment about Eric's drinking, I throw the bottle in the wastebasket. Dr. Smittley has taken out a curved needle and is wiping Eric's forehead and temple with antiseptic. It has to sting like a thousand hornets but Eric doesn't move.

Suddenly squeamish I look away. But then I imagine how Maddie would react if she saw her brother like this. For the first time I wish she'd run late.

"I'll get a bucket and clean this up."

"Let's move him over a bit and away from the blood. I need to bandage his head and don't want to get it dirty."

Together we slide Eric to the side. He feels limp as if he has no bones.

"Cold water, I need cold water," I mumble. I search in the alcove near the back where boxes and odds and ends are stored. A bucket and mob lean in the corner. Getting water from the sink by the backdoor I clean the floor, carefully avoiding the work being performed on Eric's forehead.

To my frustration, a dark spot remains while the water has turned scarlet. I hurry back and return with a brush and a sliver of soap from the bathroom. Thankfully, Maddie *is* late. She'd fall apart. I keep scrubbing the wood planks. The stain turns lighter, but I can't tell if it's gone. It reminds me of the outlines that police sometimes leave to show the position of a murder victim.

"Let's carry him to bed," Dr. Smittley says. "I know where he sleeps."

I take hold of Eric's shoulders while Dr. Smittley lifts his legs. We struggle upstairs, Eric feels surprisingly heavy and bulky in my arms. His shoulders and chest are muscular and broad. He must've been quite a hunk before the accident. The doctor is puffing for air as we reach Eric's room, sparse with a narrow bed and night stand, no rugs, no paintings or colors. Like a prison cell. Like my room at Palmer. I take off Eric's shoes and cover him with a blanket.

"I'll check on him in the morning," Dr. Smittley says. "Tell Maddie and her father that I'll be home tonight if they need me. I better go and finish dinner or the wife will be displeased." He pats me on the shoulder. "Thanks a lot, lad. You did the right thing. Maybe you better keep watch until Maddie and her father return."

"I'll wait."

Eric has not moved. Remembering the wheelchair, I head downstairs. The clock on the wall shows four-thirty. I've got to leave soon. Nobody misses the Dean's speech unless they're dead.

Folding the chair, I notice the rifle hanging from a rack in the corner. The bottom bracket, a miniature shelf, has fallen to the floor and the gun is dangling from a single clip, threatening to come loose. I reattach the shelf, pushing the barrel back into place. The bullets feel heavy in my pocket. I wonder whether I should return them to the store.

A noise comes from above. I hoist the wheelchair under my arm and climb upstairs, two steps at a time.

"You," Eric groans. His eyes below the gauze wrap are half open and a bit of color has returned to his cheeks.

"You passed out," I say, bracing for another assault.

"What're you doing here?"

"I found you, I…"

Eric stares, his eyes gathering fury as if a storm is brewing.

"Why do you stick your damn nose into other people's business?"

"Sorry." *How can Tom get along with this guy?* Uncertain what to do, I lean against the doorframe, listening to the awkward silence and the wheezing from Eric's chest.

"Fuck! My throat feels like a bucket of sand. Got a sledgehammer in my head." Eric touches the gauze. "Did you do that?"

"Dr. Smittley came and stitched you up. You have a nasty cut on your head. There was blood…"

Eric stares at me. The room turns quiet again.

"You get my chair?"

"Yeah, it's in the hall. I cleaned up the blood." I glance at Eric who remains silent. Only his eyes are glued to my face, a mix of anger and frustration.

"I put everything back in its place." I look at the man on the bed, trying to imagine how Eric was before the injury—strong, confident and handsome.

"Everything?"

I nod. I want to ask about the gun, but the words won't form. Instead I stand in the semi-darkness. Quiet fills the room…thoughts too heavy to pierce with words.

Unable to take it any longer, I begin to pace. The area is small. Three steps in one direction. Three steps back. I glance at the clock. Nearly five. I've got to leave, but I promised Smittley that I'd stay. "Dr. Smittley says, you'll be fine. Good as new." As soon as I say it, I feel foolish. How can Eric be like new when he's an invalid who'll never walk again? "I mean—"

"I know what you mean," Eric says, his voice thick with anger. "I appreciate what you did…downstairs." And then calmer. "Where's Tom?"

"Got house arrest. Mouthed off to Beerbelly this morn—"

"Eric?" Maddie's voice sounds from below. "Where are you?"

"We're up here," I shout into the hall.

"Anyway," Eric says, his eyes again intense, "I'd appreciate if you …"

I nod. "I won't tell Maddie… or anyone else."

"Thanks." Eric closes his eyes. For the first time, I feel intense sorrow. Until now I've loathed Eric, his nasty attitude, his challenging questions and him somehow standing, no sitting, in the way to Maddie's heart. A constant distraction.

"What's going on?" Maddie emerges, taking in the scene on the bed.

"He's fine, just bumped his head," I say.

"I'm fine, sis," Eric says, a small grin on his face.

Maggie has turned pale. "You look awful. What happened?"

Eric shakes his head and forces a chuckle. "Stupid me. Fell out of the chair."

Maddie rushes to the bed and bends to hug her brother. "You need to be more careful," she whispers. Eric stares back at me over her shoulder. I turn away, the knot in my throat pushing against the back of my eyes.

"I'll help Dad and then I'll take care of you." Maddie turns and gives me a quick squeeze. That's how coming home has to feel.

"Hey, I missed you so much," I mumble.

"I'm glad you were early."

I follow Maddie into the hall. "Got to go. The Dean's speech."

We embrace and for a moment I forget everything, but the feel of her body pressed against mine and the amazing smell of her hair touching every cell of my body. Her lips are soft and erotic and a wave of lust sweeps through me.

"Maddie, are you helping?" her father's footsteps clunk on the stairs.

"I'm coming," she says, pushing me away.

"Meet me next Saturday?" I whisper, fighting to get my breath under control. I lean against the doorframe, searching Maddie's face in the gloom.

"Two at the city sign," she says. "Don't forget."

I rush past her, carefully avoiding her father who's unloading boxes from a truck.

***

I sprint most of the way. It has to be super late. With every step I grow more nervous.

I can't be late.

To my horror Palmer's trails are crowded with cadets in full dress uniforms marching to assembly hall. My barracks come into view. Thank goodness they haven't lined up yet. I rush upstairs. *Damn, why am I always behind?*

Plozett is fully dressed, studying himself in the mirror. "You're late."

"No kidding." I tear off my jacket and grab a fresh shirt. My fingers tremble. There're a thousand buttons.

"Anything I can do?" Plozett glances at my wardrobe, newly stocked with this semester's clothes. "They're gathering outside now."

I shake my head. "Go ahead. I'll be there in a second."

I glance at the clock. Six minutes. As I yank on my pants, the top button pops and flies across the room. "Shit!" I'll have to cinch the cummerbund tight to hold them in place.

Tom sticks his head in the door. "How's Maddie? You okay?"

I grimace. Why is everyone interrupting when I need to concentrate the most? "Leave. Get a seat for me."

Four minutes. I pull on the jacket, fiddle with the brass buttons, a double row of twenty. The sash. Don't forget the stupid sash. I knot the fabric and grab the belt and sword. I'll buckle it on the way. Two minutes to make it to the hall. At the last second, I remember to grab my hat and rush out the door.

The paths outside are deserted. Everyone is already there. Everyone but me. I've missed roll call and will be reported which means another visit with Beerbelly and certainly demerits. What a shitty start to the year.

A few feet from the door of assembly hall, I slow, fighting to calm my breath. The cummerbund knot sucks. I'll have to adjust it after I melt into the crowd. I blink as I enter the auditorium. The room is hot and completely full. Everyone but me is sitting. I hope nobody is looking too closely at my uniform while I hurry toward the back. Tom always sits in the back. I check across the rows.

Applause erupts. The Dean. Can't the guy be one minute late for once?

"I see we're not quite ready," the Dean's voice drifts from the podium. "Shall we wait until Cadet Olson finds his place?" His voice sounds silken with glass shards piercing through.

I frantically search for Tom and the free seat. *Where is he?* I feel every eyeball on my back and face as I rush along the aisles.

Beerbelly grumbles something as I pass him. At last I see Tom's raised arm two rows back and ten seats in. I scramble into the line of chairs, stepping on feet, causing a few suppressed giggles, some curses.

"Well done. Cadet Olson has joined us." The Dean's voice drips with contempt. I shrink into my chair. My cheeks boil. Every last drop of blood has gone to my head.

"Let's move on to the business at hand, shall we?" The Dean shuffles his papers. Surely he knows his speech by heart. It's the same one he gives every semester. My hands shake. Tom pats me on the arm, but it doesn't help. Tom's hand is white. *What the…?*

My gloves. In my haste I forgot to grab them. I'm going down like the Titanic. I carefully look around. All faces are turned to the front except Beerbelly's. He's staring straight at me from his aisle seat.

I'm dead. My last year is supposed to be fun. What if I have to march Saturday? Maddie will wait in vain. It can't happen. I keep gazing in the general direction of the podium, but don't hear a word.

I'm caught by surprise when applause explodes around me. The Dean has finished. I straighten, trying to decide where to hide my ungloved hands. They feel naked.

The crowd streams into the aisles, anxious to get to dinner, ready to secretly loosen knots and buttons.

"I'm starving," Tom says behind me.

I nod, trying to locate Beerbelly through the mass of moving bodies. Maybe if I make it outside, all will be forgotten. The people in front of us are painfully slow.

"Way to go," Tony White says as I step into the aisle. "Nothing like getting on the Dean's shit list on the first day," he cackles.

"Right," I say, assessing how I can best take cover behind Big Mike's shoulders. The exit doors are creeping closer. Almost there…and through. I breathe. The air feels cool after the heat in my skull.

"You think you'll get in trouble?" Tom says.

"I forgot my damn gloves."

"You could go now and get them. You'll be back in no time. I'll keep a spot in the food line."

I nod. Beerbelly is nowhere in sight while hundreds of cadets fill the walkways. I race off, avoiding collisions along the way. Bounding up the stairs to my room, my steps sound hollow in the corridor. I yank open my closet.

The gloves are supposed to be on the top shelf, next to the folded underwear. The spot is empty. I drop to the floor to pull out my suitcase from under the bed. We're supposed to put bags and cases in the hall tonight, so the janitors can move them to the attic for the duration of the semester. The suitcase is empty. I must've left them at home, probably on my dresser. Shit.

Taking two steps at a time, I jump downstairs, out the door. Beerbelly is ambling toward me. He hasn't seen me yet. I consider turning around, that's when Beerbelly looks up.

"Olson? What's the matter with you today?"

"Sir, I—"

"First, you come late, only half dressed." Beerbelly comes to a stop in front of me, citrus aftershave filling the air. "Now you're running around campus instead of eating dinner."

"Excuse me, Sir—"

"Enough!" Beerbelly sweeps an arm. "Report to me at 19:30. And get yourself to mess hall this instant."

"Yes, Sir."

I don't remember much about dinner. We're allowed to remove our gloves while eating and I try to chew slowly and not draw attention. Out of the corner of my eye I notice Sarge moving past the food line. I keep my eyes down. In the backroom, the Dean drones on about some fancy event, interrupted multiple times by polite laughter.

"Want to get more dessert?" Tom says.

I shake my head. I have trouble swallowing as it is.

"Want me to bring you some?"

I shake my head again. Beerbelly's face appears in my mind. He's usually pretty laid back, but he was positively livid tonight. The bread in my mouth turns to sawdust and I sip water.

"I have to report to Beerbelly. I'll see you afterwards," I tell Tom as we head toward the barracks. "What's left of me."

"Be strong," Tom says. "Just another year and we'll be free. Imagine the guy in his underwear or on the pot."

I smirk. "Thanks, man."

Beerbelly's door is closed, the corridor quiet. Cadets are settling in for study hour. I knock.

"Yes."

"Cadet Olson, at your service, Sir."

Beerbelly stares from behind his desk. I notice the whiff of alcohol, not Eric's whiskey smell, but something sour like fermented beer gone stale. His face looks more flushed than usual.

"Olson, what am I going to do with you? Do you have any idea what I had to listen to from the Dean? I never ever want to see you act like this again. You're an upper classman now. A role model for the younger boys. Instead you run around like it's your first day on campus."

I open my mouth, but Beerbelly goes on. "What am I going to do, Olson?" He looks up to study my face.

"Sir, I'm sorry, Sir. I ran late because I was in town." I stop. I can't tell anyone about Eric. I promised.

"Town, heh. What're you gallivanting in town for? We can put a stop to that."

"No, Sir, I'll march extra duty. Anything, but…"

"What?"

I shake my head. "Nothing, Sir."

"You'll definitely march. The next two Saturdays. And no visits to town both weekends, period. I'm going to teach you if it takes all year." Beerbelly loosens his shirt collar. Sweat droplets have settled on his upper lip and forehead. "You won't make me look bad again."

"Sir, please, I'll march the next four Saturdays, but I must go—"

"You're hardly in the position to bargain, Cadet Olson." Beerbelly straightens himself. "You'll do as I say or I'll keep you on campus for the entire semester. Understood?"

"Yes, Sir."

"Unless you want me to send you to the Commandant? Is that what you want?"

I shudder. "No, Sir." The Commandant oversees the school's entire military and is the Dean's boss. Nobody is sent to see him unless it's life or death.

"Dismissed."

"Yes, Sir."

As Beerbelly leans forward to rummage through his desk, I close the door behind me and wonder if he's getting a drink. I could use one, too. No Maddie for three weeks. It'll be absolute torture.

Still I've got to keep it together or Beerbelly is liable to extend my sentence.

The day has been a complete disaster. I looked forward to seeing Maddie all summer, counting each day. Instead Eric tried to kill himself. I want to tell Tom about Eric, but I've given my word. I won't break it.

I wonder what Sarge thinks of guys like Eric. Vets who fought and gave their lives, their limbs, who've risked everything for their country, and live with consequences that ruin their chances of a normal life. Ruin everything. Forever. Worry is knotting my stomach. Sarge has to be livid about me infuriating the Dean. Somehow I've got to find a way to please Sarge. Impress him. Somehow.

CHAPTER NINETEEN

"You're two weeks late," Maddie says, but her arms wrap around my neck and I feel her breasts pushing against my stomach. They're high and firm and just right. I touched them through her sweater once in the darkness of the movie theatre and I'm beyond excited to think of her bare skin.

"Sorry, everything unraveled after I left here. Tom told you, right?"
Maddie nods. "Was it bad?"
"The worst part was waiting to see you." I grin down at her. "It feels like I was gone for a year." I squeeze her hand and she smiles. I suddenly feel intensely grateful.

The weeks were agony. Beerbelly appeared out of nowhere, always glaring and suspicious as if I carried a hand grenade in my pocket. I marched extra duty both Saturdays—three hours of mindless walking. Coach Briggs, mad about me missing practice, threatened to bench me for the first three games.

Worse is that Sarge hasn't said anything. He hasn't even acknowledged I exist outside regular class. This semester, Sarge teaches military strategy and at first I was excited about another chance to be near him, hear his stories. But Sarge is serious and keeps the usual anecdotes to a minimum. He treats me like everyone else, like we never spent time together. Despite maintaining a B, I no longer look forward to class.

"Guess what?" I say, drinking in Maddie's shape, the black shorts and red t-shirt. "I'm somewhat famous for being late to the Dean's speech. Some of the plebes seem to be impressed. They look at me like I'm this big shot. Some days it's hard to get out of the building for all the plebes stopping and acknowledging me. I sure hated having to stop every time an oldman appeared in the hall and I had to salute or play doorman. But this is almost as annoying."

"That's called infamous," Maddie giggles. "Let's go. I know this great place to fish." She points to a basket and two fishing poles. "You can try my brother's pole—he doesn't use it much now."

"I'll carry the basket," I offer.

We settle on the rocks overlooking a pond next to a limestone bluff. The water below looks dark and cool. Tufts of grass poke through moss, a perfect cushion of softness. The wind has picked up, but the September afternoon is still comfortably warm. Muted light filters through the birch trees, dapples the water and dances across Maddie's face.

"You ready to fish?" she asks. "I brought a few hooks and this." She opens a pouch filled with rubber lures and bobbers.

"Sure, but first I want to kiss you. You've got no idea how much I missed you all summer." I lean forward to pull her into my arms. Maddie giggles. How I love that sound. It makes me feel strong and smart…and interesting. "You need to laugh more often, Maddie. It's beautiful."

"You're silly." She smiles at me, her forefinger tracing my lower lip. "I like your mouth."

"Really? Come closer then." Our lips meet and I probe with my tongue. I feel my breath take off as we sink into each other.

It's the best thing I've ever experienced. My heart thumps and I feel the blood rush through my body as if I were drunk. Not that I've had much alcohol. Other than the wine under the bleachers, and once last summer when I stumbled across a college party in Bloomington where they served beer from a giant metal keg and nobody checked my ID. I talked to strangers I don't remember. Early in the morning I woke up on the floor in somebody's apartment. After walking home, I sneaked into my room through the window, hoping my mother wouldn't hear. My parents hate alcohol and there is none in the house or ever served when we have guests.

This is much better. I want to savor every minute. Maddie sighs.

"Something wrong?"

"No," she says, squinting at me. "But shouldn't we at least hang the line in the water. I'd like to say we fished and caught something."

"Does your dad know we're here?"

Maddie laughs. "Dad believes I'm with a girlfriend from school. He was pretty mad when he saw you hang out at the store. Though he's probably forgotten with all the worries. He loves my help in the shop and with the books. No, Eric knows. He's already asked and he looks at me funny. I'm not a good liar." Her cheeks turn pink. "See, just the thought that I'm out here with you—alone—makes me blush."

"It looks beautiful on you." I kiss her cheeks. "It's not a bad thing if you can't lie, though I sometimes wish I could. How's he, I mean Eric."

"Better. Still a bit pale, his head hurt for a week, but he's very quiet and sweet. Tom has been over and they always have a good time. Eric gets distracted and he even laughs.”

"You ever hear what they talk about?”

Maddie shakes her head. "Not really, I have to work or study. Or clean house.” She sighs again. "Anyway, I'm so glad you helped him. He's clumsier than I thought.”

"It's the stupid wheelchair,” I hurry. "No wonder, he falls out of it.”

"The chair is bad?”

"No, I don't mean buying a new chair. It's just. Well, I can't explain.” Visions of Eric on the floor, the bullets and gun return. "At school it doesn't pay to be honest,” I say, wondering if she notices me changing the subject. "They're all conniving, especially the Dean. He's a certified slime ball.”

"What does he do?”

She's taking the bait. "Nothing. He just talks about honor and glory and his smile reminds me of a wolf that has swallowed the rabbit. He's so false, it's disgusting.”

"Just a few more months and you'll be done.”

"Two long semesters and one more Dean speech.”

Maddie jumps up, her face suddenly serious. "I'm going to fix the fishing poles.”

"What's the matter?”

"Nothing.”

"Maddie?”

Maddie stops still, the fishhook useless in her hand. She shakes her head. "You talk about the time stretching. When the school year ends you'll leave.” Her voice chokes.

"Oh, Maddie.” I jump up and embrace her. "I'm an idiot. I don't mean it for us. You're the best thing that's ever happened to me. I don't know how I'd get through school…life without you. Tom has it way worse. He's hated this place from the start. Especially what it stands for.”

"You're just saying that to get in my pants.”

"You know that's not true. Please, Maddie. Forgive me. Here, I'll help you with the line. I'm an expert in knots.”

"Yeah, right. I've been fishing since I was three.” Her voice is still heavy.

"But I'm almost an Eagle Scout. I bet you don't know *this one*.” I grab the line and retrieve one of the hooks from the tackle box.

"What is it?”

I tie the line. "Eye Crosser Knot.”

"You're making it up,” Maddie giggles.

"Nope. It's a real one. Very strong…in case we catch a whale.”

"Dad taught me the improved cinch knot.”

"That's a good one, too.” I throw up my arms. "You'll be the fishing master. Come here. I want to kiss you."

Maddie moves into my arms. The sun is warm, adding a layer of heat I don't need.

"I brought apple pie," she says, coming up for air. "Made it myself from mom's recipe."

"You're the best." I bend to kiss her again. Apple pie is good, but kissing is heaven. I force myself to stop. "Let me finish the line." I attach a rubber worm and neon-yellow bobber.

After wedging the pole into a tree stump, I pull Maddie down next to me. "Where were we?"

We kiss and my hand wanders across her shirt toward her breast. I can tell she wears a bra and I long to open it. During the summer I secretly checked my sisters' underwear drying in the basement. They seem to unhook in the back, but I don't want to rush and make Maddie angry. Instead I stroke the fabric on top of her breast.

Maddie sighs again and our kiss turns into a dance of tongues. Electrical currents charge through me with such force I feel lightheaded. A bit of skin shows on her stomach and I caress the smooth area with my finger.

"You want to eat?" Maddie says. She looks flushed, her eyes bright blue against the red of her shirt.

"Sure," I say, though I'd rather investigate the skin under her sweater.

The pie is delicious and still warm with butter streusel on top. "It's so good," I say, savoring the crumbs in my mouth.

Maddie jumps up. "We have a bite." The bobber dances and disappears beneath the surface. She pulls and a sunfish with bright blue and orange spots struggles on the line. With a quick twist she removes the hook and places the fish in the grass.

"Now we have an alibi," I say. "Come here. Leave the fishing. I have to get back soon." I'm furious because we have drills this afternoon, a new idea from the Dean.

Maddie kneels in front of me and places her hands on my shoulders. "Why do you have to go so early?" Her lips meet mine, soft and sensuous and I close my eyes. My hands are on her back and slide below her shirt, her skin like silk, warm from the heat and fresh sweat. The bra opens without a hitch and my fingers travel toward the back of her neck. Maddie sighs, pushing herself against my chest.

"The Dean's brilliant new plan," I mumble, kissing her neck. "We march every Sunday afternoon to practice for some stupid parade." My hands wander to the front and climb underneath the loosened bra until they meet the soft mounds of her breasts. I stroke until her nipples turn into pearls. She sighs again as I begin kissing her throat. A voice tells me to stop, that I'll be late and that trouble will surely follow. But it's impossible. Her hands are moving across my back and every touch feels like fire. A terrible urge begins to grow inside me and my pants are too tight. I want to rip off her clothes and kiss every inch of her body.

Just then Maddie pulls away. "You'll be late and I don't want you to blame me later. Remember what happened last time. So better go." She straightens and fastens her bra. "That was a nice trick. Like you've done it before."

I leap up, hoping the hump in my pants is disappearing fast. "I swear I've never done this. You're the first. One more kiss? Then I'll go."

"One more." We embrace. "Now scoot," she laughs and slaps me on the bottom. "I'll see you next week, same time."

"Same place," I yell, jogging into the woods. "I miss you already."

"Miss you, too."

CHAPTER TWENTY

Sweat runs down my face, soaks my uniform. Marching practice is ridiculous. We walk back and forth, carrying rifles, creating formations. We march the same patterns over and over until my feet throb and I want to scream.

Maddie's face floats in my vision, her soft skin and body, but I've got to pay attention, count steps and watch my classmates. The Dean keeps stopping by, evaluating our progress and I can't afford another disaster.

By the time I get to my room after dinner, I want to sleep or at least rest my legs for the upcoming weeks' worth of football practices. Instead I drag myself to study. Beerbelly has been making surprise visits and is apt to catch me. Besides, another English report is due tomorrow. I rummage through the drawers in search of clean paper.

Tom blasts into the room and towers over me. "I can't believe you didn't tell me." He looks pale and squints down, his lips pressed into a straight line, his eyes furious slits.

"What did I do?" I look at my friend who seems angrier than I've ever seen him.

"You were jealous," Tom continues. "You couldn't stand it that *I* was close to Eric and you weren't. Did you ever consider he may have needed *my* help? That I should've been there." Tom's breath rattles as if he's inhaling through a sieve.

"What're you talking about?" I suppress the urge to kick Tom's butt. Instead I close the door. We're forbidden from leaving rooms unless we study at the library or have a really good excuse—like being dead—*and* have a pass. Surely, Tom has neither. Thankfully, Plozett is at the library. "Can we start over? What did I do?"

"You didn't tell me about Eric." Tom's voice is calmer but his eyes still blaze. He looks hurt. "What he did."

I look up in disbelief. "Are you talking about when I *found* him?"
Tom nods.

"You've got to be kidding. He asked me to keep it quiet. You should've seen him. It was embarrassing. When he finally realized what had happened... He was worried about anyone finding out. Besides, you had house arrest."

"Yeah, Eric didn't want Maddie and their father to find out. He was okay that I knew."

"How was I supposed to guess that? I can't read minds and I'm not a snitch."

Tom shakes his head. "You could've said something. It would've been okay. Eric mentioned it, thinking I knew. He hinted something and I sat there like a dumbass. He'd assumed you'd tell me and instead I asked all these stupid questions, making him upset again. You're a self-centered prick."

Fury rises in me, a low heat that brews in my stomach accompanied by a strange ache, almost like pain and I wonder about the guy in front of me. I wonder how we've been friends when Tom has gone crazy.

"You're just mad 'cause you were stuck on campus that day. That was your own fault."

"You wanted to be his friend and step between us," Tom says, pacing the room. "Have a secret, something I didn't know."

"I don't get it. He obviously told you, so why are you so angry. When he came out of it, he said not to mention it and so I didn't. He looked super...upset, angry and I don't know—"

"You never thought it'd be important, that I could help ... You're just too thick. You're turning into one of those military assholes who don't think worth a loaf of bread."

"Bullshit! Shut up, I've heard enough." The ache in my stomach grows. "If you're unable to see my side I guess we don't need to talk anymore."

"I'm leaving." Tom takes three long steps and yanks open the door which smacks against the wall with a thump.

I stare at the gaping doorframe and can't move. Tom's words echo through my head like a song of shrill trumpets. I lift my hand and watch my fingers shake. I haven't had a fight like this in years. Not since getting into it with my sister Mary. Certainly not with Tom. I lean back.

Here I thought I'd done the right thing, not betraying Eric's actions that he wanted to keep private. I obviously underestimated how close Tom and Eric are. Except I didn't realize, not at all understand how important Eric is to Tom.

But damn, I tried to be honorable. Suddenly, I wonder if Tom has thought about suicide and wishes for someone to know and understand. I try recalling past conversations, hints and Tom's complaints. Maybe Eric wasn't serious either. Just wanted help, somehow get a grip. It seems impossible to tell what goes on in Tom's head. Or Eric's. I thought I knew Tom. Obviously I don't understand anything.

***

Weeks stretch into a month. I keep watching Tom who looks paler than usual and sticks to himself. Sometimes I see him hang out with Markus and a couple other sophomores. In math and English we sit next to each other, and I try to gauge Tom's mood.

Except for the occasional one-word communication necessary in class we don't speak. I want to pat Tom on the back and say something like let's quit the bullshit and be friends, I miss talking to you. In my mind I do it a hundred times, but somehow I never actually do it. The words stick in my throat.

Then the moment of opportunity passes and we rush off to different classes. During tattoo Jimmy Hendrix's *Wild Thing* thumps down the hall. I know it's from Tom's room. He brought a tape player after summer break. I plan to casually walk by, but I never can make my legs move. Secretly I'm afraid of Tom's rebuff. Plozett asked me to join their poker game and I spend most of my free time in the cave. I'm a dollar ninety ahead, but I honestly don't care.

I don't even try when Tom gets mad and causes a nasty shouting match. By the time I arrive in the cave, Tom is red in the face.

"Damn killers," he yells. "They slaughtered an entire village. Even the kids. How do you explain that?"

The entire senior class is there, including Tony White with his friends, Muller and his cousin from the cavalry.

"Liar," Bloom says. He's sharing a cigar with Tony blowing smoke rings.

"It's fact," Tom yells back. "If you read the paper you'd know it's true. *My Lai* really happened. More than eighteen months ago. Except they never told us. The American people only sacrifice bodies and minds and finance the whole thing. Damn liars. The army was covering it up. Disgusting!"

"I don't believe it." Tony steps in front of Tom. "*I* haven't heard anything."

"You don't keep informed." Tom stares straight back. They're eye-to-eye but Tom looks thin and small next to Tony's muscled chest.

"Are you calling me stupid?" Tony blusters.

"Those are your words," Tom says, refusing to back down.

"But seriously, how do you know?" Bloom interjects. "I haven't heard anything either."

"Me neither," Big Mike yells.

"You're just a liar," Tony says. "A hippie traitor."

"Hippie traitor," some of the others yell. Though I want to ask details, I just watch. I can't imagine Tom making it up. He must've learned it from Eric who watches all the news and reads the *New York Times* and *Newsweek*. I feel like a wimp.

Tom shrugs. "Just wait, you'll hear." He turns and heads out the door, ignoring me. It feels like a slap in the face.

***

Despite seeing Maddie, I've never felt this alone. I know Tom goes to town on weekends just like I do to meet Maddie. I see him and Eric in the backroom talking. Sometimes Tom pushes Eric's chair on the sidewalk while I pace the silent streets with Maddie, trying to figure out where we can be alone.

The weather has turned wet and cold with occasional night frost. Fishing is out of the question. So is staying at the store. Maddie's father glares at me as soon as I show up.

I'm looking forward to tomorrow's matinee. At least we can hide in the dark, it's warm and I can sneak my hand under Maddie's sweater.

"What's with you two?" Maddie asks. We're squeezed into the recessed entrance of a shoe repair shop to take shelter from the whipping wind. "Tom arrives by himself and then you show up. You never speak to each other and leave separately."

"We had a falling out."

"You want to tell me about it?"

Remaining silent, I take Maddie's face between my hands. I want nothing more than to forget and kiss the lips in front of me. Lately, I'm horny all the time. Maybe the anger makes it worse. My body aches with longing.

"Andy?"

"What?"

"You want to tell me what happened?" Maddie pushes away my hands. The last rays of a late November sun disappear behind the roofline and plunge us into shadow. Still it's hard to believe that winter is nearly here. I blink and open my mouth, but then I shake my head.

"I can't." The ache in my stomach is back.

Maddie looks at me, her eyes large, her face a sea of hurt. "What do you mean you can't? I thought we were honest with each other and didn't have secrets."

"I am and I don't. Except this is complicated." I take hold of her hands, but Maddie pulls them back.

"I don't understand." She looks away. "Either you are or you aren't. And if you are, if we don't have secrets, you can tell me."

I sigh. This is getting worse by the second. First Tom and now Maddie. It's all Eric's fault. But then how can I blame Eric? I may want to kill myself too if I had to sit in a wheelchair. I rack my brain for something to say, some other idea why I fought with Tom, but my mind remains blank. It's hard to lie when I've tried to do the right thing all my life. Except for a few white lies at home, covering my tracks with my super strict parents, I've prided myself in being honest. No, I can't tell Maddie what really happened.

"Let's take a walk," I offer. "Maybe we can get a piece of pie at the diner."

"Eat your pie alone. I'm going home," Maddie says. She looks at me strangely. "You can speak to me when you're ready to tell the truth."

"Maddie, wait!"

But Maddie runs off. I can tell by her shoulders that she's upset, probably crying while I stand rooted to the ground. Life is one big nasty joke.

I stroll down the street toward the woods, my eyes drawn to the store and the checkered curtains on my right, my mind fighting to look straight and ignore the cause of my pain.

When the school's auditorium appears behind the trees, I turn and continue down the path toward the creek where I got lost the first year. I keep walking until I find myself on the banks of the river. It's still low and I contemplate jumping across the rocks to the other side. But then I just sag to the ground, my legs weak and tired. I grimace. At least I won't get lost here anymore.

The sun disappears, its last glow turning trunks and brush into orange fire. The strange light and my mood give me a sense of impending doom. My stomach twists, a dull throb that spreads to my throat. First Tom, now Maddie. I'm alone once again. Just like the night of the hazing. Actually worse, because back then I had Tom.

I stretch on the ground and stare into the graying sky, the leaves below me rustling. It's obvious that Tom isn't going to come to me. He can be stubborn and I have obviously hurt his feelings. But Tom is such an idiot, believing that I would divulge a secret. I misjudged the entire situation, but I've got to be strong and do something about it.

Maddie's hurt expression drifts into my vision. There is the other problem. I'd either have to lie about the cause for my fight with Tom or remain quiet and never talk to Maddie again. Neither is an option. Besides, even if I did lie, she'd know. I'm a lousy liar.

I turn to my side. Oak leaves, now brown and dry, crunch against my cheek. The wind has picked up and a layer of clouds snuff out the last light. It smells like snow and I shiver. It's hard to tell what time it is, but I know what I've got to do. Breaking into a jog, I head for school.

I finally have a reason to see Sarge. What did Tom say about the cover-up? Surely Sarge knows. Then I'll catch Tom and apologize.

A Different Truth

I want my friend back.

CHAPTER TWENTY-ONE

The administration building is only partially lit and deserted. Most of the faculty live in the faculty dorms or in the houses for married couples. I wonder if Sarge will even be there.

I knock and listen. Nothing.

I'm about to turn away when the door swings open.

"Olson? Come in," Sarge barks.

I rush inside. I'm freezing, my hands stiff with cold, my palms muddy. I hide them behind my back and straighten.

"Cadet Olson, at your service, Sir."

"Sit your ass down." Sarge points to the lone wooden chair in front of his desk. He's chewing another cigar. "What's on your mind?"

I plunk into the chair. What has seemed plausible just minutes earlier, appears absurd now. Why haven't I gone to dinner instead?

"I see you've been in the woods again." Sarge's eyes lodge on my chest.

I look down. To my horror, a leaf sticks under the lapel of my jacket. I crush and stuff it into my pocket.

"Sorry, Sir, I needed time to think."

"Spit it out, Olson, I don't have all day. Mess hall duty. Not even time to smoke this damned cigar."

"The reason I came here… I had a question," I stumble. Sarge's face remains still… waiting. "I heard about My Lee or something…I mean Tom, Cadet Zimmer said there was a massacre and I wanted to…"

My voice fizzles. I've got to be mad to ask Sarge about this. Of all people, I should've gone to see someone else. Even Eric would've been a better choice. Sarge's eyes are glued to my face, his cigar circling from left to right and back. It's impossible to know what goes on behind the broad forehead.

I open my mouth to continue, but don't know what else to say so I jump up. "I'm sorry, I made a mistake. I better go."

"Sit down, Olson. You're a nuisance bar none." Sarge leans forward. The leather chair creaks as he grabs a matchbox and lights his cigar. Sucking noises erupt into a cloud of smoke. "Damn war."

"I can leave," I offer, though my legs are filled with lead.

"You asked for it, now let's talk," Sarge says as if he knows my thoughts. "I'll tell you what I know. I assume that's what you're here for?"

I nod. I can't speak.

"First of all. My Lai, l-a-i and more correctly Son My, is the name of the village where it happened."

The cigar fog reaches my nose and I cough.

Sarge clears his throat. "In a nutshell: Intelligence assumed the village harbored enemy soldiers, you know, hid them underground. They were wrong! Looks like Charlie Company, the platoon in charge, went in there and instead of fighting the VC, killed hundreds of civilians—women, children, old men, even the livestock. Everything that moved." Sarge spits into the wastebasket. "Carnage."

"What happened to the men? I mean the soldiers that killed..." My voice is barely audible. Tom was right. As usual. Why did I ever doubt Tom's story? I remember the scene in the cave. I should've said something, supported Tom.

"One is on trial for murder." Sarge clears his throat again. It sounds like a growl. "Rightly so. There'll be more court-martials. I'm sure of it. Some have since died in battle."

"Why didn't we know? I mean didn't this happen last year?"

"Last March. Good question, Olson. I can only guess that the right people didn't come forward. War is nasty business. People are killed every day though this was horrific. It takes leadership, strength of character to recognize the wrong thing and do something about it. What we try to teach you here."

"Did *you* know—earlier?"

"I heard about it in the spring. One of the men from Charlie Company sent letters, there was talk, rumors. I didn't hear the entire story until recently. Like everyone else."

I nod.

"Look Olson, I won't lie to you. Soldiers shoot. They die. Civilians shoot. They die. Killings aren't fair, our men murder their own by mistake—friendlies—but most men try to do the right thing. When your life is on the line, you sometimes overreact. Especially when you're inexperienced. Like you ran out to the woods when you got upset about the letter. Got lost. Overreacted. Imagine you're angry, scared for your life. Add tired and miserably uncomfortable. Your nerves are shot."

I nod again.

"That's why we do things in teams, train you the right way. To stay calm, to keep your ears and eyes open. Work together. Your buddies are what keep you alive. Understand?"

"Sure." I want to ask what Sarge thinks of the war, about his role.

Sarge sends another puff of smoke across the desk. "I'm late."

"Yes, Sir." I jump up. "Thank you."

"No problem, come and see me again." Sarge stabs his cigar into the ashtray, flinging pieces of tobacco and ashes across the polished oak.

"Yes, Sir."

I jog toward mess hall. The second dinner shift is starting. I scan the tables but don't see Tom. Maybe he already ate or he's still in town with Eric. Curfew isn't for another hour. Slightly disappointed I load my tray, fried potatoes, peas, two burger patties dripping with grease and strawberry Jello. I'm starving. And though I've got to prep an analysis of *A Separate Peace*, the last English project of the semester, I'm relieved because tomorrow is Sunday and I'll catch up with Tom. I'll ask him about My Lai, but mostly make up for being stupid. I whistle. For the first time in weeks, I feel happy.

***

I stick my head into the washroom where a half dozen guys are getting ready. "Has anyone seen Tom?" Everyone shakes their head.

It's Sunday late morning. A hard sun shines outside. Blue lights reflect off the whiteness of the season's first snow. It's just a dusting and too early to go ice-skating, one of our favorite pastimes. The lake has crusted over around the edges, but the middle is still open water.

I woke earlier than usual, excited about the prospect of seeing Tom, renewing our friendship. Maybe we can visit town together, see Eric and Maddie.

"Tom, where are you?" I mumble under my breath. Now that I've made up my mind I'm eager to talk. I expect to find Tom at breakfast, devouring a mountain of scrambled eggs. Few cadets are up. Tom is nowhere in sight. I recheck the bathroom on my floor.

There are few places cadets can be outside of class. On the weekends, life plays in the halls of our barracks, the cafeteria and the cave. A handful of first-years hover around a monopoly game in the corridor.

I knock on the doorframe of Tom's room. "Have you seen Tom?"

Toad is sitting at his desk, his face hidden behind a folder. He glances at me and blinks behind the glasses as if he's been asleep. Then he shakes his head.

"Come on, Toad, you must've seen him earlier."

"Actually," Toad looks confused, "I haven't seen him all morning. I thought he was already gone when I woke."

"Think, man," I say, "Did you see him last night?"

"Actually." Toad puts down his folder, but his eyes remain stuck to the desk in front of him. "I can't remember."

"What do you mean, you can't remember seeing him or you can't remember what happened last night." I move next to Toad's desk. I want to shake the guy. "Think, Toad. What happened?"

"I must've fallen asleep." Toad's voice turns whiny. "I did see him around 22:00 when I was getting ready for bed. But I don't remember after…I don't know."

"After what?"

"He went to the bathroom and—"

I still want to slap him. "And?"

"I don't remember. He could've been there or he could not have."

"It didn't cross your mind to check or tell anyone?"

"I thought… I mean I got busy with my book, it's a really great story. I read with my flashlight under the covers."

"Never mind." I hurry out the door and jog to the library, a square limestone building with two floors connected to the classrooms via a long corridor.

When I burst through the door, the librarian, a gray-faced woman of indefinable age, stares at me with a scolding look. I don't really expect to find Tom here, but then I haven't been around him for weeks. Who knows, maybe Tom is picking up another volume of Shakespeare. I grin, remembering when Mr. Brown tried to pick on Tom in English without success.

I rush along the aisles, check the few lowered heads at the desks and benches, the endless shelves loaded with everything the English language has to offer. Palmer has an impressive library, even a separate temperate-controlled room with rare books only available to the faculty and to be handled with white gloves. I make a loop around, but don't see Tom.

"Where are you," I mumble. I head back to mess hall. It looks deserted, the kitchen staff wiping tables and stacking trays and silverware in preparation for lunch. Maybe he's taking a walk. But that's unlikely. It snowed last night, just a dusting, but the air stings with frost. Still, I jog along the paths, winding like ribbons between buildings. Barely anyone is out. Has he gone back to town to see Eric? It's possible. After all, besides me, Tom has few close friends at Palmer. I decide to return to Tom's room.

Toad still sits parked at his desk, one hand in the drawer sticky with caramel. He's stuffing a candy bar in his mouth when I enter the room. *No wonder you're fat.*

"Has Tom come back?" I ask, unable to keep the irritation from my voice.

"No." Toad turns on his chair. A fleck of chocolate has melted and clings to his upper lip like another mole.

"Have you been here the entire time?"

"I went to the bathroom, but otherwise."

I plunk on Tom's chair, struggling to control my temper. "What about last night? Think!"

Tom's bed is unmade, the wool blanket roughed up, the sheets pulled out. It's impossible to tell if Tom has spent the night or if he messed it up last night and didn't return. Either way, he wouldn't leave it unmade.

"I already told you." Toad sounds exasperated. "I read and can't remember."

"Did you get up in the night, go to the bathroom?"

"Yes, but what's that have to do—"

"Did you notice Tom then?"

"I was half asleep, it was dark. You think I can see in the dark?"

"Never mind. What about sounds? Does Tom snore, did you hear anything?"

"He's pretty quiet. Most of the time I don't hear him at all. He says I snore a lot, but I can't help it."

Who cares, I want to scream. What a pathetic character Toad is.

"When was the last time you saw Tom?"

"I already told you. Last night some time, shortly before taps."

"When you read under the blanket."

"Right."

"He wouldn't have left this morning without making his bed." Beerbelly or one of the senior officers is bound to inspect anytime. Tom won't risk demerits for something that obvious.

Toad shrugs.

I jump up. Frustrated and angry I check the clock. It's nearly noon. Worry creeps up in me like a slimy insect. Something is wrong. Something I can't put my finger on.

I head for Beerbelly's apartment on the first floor. I hate to see him, but I've got no choice. What if Tom has done something like Eric? He'd do it right. He'd succeed. After all, he's been all alone with a father who doesn't care and a mother who's lost her mind. Worse, because I'm a self-centered ass.

I knock on the counselor's door. Straining to keep my voice level when Beerbelly opens, I say. "Sir, excuse me, Sir. Cadet Zimmer is missing. He's been gone from his room since last night."

New doubt creeps up in me. Maybe Tom was there and Toad just missed him. Toad seems to operate in a permanent state of distraction. Hard to imagine how he gets through school.

"What makes you think Cadet Zimmer is missing?" Beerbelly starts a coughing fit and I cringe. He's obviously sick because he looks like a mess, his hair disheveled, his shirt unbuttoned at the top, showing tufts of gray hair. He waves me inside and sags behind his desk. "Maybe he went for a walk. To town. It's Sunday after all."

I shake my head. The feeling of doom is back. "No, Sir. I believe something is wrong. He didn't make his bed this morning. He'd never leave…"

Beerbelly leans back in his chair. "What would you like me to do? Campus is huge. Did you check everywhere? Could he have left? Maybe gone home early? Winter break isn't far off. I don't want to alert the Dean for nothing. Not after all the crap you've pulled."

"Didn't you hear what I said?" I hear my voice rising into a scream. Is the entire school stupid? "He went missing last night or this morning. No way, he left." To Tom home is worse than Palmer. He'd rather live in a tent than go home early.

"Calm down, Olson. I'll alert a couple of teachers. Maybe he's gone to see faculty." Beerbelly straightens with a sigh. "If warranted I'll see the Dean. You go and organize a search detail. Pick ten men from your floor. Cadets who know Zimmer."

"Yes, Sir."

I race off, glad for something to do. The second-floor corridor is quiet and I hope to find enough guys in their rooms. I knock on doors, explain and have them assemble in the hall. Despite Tom's outspokenness against the war, most of the younger cadets like him for his quiet intelligence, his genuine ways. He's never mean like Muller or Big Mike and he's always willing to help people with study prep. The few that don't like him are idiots anyway.

The nagging in my stomach grows. Against all hope I go back to see Toad. But the room is empty, Toad undoubtedly at lunch. Nothing indicates that Tom has been here. Maybe I should make Tom's bed. In case he returns and simply forgot. He'd be happy I covered for him.

But then, what if it's a crime scene. I step closer to examine the sheets and pillow. There's nothing on it except for a couple of short dark hairs. Hardly evidence. I shake my head remembering the boys I'd asked to assemble and rush into the hall.

They slouch in the corridor, leaning against the walls. "Listen," I say, struggling to sound confident. "Tom hasn't been seen since last night. Pair up in twos and check every building."

Markus looks worried. "What if we can't find him?"

"You must. He has to be somewhere. Ask everyone you see. We'll meet back here in one hour."

We fan out across the barracks, the school buildings, mess hall and the gym. I run across the lawns to barracks C, the air fresh and icy attacking my nostrils, when I notice tracks in the snow, leading toward the woods. The ground crunches underfoot. It snowed last evening and these look new. Abandoning my plan to visit the barracks, I hurry toward the trees which look thin and dark against the brightness of the snow. I remember getting lost. It seems ages ago.

Squinting against the glare, I hug myself to ward off the frost and the wind that always picks up across the lake. I follow the tracks up a shallow hill and down the other side, wondering what people are doing out here. Holly and shrubby cedars form a semi-circular thicket like a room. *This is stupid. Why would Tom run out here? He doesn't care to exercise and these footprints are from at least three people.* The tracks have gotten deeper and are easy to see. As I round the holly trees, I notice a trampled area in front of me.

When my eyes lift from the ground, a pair of shoes comes into view, dark blue pants, Palmer's shirt and Tom's face.

Except, it doesn't look like Tom, rather a bloody, swollen lump where his face used to be. His head hangs to one side as if he's asleep. Held by a rope, his hands are clasped back around a big oak tree he's leaning against. A piece of fabric, what looks like the remains of one of Tom's handkerchiefs, is stuffed in his mouth. Tom owns an infinite selection of colorful handkerchiefs and is always happy to share them with me.

"Tom!" I yell. "No, Tom. Wake up!"

A groaning noise escapes from behind the cloth and I yank it out of Tom's mouth.

"Hey," Tom says, his face turning into a grimace.

"What happened?" My fingers shake as I untie the rope around Tom's hands. They look purplish blue. Tom groans again and falls forward. I catch him in my arms, trying to stand him upright.

"Can you walk?" I ask. "Come on, I'll help you."

Tom grunts while he tries to set his feet, but his ankles give and he falls into the snow, his bluish hands uselessly at his side.

"Tom, please," I'm crying. "Get up!" I shout like giving a command, rubbing and pulling Tom's arms and trying to lift him. But Tom is too heavy even for me and his long limbs provide no traction. "Listen," I say, "I'll get help. Don't go anywhere. I'll be back in two minutes." Tom's eyes are closed and I don't know if he's heard me.

I race toward the sick wing, a section in the administrative building. I've never felt so slow in my life as I sprint across the white-powdered lawns, ignoring the hammering inside my chest, a silent scream trying to burst into the morning's stillness.

"Help," I yell, shoving open the door, almost falling when my wet soles slide across the linoleum.

Tom lies unchanged in the snow, a heap of twigs not much different from the fallen limbs of diseased trees as we, the doctor and Sarge draw near. The procession back to school goes quickly, Sarge carrying Tom as if he were a mere child. A crowd watches us from the lawn in front of sick bay.

"Make room," Sarge shouts. "You better go to your dorm, son," he says to me after carefully placing Tom on a bed. "We'll take care of him."

Our eyes meet. I struggle to keep the surge of tears from unleashing. All I can do is nod.

The afternoon drags in terrible slowness as a hush falls over the second floor of Barracks B. The usual banter, joking and play-fighting has stopped. Instead I hear the other cadets visit each other to go over the morning events.

"I can't believe Tom's roommate didn't see anything, didn't even notice that Tom wasn't around. I mean, is the guy blind?" Markus comments next door.

"Who'd do such a thing," someone else says.

Who indeed? I'm pacing in my room, unable to sit or study. I want to visit Tom and talk. Ask him a hundred questions.

They've turned me away at the door three times. "Tomorrow," they told me. "Give it time." I tried again anyway, hoping to get through the nurse playing sentry.

On the way back I stop by the cave in search of distraction. I don't feel like playing games or watching TV. I want to see Tom and find out what happened. The thought of Maddie crosses my mind.

I push it away.

CHAPTER TWENTY-TWO

Monday I stop by sickbay before breakfast. I can't take it any longer, I'm worried about Tom and that he'll die. The day nurse at the desk looks at me inquiringly.

"Yes?"

"I'm here to see Tom."

"Tom is in no shape to have visitors." I've only heard of Nurse Mellon and that she's strict and none of the boys like her. She's good at sniffing out fake colds and stomach aches around exam weeks: thermometers heated on radiators, diarrhea caused by laxatives and self-inflicted skin rashes. Despite the situation I suppress a grin, thinking how her name matches her huge boobs, and imagining her hovering over me.

Her face is as round as her breasts, large cheeks only disrupted by a dimpled chin and thin lips without the faintest hint of lipstick. Her eyes are light blue, too pale to leave an impression but missing nothing.

"I've got to see him. Please."

Nurse Mellon's pale eyes scrutinize my face. "Why don't you come back during your lunch break? By then, Tom will have been examined by the doctor and, provided all is well, you may see him for a few minutes."

***

I can't concentrate, not even when Sarge presents me with the advanced sharpshooter's award. I completely forgot about the rifle shooting contest last week.

Sarge has me come in front of the class and attaches the silver pin, a miniature cross, to my chest. "Great job," he says, shaking hands. "See what a little hard work will do for you."

I return to my desk. To my surprise I don't even care about the new pin. A week ago I would've been ecstatic to get Sarge's attention, adding the coveted award to my meager collection. Some of the boys have a dozen medals for various achievements while moving up in rank. Of course, most of them make better grades. I figured out that the only way to get ahead is to be an A-student or have a father with lots of cash. Neither is going to happen. All I want now is for the hour to be over so I can visit Tom.

I grab two apples and three rolls from the lunch buffet and sprint to sickbay. The reception desk is deserted. I look down the hall—nothing. The linoleum gleams, reflecting the high efficiency bulbs overhead. I might get in trouble, but didn't Nurse Mellon say I'd be able to see Tom? Better apologize afterwards than waste time asking.

I push open the first patient room: empty. The boy behind the second door has a broken leg. I don't know him. Behind the third door, I recognize Tom's long frame beneath the sterile white of hospital blankets.

He looks pale and asleep, the left side of his face covered under tape and bandages. I quietly walk to his side and stand, indecisive whether to wait or leave. For a second I worry if Tom is still breathing. I bend lower until I hear a slight rattle from his throat.

Whether it's because I'm noisier than I thought or that we share a deeper connection, Tom opens his eyes.

"Hey."

"Hey." I fight a lump in my throat. "How you doing?"

Tom moves his head to focus on me. "Sort of lousy. What're you up to?"

"Not much, boring English and math, messed up my report pretty good, but I don't care."

"I see."

"Tom, listen." I pause, contemplating whether to put my hand on Tom's arm which looks white, almost translucent.

"I was an idiot," Tom breathes.

"*I* was the idiot," I say. "I—"

"Bull, you honored a secret. I understand that now." Tom's good eye moves toward a smile, but gets somehow stuck showing pure remorse.

I nod. "I did but I should've been more aware of your friendship with Eric. You, I never…"

"I know you aren't taking Eric away from me. I was stupid."

"I saw Sarge and he told me. It's all true. I should've taken your side…in the cave."

"What's true?"

"My Lai. The killings. You were right all along."

"You'll have to figure out where you stand for *yourself*," Tom coughs, straining for air.

"I mean I should've stood by you," I say, "all along…" my voice fails as I remember watching Tom in the cave, arguing with Muller…alone. I could've said something then… all the other times. A bead of sweat rolls down my temple. I remember my own family, how they never cared what I had to say. "I'm sorry, no matter what," I mumble.

"I know."

"Who did this?"

"Already talked to Sarge," Tom says, his face turning into a grimace. "I don't know. They put a blanket over my head. It was dark outside."

I want to hit someone. "What happened?"

"Guess I must have real enemies. Thought they were in Vietnam." Tom's laugh sounds like a croak.

"I'm sure glad you're tough." I pat his arm after all. It seems thin and cold. "What happened after they carried you out?"

"There were at least two…they whispered. Study hour was almost over and I was heading for the john. I was just thinking about my visit with Eric and next thing I know, someone grabs me from behind. They herded me outside and tied me to a tree. It was dark, new moon, just flashlights pointing at me. I couldn't see anything."

Tom pauses, his face almost as white as the gauze. "They smacked me around and I finally passed out. When I woke I was alone. It was so cold. I tried to yell but they'd stuffed a cloth in my mouth. I knew nobody would hear me anyway. I thought maybe Toad would notice…The forest was spooky."

I nod. Just like the hazing. Cowards that beat up people over nothing…because they're new or different or have other beliefs. Tears press in the back of my throat, spurred on by sorrow for Tom, but mostly by fury that threatens to boil into rage. I want revenge. Not since the first hazing have I felt this angry. Not even Muller's abuse comes close. I jump up and begin to pace.

"I'm going to find the sons of bitches," I whisper. "You get well. I'm going to sniff them out."

"You watch yourself." Tom closes his eyes.

I turn at the door. "I'll be back tonight." But Tom doesn't seem to hear. Though I want to run and scream, I force myself to walk. I slow down near the office adjacent to the nurse's desk. Nurse Mellon is still gone, but I hear voices from beyond the door of an exam room.

One of them is Sarge's, gravelly and capable of carrying through cement walls. "…do an inquiry." The other voices join, but are too soft to understand. I think I hear the Dean. One has to be the doctor and the other nurse Mellon.

When somebody moves beyond the door I jump around the corner and hurry outside. I'll do my own inquiry, I'll see to that. I race back to the school building. Class is about to start. I'll have to force myself to concentrate. It'll be a long afternoon.

That evening I make a list of possible suspects, who would be capable of doing it and anyone with a potential motive. I remember Big Mike who was angry at Tom after the Evansville trip. There is Muller's outburst in the cave, Bloom, the fight with Tony about the massacre. Maybe there are others Tom has offended with his liberal views and his obvious dislike for military life.

After dinner I return to see Tom. The night nurse lets me in. "Five minutes and nothing exciting," she whispers as we enter Tom's room. The light on the nightstand casts a milky glow across the top of the bed. Tom's eyes are open and very bright. His good cheek glows pink in the whiteness.

"Hey," he says.

"How you feeling?" I ignore the chair next to Tom's bed.

"Freezing, can you get me another blanket? Over there in the drawer."

Glad for something to do, I jump to rummage for the cover. "It'd really help if you could remember something about the night. Something must have been familiar."

Tom shakes his head. "I already told Sarge that it was too dark and that they only whispered. You know I'm quite famous now. The Dean stopped by and almost all the teachers. Someone brought cookies. You want some? I'm not too hungry right now."

I shake my head. "Keep those until you're ready. Fatten you up."

"Time to go." The nurse hovers in the door.

"Just one more second." I nod at the woman who stubbornly remains waiting. "Do you remember what time you went to the bathroom?"

"Before ten. Close to tattoo for sure."

That matches what Toad said. "I'll be back tomorrow," I say aloud. "We'll find them. Don't worry."

Tom nods. It seems like an effort.

When I return to my room, Plozett looks up from his desk. "Toad was here looking for you."

"Did he say what he wanted?"

"No, but he said he'd check back. I didn't know where you were."

"That's okay, thanks anyway." I head out the door. I'm supposed to study for a math test but feel pretty confident. So what if I don't get an A. I got Bs and Cs in most subjects anyway.

I enter Tom's room. "You're looking for me?"

"Yeah." Toad abruptly throws his history book shut, but I notice the paperback inside about some crime story set in space. "I remembered something. I thought you might want to know. I was going to tell Sarge but then I thought—"

"Never mind, what is it?"

"The night Tom disappeared, I mean earlier that day, I saw a couple of jocks leaving our barracks. Thing is, they were cavalry and don't live here. Maybe it's nothing."

The members of the cavalry, called horsemen, typically come from wealthy families that can afford additional tuition so their offspring can ride and jump the three dozen white Lipizzans the school maintains. The horses are gray at first and turn white by the age of ten.

A horse adorns Palmer's signature logo and is plastered on the school's crest and all our insignia. Cadets from the cavalry hang together and rarely socialize with common infantry men like us. Except for Muller whose cousin is in the cavalry. But then Muller doesn't really mix with us either. He obviously believes alienation is the price of leadership.

"Did they carry anything or act strangely?"

"I didn't notice anything."

"What time was that?"

"Before dinner, I think." Toad looks at the ceiling. "Yes, I was headed outside when I saw them. I always go early to—"

"What time?"

"Before six."

I sigh. "Thanks Toad. Let me know if you remember anything else."

I go over the evidence I've collected so far. It's thin and doesn't make sense. I'm frustrated about the lack of time and opportunity to snoop around. Days are filled with classes. Football training has resumed with weight lifting and sprints, not to mention the mandatory study time which forces me to remain at my desk or in the library every night.

I carry a notebook to jot down clues or new ideas, but my questions have yielded little and the pages remain bare. Only in the movies do the private investigators find things in a logical string of events. Real life is much different.

When I return to visit Tom the following day, I'm sent away.

"Sorry, Tom needs to rest." Nurse Mellon's lips are firmly set. She's the only one at school ever addressing us by our first name.

"What about this evening?"

"Not today."

"I don't understand. I saw him yesterday and he was fine. Why isn't it okay today?"

Nurse Mellon sighs.

"Please, I won't stay long."

"Tom is sleeping most of the time. His fever is pretty high. He needs to get as much rest as possible."

I nod. "I'll be back tomorrow then."

But the next day I don't get any farther. Rumor has it that Tom has pneumonia and lies under a plastic tent to keep the air clean and filled with oxygen. Someone else says Tom will be moved to a hospital in Evansville. I remember how Tom loves visiting Evansville and its movie theatres with double and triple shows of the newest Hollywood films.

By Wednesday evening, I can't take it any longer and burst into Sarge's office. "Is Tom going to die?" To my embarrassment my voice shakes and I feel tears at the back of my throat.

Sarge sits behind his desk, grading papers with a thick red pencil. For a second he looks ready to yell but then his face softens.

"Sit down, Olson."

"I don't want to sit, Sir."

"Fine." Sarge rises from his chair and begins to pace around the room. "I know you two are best friends and what I'm going to tell you now needs to stay in this room. Understand?"

I nod. My knees suddenly wobble and I wish I'd followed Sarge's order to sit.

"Tom is very ill. When we found him, it looked like he'd be fine. But he spent an entire night in the woods at freezing temperatures and he isn't built like you and me. Tom has pneumonia. He's having trouble breathing. The doctor asked for help from the Evansville hospital and they sent an oxygen tent. He's stable but it wouldn't hurt if—"

"What does that mean?" My voice is shrill. "Stable."

"It means he's no better and no worse—for the moment."

"Did you find out anything? Who did it and why?"

"I'm working on it. We'll find them, if it's the last thing I do at this school. Why, do you know something?"

"I'm not sure, Toad, I mean Cadet Todd, saw several men from the cavalry leaving our barracks. They never do anything with us."

"Unlikely." Sarge waves an arm to cut me off. "Anything else?"

"Yeah, remember the trip back from Evansville when Big Mike threatened Tom? What if he made good on it?"

"Possible but I've already checked on him. He was prepping for an exam with Tony. They were in the study room of Barracks D."

All barracks have a study area on the main floor, outfitted with a couple of desks, extra chairs and a table, meant for group projects and to foster teamwork.

"Big Mike studies on Saturday night?"

"I know what you mean, but his voice is quite loud and he was definitely in that room."

I feel deflated. Big Mike has been my prime suspect from the beginning. I didn't tell Tom, but I talked to Big Mike after practice one day when we were the last ones leaving. "Why don't you leave Tom alone?" I'd tried to sound casual. "He's not a jock like you, so what's the big deal?"

"You worried for your skinny friend," Big Mike said, his face turning into a nasty grin. "A word of advice, you should pick your friends more carefully."

"Just leave him be," I said. "He's a good guy."

Big Mike ignored me and walked off.

"Son, you listening?" Sarge is staring at me. "I said I'll let you know if anything changes… on either front."

"What about Muller?" I blurt.

"What about him?"

"He threatened Tom in the cave. Said someone should teach him a lesson. Many of us heard Muller say it."

Sarge falls into his chair. The room is quiet except for the radiator creaking in the corner.

Encouraged by Sarge's silence, I go on. "Muller can't stand Tom's antiwar talk. He has always been over the top. He's extreme and believes he's perfect, but really he's cunning and enjoys when others suffer."

"You're referring to your duel with Muller?"

"He wouldn't do it to me, I'm too strong."

"I don't know." Sarge shakes his head and refocuses on me. "Listen, son, I know you're upset and angry but you can't go around accusing people. They may all have faults, but we need to be doing this the right way."

"But, Sir."

"No buts. Dismissed."

"Thank you, Sir." For nothing. What in the heck is the *right way*? Somehow I expected Sarge to help. I think about the My Lai massacre and what Sarge said about it. He'll protect the establishment. He's too close to it. I head for the door, my stomach churning with revulsion and disappointment.

"Olson?"

"Yes, Sir?"

"Promise to come to me when you hear anything. I'll let you know what I learn."

"Yes, Sir."

CHAPTER TWENTY-THREE

I awake soaked in sweat, my heart racing. Big Mike chased me across the frozen lake wielding a saber. Everything was milky and foggy. The edges between ground and air fused into white clouds like wafts of frozen nitrogen. The farther I ran the thinner the ice became while Big Mike's laugh grew louder and closer behind me.

I tried circling back and avoid the open area in the middle of the lake, but Big Mike's friends materialized from the fog carrying sabers. Suddenly Tom was there, wearing a hospital gown giggling while he watched his bed break through the ice. Then Tom was on the bed, flailing his arms for help as it disappeared from view into the glassy water.

I screamed, torn between rescuing Tom and saving myself from the sabers, when I felt the ice break, thin lines forming ragged edges, faster, then the breaking sound, a sharp snap as I sank, Big Mike standing above, waving at me. Tom in the clear water, his eyes open and staring without expression.

There's no way I'll go back to sleep now. I get up and traipse to the washroom for a drink of water. The night light is dim but I have no trouble finding the sink. A sound like a tiny whimper makes me stop.

I listen. Nothing.

"Anybody in here?" Nothing except for the dripping faucet. Still worked up about my dream, I feel foolish standing barefoot on the tile floor. "I'm hearing things," I mumble and head back to my room.

***

During the next four days, I race to sick bay between classes, hoping to be allowed in or to find the reception desk vacant. Every time, one of the nurses stares at me, shaking her head with tight lips. "Maybe tomorrow, be patient," they mumble until I turn away.

Saturday, Tom's father materializes in my room.

157

"I hear you're friends with Tom," he says. He's as tall as Tom with the same long features except for a roundish belly and a layer of flab underneath his chin. His eyes are green and hard like polished marbles. "I'm Tom's father, Thomas Zimmer."

It sounds strange to me that Tom's dad has the same name since they have so little in common. "Nice to meet you."

"Tom is very sick. We may need to move him to a hospital. The Dean said you'd assist me preparing his things."

"Yes, Sir. His room is down the hall, number 222. I'll show you."

We walk along the corridor. I search for something to say, but the silence between us is too thick to penetrate. I glance at the man at my side who looks pale and whose lips are pressed tight.

"This is it." I open the door to Tom's room, relieved Toad is out. "His things are on the right. I'll have to ask Beerbelly, I mean the barracks counselor, to get the suitcase."

"No need, I brought an extra bag. We'll only take his pajamas and a few personal items for now. I expect he'll be back soon once he's better." Zimmer Senior stands in the room like a foreign object while I collect Tom's toiletries and a few favorite books and movie magazines, wondering if Tom will be able to read anytime soon.

"That's all." I hold up the bag. "When will he be moved?"

"Monday. The ambulance will take him."

I nod. I've run out of things to say. "I'll be in my room if you need anything."

"Thanks, Andy." He hesitates. "Tom always talks about you."

I nod again. The lump in my throat is growing.

"Say, you wouldn't have any idea who did this?" Tom Senior's face shows a dimension of pain, I've missed before.

"No Sir, I'm sorry, I've been searching myself and Sarge..."

"Of course, thanks Andy." Thomas Zimmer Senior walks down the hall, his steps hollow and lonely.

In my room I stare at the wall. Something is nagging me, but I can't figure out what it is.

My last two finals are Monday and Tuesday. I'll be picked up Wednesday for Christmas break. My mother wrote. They're all looking forward to seeing me. I bought a few small gifts from Maddie's shop in November, now stacked inside my desk drawer. I wanted to buy nice things, but money was even tighter and now I'm broke. Going out with Maddie and Tom, to the movies and stopping by the store is expensive.

Maddie. All fall I hoped for an opportunity to meet her privately, but we had no place to be alone. Though she attends the local high school, I can't visit there—Palmer cadets don't mix with townies. The biannual dances the school arranges for us are a big deal and attendees from the classy girl's academy in North Bend are driven down in a bus. The dances start in the early afternoon and are over by 21:00 to allow the girls to return to their school.

The girls' painted faces and piled-high hair, fancy dresses and long gloves and lacquered shoes are nothing like Maddie. At the last dance a blonde circled around me, but I felt awkward and tongue-tied. I don't look forward to the next dance in February. All I can think of is Maddie. It's been two weeks since our fight.

It occurs to me that neither Maddie nor Eric know about Tom. *Eric is probably going crazy wondering where Tom is. And Maddie?* She was upset with me, but she probably wonders why I haven't stopped by, what I'm doing. Why I haven't tried to change her mind. Why I'm not making up and winning her back. *I'll go tomorrow to tell them.*

I think about Tom in his hospital bed and that he'll miss his finals. But Tom is a good student and will catch up in the spring.

After sleeping late on Sunday and missing breakfast, I head outside for lunch. The mess hall is nearly empty since many cadets embrace the freedom of a discretionary meal. The food line short, I take a tray and scan the offerings of meatloaf and fish filets. Opting for meatloaf, I sink my fork deep into the mashed potatoes, one of my favorites, when Plozett rushes into the door.

"Andy. Did you hear?" His customary laid-back attitude is replaced by a strain on his face.

"What?"

"Tom's dead." Plozett's voice sounds metallic.

I watch my roommate's mouth open and close, but no other words reach my ears. Blood rushes through my skull in crashing waves. I shake my head. Several cadets from other years begin to crowd us, digging for details to replace the dullness of Sunday afternoon.

Plozett places a hand on my shoulder and I come to. "Sorry, man, I know you were best friends."

Ignoring him and the growing mob, I push away my tray and hurry outside. It can't be. Tom can't be gone. I sprint to the infirmary where several cars are parked in front. Men and women in civilian and military clothes hover in the corridor. The reception desk deserted, I race down the hall.

Tom's father stands in front of Tom's room. Head bend, he listens to the Dean whose voice is too low to hear. A plump woman with bleach-blonde hair hangs on Tom senior's arm, her eyes large and worried but dry.

"…launched an inquiry…regretful accident…all under control," the Dean says as I draw near. The Dean pats the woman's arm like he's done a million times.

"What happened?" I ask. It sounds like someone else.

Tom's father looks up, his polished eyes wet. "Tom passed away this morning. He... the infection was too strong."

The school's doctor appears from Tom's room and nods at the Dean and then Tom's father. "You can go in now."

Tom Senior's eyes meet mine. Then he turns and enters Tom's room. I follow.

"You don't have permission." The Dean's fingers claw my shoulder.

"But he was my best friend." I feel the familiar anger choke my throat.

Tom's father turns. "It's okay, he can say good-bye."

Tom lies in bed in a new blue and white striped pajama as if he were sleeping, the oxygen tent folded to the side like a discarded umbrella. He's pale as usual except for the purple bruises around his right eye and cheek and a yellow tinge that has crept into his cheeks.

Tom's long face looks peaceful, his mouth relaxed with a slight upward curve as if he's had a last laugh before forgetting to breathe. His hands lie folded on his chest in a praying position though I never saw him pray. Chapel is mandatory for all cadets but I'm pretty sure Tom was an atheist. A minister hovers to Tom's right, mumbling into a gold cross he holds in his palm.

I look away. What a farce. Suddenly unable to stay another second, I push past them and race down the corridor, my steps loud and lonely on the linoleum.

Tom is dead.

It's impossible to think of Palmer without Tom. For the past few weeks, I functioned on autopilot, always thinking how I'd tell Tom this or ask Tom that. Now Tom is gone.

I continue running. It's freezing but I keep going, my feet carrying me toward the woods, my legs mechanical windup toys without feeling. The air burns my face, my lungs hurt. I can't stop.

Because if I stop I'll have to think. My legs ache, turn to agony. Still I run, the trees above me silent—indifferent. There is no place to feel better. I remember coming here, being upset about my mother's letter. It's so trivial. In fact I realize that I don't care. I'll soon get my own place anyway.

Tom's face is back, pale with eyes closed. I zigzag through the forest, across the paths, blind to everything. I begin to wheeze.

I want pain. Yet I feel nothing, a robot moving his legs, up and down, left and right. I gasp as the wheezing increases. Still I can't stop. Another direction. Downhill. Into Garville.

The town looks even more deserted on Sunday, its streets void of cars except for Dr. Smittley's Cadillac in the carport and a red truck with rusty fenders in front of the tavern. My legs scream, my lungs roil with every breath. I have to slow down or collapse. The newest poster announces Easy Rider, Peter Fonda staring across some canyon. Relaxed. Indifferent. Who gives a shit?

Tom is dead.

My lungs aching, my legs numb, I begin to sob. My body is a sack of cement that slowly sets and now holds me in place until the effort to move one more step becomes too great.

I crumble to the curb. Tom is gone. I push to force air through my lungs as scenes with Tom flash by: our first encounter, Tom discussing the war, throwing his arms in the air, Tom drinking wine behind the bleachers, Tom in the old chair with Eric, Tom passed out in the woods. Somebody did this. Someone murdered him.

"Andy?"

Maddie's face hovers in fog. I wipe my eyes with my sleeves and swallow the torrent of slime and wetness in my mouth.

"What's wrong?" Maddie's voice is full of concern. I notice Eric waiting a few feet away as more people leave the theatre. I shake my head. It's hard to form words and say it out loud. I clear my throat. Maddie waits, her blue eyes glued to my face. "What's the matter? Do you need help? Please tell me."

I shake my head again. "Tom…is dead." Fresh tears spill as I hear myself say it. It seems somehow more real.

"Oh, no." Maddie cries, her face turning pale. "What happened?" She begins to weep. "He was fine two weeks ago."

Eric's wheelchair edges closer. The rest of the Sunday crowd has dispersed to leave the road to its sleepy ignorance. "What happened?" he growls. His eyes have turned to blue ice, but I can all but breathe. "Why don't you come to our house?"

I sit there and stare.

"I'll make you a cup of tea. You don't have to talk if you don't want to." Maddie places her hand on my arm. Her fingers are thin and long, her fingernails painted a pearly pink. I straighten. Old men have to feel this way right before they die. I keep staring down as we shuffle toward the store, the squeak from Eric's wheelchair the only sound.

Maddie rushes into the backroom. I hear whispers and a moment later Maddie's father appears, his face a mix of curiosity and shock. He carries Eric upstairs. Maddie hoists the wheelchair to the apartment on the second floor.

It seems like the most normal thing in the world. Thankful for the distraction, I slump into a couch with wide arms and red pillows. The familiar sounds of the kitchen remind me of home. Water running, cabinet doors opening and closing. Reality returns …crashes. *Tom*.

"Black or peppermint?"

"What?"

"The tea, you want black or peppermint."

"Black," I say, becoming aware of Eric near the window watching me. Nobody speaks and the noises from the kitchen fill the room.

Maddie places a ceramic mug in front of me. "Here."

"Thanks." I don't care much for tea but it gives my hands something to do. I remember that I haven't eaten since last night, yet I feel no hunger. "Somebody killed him," I say into the silence.

Eric rolls his chair to the couch. "At Palmer?"

"Yes, they haven't found them yet."

"Why don't you tell us from the beginning?" Eric speaks gently. Only his eyes burn.

I recount finding Tom bound to the tree, Tom getting sick and me unable to learn any clues. I stop. I can't bear to tell about this morning, the Dean, the people outside the room. I'm going to throw up.

"When...?" Maddie holds my hand.

"This morning he…"

The room turns silent again. Hammering sounds come from downstairs. I keep swallowing. I'm crying inside.

"I bet they'll sweep it under the rug," Eric says. "They don't want to create any waves, keep Palmer out of the news, even if it means the bastards are getting away with it."

"Not if I have anything to say about it." New tears threaten. "I'll get them if that's all I do."

"Let's review the details," Eric says. "Maybe we can figure it out. There have to be clues. Did Tom have enemies? He seemed pretty outspoken. We—" Eric's voice falters. He clears his throat and wipes a forearm across his eyes. "Fucking assholes." He rolls to the window and turns his back. "He was here just a couple of weeks ago," he continues. "We discussed My Lai. His plans. He wanted to go to Stanford, had already applied…" Eric shakes his head.

"Tom's only fault was that he was honest and didn't play stupid games," I say. "He made some people mad with his stance against the war. He stood up for what he believed in. He hated what the government had done in Vietnam and people knew it. He had arguments with a bunch of people like Muller and Big Mike.

"Who's Big Mike?"

"Dumb football jock." I grimly chuckle. How strange I sound—like a sick cocktail of laughter and sobs. "I guess I'm one, too, but I'm not dumb like that guy. Mike is huge and he's pretty mean, on the field and off."

Eric nods.

"He has an alibi. I just have to keep asking and digging."

"What about Tom's roommate? Didn't he see anything? Don't you guys keep track of each other every second?"

"Toad didn't see anything except a few guys from the cavalry who seem an unlikely choice. They don't even know us, we're so far below them. And Toad was reading and didn't pay attention."

"Come on, wouldn't you know if your roommate was missing?"

I keep thinking if I'd realize if Plozett were gone. We aren't friends and have different interests. Still, wouldn't I sense if the bed six feet away were empty? I'll ask Toad again. I go over the events of the past few weeks, but nothing else comes to mind. I'm exhausted and my head throbs.

"I better go," I say, climbing out of the cushions. "Thanks for the tea. I need to eat something and get busy studying."

Maddie walks me downstairs. "Come back soon. I…we want to know." We hug but it feels strange. "I miss you," she whispers.

"I miss you, too." I nod at the girl in front of me. I want to kiss her, but am confused about feeling the urge and being sad about Tom. Somehow I've got to honor Tom and not think about sex. "I'll stop by after the break. We're going home Wednesday."

"Later, man," Eric yells from upstairs. "Write to us."

"Be careful." Maddie's eyes are anxious, her hand on my shoulder smoldering heat.

CHAPTER TWENTY-FOUR

An hour 'till Sunday dinner. I stare at the English paper on my desk. My writing looks like chicken scratches. I've got no idea what it says. My mind moves in circles, bits and pieces of today's events, Tom on the bed, his pale face. Had Tom been in pain? What had his last thoughts been? Had he believed I'd find out who did it?

"You got a minute?" Markus Webber, the blond kid from next door stands in the door. He looks scared as usual, his eyes wide, his hands in a flutter.

"What's up?"

Markus takes a few steps and stops by my desk. "I noticed something and thought you should know." His voice jumps into a squeak and his cheeks turn red. "I'm so sorry about Tom."

I nod. I can't speak.

"I was wondering who'd do a thing like that," Markus says. "I overheard something the other day and I wondered…Maybe you could tell Sarge or I mean…"

"What did you hear?" I only half listen. Markus runs around in a state of permanent excitement.

"It was in the library. I was putting away a book and saw Tom. He was reading. He helped me with English a few times, so I didn't think much of it when Big Mike showed up by his side. I mean that was unusual since Big Mike never talks to anyone but his football friends."

"Go on."

"Big Mike asked Tom to help him with English. He had a paper due… Macbeth."

"What did Tom say?"

"I couldn't believe it, but he refused. He just shook his head and said he couldn't do anything for Big Mike. Big Mike said, 'come on man, I need this. It's due tomorrow. I'm on the verge of a D. My father will kick me in the nuts.' Tom said he couldn't help. Not even sorry."

"And Big Mike?"

"He got all red in the face, like he was going to smack Tom. He said he'd expected as much from a traitor."

I lean back in my chair. "Did anyone else hear?"

Markus shakes his head. "It was Sunday night and he sat in a corner. After that Big Mike had this mean look every time he saw Tom."

"Thanks, man. Keep your ears and eyes open."

After Markus leaves, I take out my notebook. Big Mike is certainly strong enough to attack Tom. But then he has an alibi. Dead end again.

I jump up and head outside. No point trying to study. I hurry along the cleared path lined by neat piles of snow. I forgot my coat, but don't care. The cold makes me feel more real. I've got to feel pain like Tom.

What does it matter that I'm freezing when Tom is dead. Dead!

I end up in the educational building where most teachers have offices. I scurry down the stone-tiled corridor, a row of somber looking administrators and benefactors watching from their black and white photo frames.

A thin strip of light filters from underneath Sarge's door. I knock.

"Come in."

"Cadet Olson, Sir, excuse me," I falter.

"At ease." Sarge's voice is surprisingly soft.

"I came to ask about Tom... Cadet Zimmer." I stop. "Are the police going to investigate? It's murder and I was wondering…"

"Right, Olson. Sit down and listen to me. Like I told you, we're looking into it. The Dean doesn't want to involve the police."

"But Sir, Tom—"

"Olson, leave it alone. We'll take care of it. It's too late for Tom, but we'll find the sons of bitches."

"Wouldn't the police…?"

"The Dean is adamant," Sarge says. He leans forward and selects a cigar from a wooden box. "We're in charge. Did you learn anything new? Tell me."

"No Sir, I talked to the cadets on my floor but nobody has seen anything."

"You leave the rest to us, now, you hear." Sarge stands up and I follow suit. "Go home and take a break. See your parents. It'll give us time to go over the evidence, talk to people. We'll reconvene after the holidays. Dismissed!"

I stop at the door and turn. "Sir, I—"

"Olson, we *will* find them."

"Yes, Sir." I leave.

How can they talk to people if everyone goes home? They won't investigate while cadets eat turkey and open Christmas gifts. Now is the time to act. Eric was right. The Dean will sweep Tom's murder under the rug. Nobody will care after the break. Life will go on as usual. How convenient.

I fight for breath as new fury sweeps through me. I won't give up, not now, not ever. To heck with my exams.

I head for the cave. Everything seems as usual. Few cadets hang out today, most are studying for finals. The air reeks of cold tobacco smoke. I slump into a chair, listlessly rifling through a car magazine. Without seeing anything I throw it back down. I won't get a car any time soon. Not until after college. If I even go. I notice the TV, jump up and twist the knob.

A guy in a military uniform appears, his mouth opening and closing in silence. I fumble with the volume. General William Peers, it says on the screen.

"…the American public can rest assured that we will investigate fully the events in My Lai and will bring to justice those responsible for this terrible tragedy."

My ears perk up. I was here when Tom talked about it. Nobody believed him. Not even me. Suddenly I wonder if things would've been different if I'd helped Tom, taken his side publicly. Not been such a coward. Maybe Tom would still be here. Maybe …if we hadn't fought, I'd have seen Tom's side…understood.

"…the truth will come out and we will spare no-one…"

Tom knew the truth.

I swear to myself I'll learn all I can. About the government, the military, the war and what's going on at this school. I'll never again be stupid. I'll learn and then I'll make up my mind. For good.

And I'll find the killer.

CHAPTER TWENTY-FIVE

Bloomington has disappeared under a foot of snow. Every morning and evening I open my notebook to go over things. I barely notice the Christmas tree that pokes the ceiling. Not even the red and silver packages underneath interest me much.

All I can do is think about Tom. While I've always missed him during break, this is different. I can't imagine going back and not finding Tom in his room at the school. He'll never be there again.

The air inside stifles me and I often take off trudging through the snow into the woods behind the house. My parents know. A letter arrived, explaining the "unfortunate event" and assuring worried parents that their children are safe. Bullshit!

"Wasn't that your friend?" my mother asks. My throat tightens into a knot and I gulp for air. I want to scream at her. They murdered him, Mother, and nobody is doing anything about it. Instead I grab my coat. I only want to go back and find the killer—if I can just make it through break in one piece.

***

Palmer is indeed quiet when I return. Nobody speaks of Tom as daily schedules keep everyone too busy to follow independent thought. Toad has a new roommate and life goes on as usual, except for me who feels Tom's absence like a festering sore.

"You were right," I say. I'm in town to see Maddie and find Eric in the backroom. "The school is covering it up. It's inconvenient and we're all kept busy."

"I'm not surprised." Eric is sorting through a stack of invoices. "What're you going to do about it?"

I look up. What can I do if not even Sarge wants to support me?

"You aren't going to give up on your friend, are you?" Eric's eyes are attached to my face. They're like blue coals and I look away. "He was my friend, too. You're going to drop it like the school wants you to?"

I cough to find my voice. "I guess I—"

"Listen to me." Eric pulls his wheelchair close, our knees almost touching. "You were Tom's only real friend in that place. If you don't look for the murderers who will?"

"You're right. But I don't know what to do." I pause. "You were his friend, too. Maybe more than I ever was," I say quietly.

Eric shakes his head, his eyes wet. "He always talked about you. Tom was an amazing guy. He had real strength. He deserves to have justice. You were his best friend. No doubt." Eric's hand feels warm on my forearm. I fight the torrent of emotions that threatens to spill over. That I've choked back all week. I swallow. It sounds as if I'm under water. "All I'm saying is not to give up. Go over everything again. Ask questions. Talk to people." He sighs. "I wish I could get out of this damned chair and march straight in there."

"You can still do lots of things," I say. "Life is worth living."

"What would you know about it?"

"Not much, I guess." He's right. I don't have a clue about anything.

"Hey guys." Maddie stands in the door. "What's going on?"

"Just talking about Tom." I rub a sleeve across my face, clearing my throat as I jump up. "I missed you terribly."

Maddie smiles. "Can you help me carry these groceries upstairs?"

"Sure."

"Keep me posted," Eric calls after us.

"Put them on the counter." Maddie looks at me. "You okay?"

I shake my head. "I'm going to find the sons of bitches." I put down the bags and glance at the girl who stands silhouetted against the window, her hair a black frame around the blazing of her eyes. I want to walk over and grab her, pull her close and kiss her into oblivion—until I've forgotten everything.

Instead I'm frozen, my back pushed against the counter. Sadness and excitement tangle inside my head, fighting for attention. The moment passes and Maddie begins emptying the paper sacks.

"It's late. I better head back."

"Could you carry up Eric before you go? Dad is at the tavern for a bit and I can't do it by myself."

"Thanks, man," Eric says as I lift him into my arms. It feels strange to be so close to this man, an intimate gesture of carrying him like a child. "I know you mean well. It's just that..."

"I know." I place Eric in the chair. "I'll let you know what I find out."

I hoped Maddie would walk me downstairs but she's peeling potatoes. I kick myself for missing the opportunity to kiss her. It won't happen again.

"Come and see us anytime," Eric calls after me.
"Next week," Maddie yells.

CHAPTER TWENTY-SIX

When I return the door to Tom's room is ajar, Toad staring into a book, his nose nearly touching the pages.

"You got a minute?"

Toad looks up reluctantly. "What?"

"I want to talk about Tom."

"What about Tom? I already told you what I know *and* Sarge *and* the Dean." Toad disappears behind the book.

"I want to hear it one more time. We must've missed something." I lean against Toad's desk which is littered with Hershey's chocolate wrappers. Cookie crumbs cover his files and papers. How can Toad get away with being such a slob?

Toad continues reading.

"Come on, man. Your roommate is dead. Even if he wasn't your friend, don't you feel it's important?"

Toad looks up, his face crunched into a frown. His cheeks round like buns, only his eyes and eyebrows move together. I wonder what goes through Toad's mind. I've never thought about Toad until now, how he spends his time and gets along.

"I don't know how I can help," Toad says. His voice seems several notes too high.

"Let's just go over the evening again. What time did Tom arrive?"

"After dinner, about 19:30."

"What did he do after he came in?"

Toad moves the mass of his body into an upright position. "He was reading Shakespeare." He shakes his head. "I never understood how he could read that stuff for fun. I mean, I like to read—"

"What happened next?" I ask.

"He left the room."

"What time was that?"

"Before ten, I think."

"You think? Did you check the time or how did you know?"

"I didn't but I sort of know. I'd checked about ten and gave myself another fifteen minutes to read before getting the flashlight."

"And?"

"I read under the covers. Don't tell anyone. I—"

"Back to Tom. So he left to take a leak. Then what?"

"I… don't know. He didn't come back. I was under the covers reading and fell asleep."

"But before you got your flashlight. Did you hear anything? Did Tom return?"

"No," Toad shakes his head. "I only know I got my flashlight and continued reading. I get really into it when I read and don't pay attention. He may have returned…"

"But you said earlier, he didn't come back."

Toad pulls himself up, a considerable effort from the low position of his chair and starts rummaging in his desk drawer. "I need candy."

"You already had three. Come on, answer the question."

"I told you, I don't know, he could've returned without me knowing." Toad retrieves a chocolate bar, sticking half of it in his mouth.

I get up choking back my frustration. "If you remember anything at all, you come and see me. I'll get you more candy bars if you have anything important."

Toad slumps on the chair and grabs his book.

I turn to leave. At the door, I look back. Toad appears to be reading, his nose inches from the page except the book cover is turned upside down.

Deep in thought, I return to my room. Toad knows something but he isn't talking. *Why?*

I take out my notebook and begin jotting down the date and my conversation with Toad. My gut tells me that I've got to dig deeper. I'm missing something.

My next target is Muller. Except Muller won't be as easy. But I sit next to him in German class, not my choice of a seating arrangement, but maybe an opportunity for conversation.

"We're going to the lab," Herr Heinrich announces Monday morning. A native German, his English accent is thick as he pronounces each word sharply. "Take your workbooks."

"Muller, wait," I say, catching up with him in the hallway. He always walks like he has a broomstick down his spine. "Got a minute?"

"We're in class," Muller says, turning his head slightly while marching perfect steps.

"I know but we can talk while we go to the lab, right?" I feel like punching Muller's face but force myself to sound pleasant. "Look, I'm trying to figure out what happened to Tom."

"Why don't you leave that up to the authorities? Sergeant Russel and the Dean will take care of things."

"But I want to help. I wonder if you saw anything. I mean you're always on top of things, you know, really good at everything. Observant." I wonder if Muller sees through my sickening pleasantries.

"Yes, I do know quite a bit." Muller seems to go for it. "But I can't say that I saw anything. I was actually in the library that night. Studying for an English exam."

"Good for you," I say. "Who else was in the library?"

"I don't remember seeing anyone. I'm pretty dedicated, don't want to ruin my perfect scores."

I want to thump him again, but force my voice to stay calm. "Glad to hear it. Do you remember what time you returned from the library?"

"Must have been after ten. I always take a shower before bed so I closed my books at 21:50 which would have put me back at the barracks at 22:00." Muller looks at his watch as if he can read the length of time it takes to walk between the library and the barracks.

"That would've put you outside about the time Tom was taken."

"I suppose," Muller says. "But I didn't see him." We enter the lab. "I have to study now."

I open my mouth to ask about Toad, but Muller plops down and opens his book. I'll have to continue later.

It looks as if both Toad and Muller were near but neither saw Tom. Either Muller lies or Toad, maybe both. It's more likely Toad. But then Muller threatened Tom in the lounge. Maybe he lined up help to teach Tom a lesson. He was alone in the library, so no alibi.

I try focusing my attention on the microphone. The foreign language lab is first-class. Thirty seats are outfitted with the newest recorders.

"Ich heiße Peter. Wie heißt Du?" I chant before listening to the playback with my headphones. It sounds ridiculous like a snake's hiss. I hate my voice, but keep speaking and listening until the hour is over. Again something nags in the back of my head, yet I can't figure out what it is.

***

Every night I consult my notebook until I know every letter and word by heart. Still nothing has changed. What I've learned is minor. I keep turning the pages until my head hurts. I watch my classmates for signs of suspicious behavior just like I did after the hazing in junior year. Most act like regular shitheads and as if nothing has happened.

As week after week passes I'm more and more discouraged. Instead of lessening, the pain in my heart grows—until I feel it in every step and every activity. It's an emptiness, a hollow space inside me that hurts all the time.

I lie awake thinking about Tom and I go to sleep thinking about him. *Who did it? And why?*

If I felt isolated when I arrived here, it's worse now. Sure, I hang out with the guys on my floor, but it's not friendship, not what I had with Tom. I get the sense nobody really cares about anything. The only time the pain lessens is when I see Maddie. She's my savior, the one person I feel really close to.

Worse, I can't shake the feeling that I'm being watched. It's nothing specific, no obvious footsteps following me, no stares, just a subtle creepy sensation that makes the hair on my neck stand up. Maybe I'm losing my mind.

I go to town every chance I get, discussing Tom with Eric, taking long walks with Maddie and looking for clues. But Eric knows none of my classmates or faculty and our discussions lead nowhere. We're going over the same old tired chain of events.

Time is running out. I'll graduate next month. I can't think about that now because once I leave, it'll be all over.

I've got to dig deeper. Quickly.

During afternoon football practice I watch Tony and Big Mike, trying to come up with an idea on how to ask about Tom. I know they didn't like Tom. Especially Big Mike. At least that's what Markus said. Though I played many games with them, I feel no more comfortable talking or hanging out. I've put it off for weeks, looking for an opportunity. Maybe I should ask them separately. But they're always together.

After practice I hang around the locker room. Big Mike takes half-hour showers and Tony returns alone dripping with a towel around his waist.

"Hey, Tony," I say hoping to sound casual. I'm dressed and slowly packing my sticky sweatpants into the laundry bag.

Tony is inspecting his fingernails. "What?"

I swallow against the pressure in my stomach. No more wimping out. I'm doing this for Tom. "I want to ask you something about Tom."

"Tom is gone," Tony says. "What's there to talk about?"

"I want to know what you did that night." There, it's out, the words I've mulled around in my head for weeks.

Tony looks up. His eyes widen but then narrow into angry slits. "What's it to you, Olson? None of your business."

"I'm helping Sarge."

"Your buddy, Sarge, hah," Tony mocks, spinning around to inspect the clothes hanging inside his locker. "You're turning into a regular brown-noser."

"Well, what did you do?" I ask, glancing nervously at the door to the showers.

"I already told Sarge I was working with Big Mike in the study room."

"What did you study?" My voice is soft.

"Don't remember, some exam the following Monday."

"What's going on?" Big Mike's bulky frame appears next to Tony, the towel around his middle barely long enough for a knot.

"Olson is digging around about Tom," Tony says, still inspecting his locker.

"What about that ding-a-ling?"

"Tom wasn't a ding-a-ling." Heat spreads through my cheeks and neck. I've got to remain calm.

"Whatever you say," Big Mike barks. "You're not getting it, Olson, because you're a loser just like Tom and on top of that you're gullible." He grins at Tony. "Right, Tony?"

"What do you mean?" I ask though I want nothing more than to leave.

Big Mike sweeps a paw through the air. "Like everything, brown-nosing wannabe's like Sarge, and hanging out with ding-a-lings like Tom, losing the race." He slumps on the bench. "Let me give you a piece of advice. If you want go somewhere you've got to seize power and be willing to use it."

I stare. It's the most I've ever heard Big Mike speak. "What about the race?"

Instead of answering he shoves Tony and chuckles. "Good old Tony here fixed you right up and you didn't even have a clue." He slaps himself, initiating a tidal wave of flesh on his stomach. "Man, I'm hungry. Wonder what's for dinner."

"You sabotaged my canoe." I notice Tony throwing an angry glance at Big Mike. It all makes sense now. The way Tony acted after the race. His glee. I'm so furious I could explode, but the voice in my head says I've got zero chance to fight either one of them, fighting both is suicide. I've got to concentrate on Tom.

"Tony said you two studied the night Tom died," I say, my voice trembling. Though strangely it's not from fear. I'm no longer scared, only disgusted. I realize I'll never be part of them, the wealthy who seem untouchable, above the law. Tom was rich, too, but never used it for his own gain or to push guys like me around. To my surprise I produce a smile.

Big Mike turns around, his bulky chest nearly touching me, his face only inches above my face.

"Olson, quit nosing around. It's unhealthy."

I ignore Big Mike's eyes spitting fire.

"You remember what exam you studied for?"

"I don't remember. Now, cool your chops." Big Mike turns and yanks open his locker, making the entire row of cabinets groan in metal-screeching protest. I move to the door and turn around.

"Why didn't you like Tom?" I ask.

Big Mike shrugs. "He didn't belong."

I notice that Tony has returned to staring into his locker as if to avoid Big Mike's eyes.

Something is up. But these two will never talk. I look at the wall clock. There is still time to see Sarge before dinner.

***

"Enter," Sarge's voice vibrates through the wooden door.

"Sir, excuse me, Sir." I feel suddenly tongue-tied.

"Olson, you in trouble again?" Sarge leans back in his chair.

"No, Sir, I wanted to talk about Tom."

"What about?"

"I wonder if you learned anything new." I look straight ahead, trying to concentrate on my body remaining at attention.

Sarge sighs. "Olson, for goodness sake. Sit down."

I rush forward to grab the wooden chair.

"You should be studying, not playing Sherlock Holmes. I don't know anything new. We're still asking around, but the Dean doesn't want the school routine interrupted."

I wait for Sarge to continue but he remains quiet.

"I'm just wondering. I've been asking a few of the suspects."

"Who are your suspects?"

"I talked to Toad, and Muller. I just spoke with Tony and Big Mike."

"The football players?"

"Yes."

"What did you learn?" Sarge opens his desk drawer and pulls out a notebook.

"Toad is pretty suspicious. He pretended to read but I could tell he wasn't. And Muller, he said he was in the library but he really doesn't have an alibi. Nobody saw him. And Tony and Mike, they supposedly studied. Markus said Big Mike got really mad after Tom refused to help him with a paper."

"Well, White and Stets have an alibi." Sarge rifles through his book. "I wrote down that they were in the study room in the barracks. There were witnesses."

I nod. "But Toad—"

"Olson, this isn't going anywhere. Do you really believe Cadet Todd attacked Tom? He can barely move himself across the room, let alone drag a person into the woods." Sarge's fingers drum the desk. "Besides, what would be his motive?"

"They're roommates. Maybe Toad hated Tom."

Sarge shakes his head. "I suggest you work on your classes so that you can get out of here in a few weeks. Your life is just beginning. Don't waste it on things that can't be changed."

I don't believe my ears. Sarge is talking like Tom is a cup of spilled milk. No big deal, just a nuisance you can wipe away.

"But, Sir."

"No buts, you better get to dinner." Sarge looks at his watch. "And I'm late for it, too."

I slowly get up.

"Go on, Olson, hop to it. I'll let you know if I hear anything."

I nod, the words refusing to form as I walk out. Sarge isn't going to do anything either. He's giving lip service just like the rest of them. Eric is so right.

And Tom? A wave of emotion sweeps through me as I remember Tom talking about the establishment of the school, the rich elite. That they're above the law. Tom was inconvenient, a smart boy seeing right through it all, when all he wanted to do was graduate and head to California. I feel like choking and run outside. A tear drips on my hand and I wipe it on my pants. *Damn them.*

I *will* find out. A voice in the back of my mind begins to nag.

What if you can't?

CHAPTER TWENTY-SEVEN

"Olson, report to the Dean." A second-year cadet stands in the doorframe to my room.

I shut my physics book. "What about?" Reporting to the Dean is highly unusual. The Dean only greets parents and gives speeches to the cadets at the beginning of each school year. The rest of the time is a mystery.

Though I welcome the interruption of study hour, I feel a wave of jitters move up my legs. It gets worse as I head toward the Dean's villa. I remember crawling out of the grate in front of the living room window. It was the closest I've ever been to the Dean's house.

"Cadet Olson to see the Dean," I shout when the maid opens the door.

"One moment, Sir, come in." The maid curtsies and disappears down the hall. I wait inside the door, afraid to move across the Persian rug.

"Cadet Olson, this way," the Dean calls from the end of the corridor.

"Yes, Sir." I march down, my shoes silent on the thick wool carpet.

"Shut the door." The Dean sits behind a mahogany desk, bare except for a few silver-framed photos and a single folder in front of him.

I close the door and wait. It's stuffy in here and I feel my armpits leak into my shirt.

"Cadet Olson," the Dean folds his hands and stares at me through horn-rimmed glasses, "I hear you're asking about Cadet Zimmer."

"Yes, Sir," I say. "I want to find who took Tom, I mean Cadet Zimmer." I can't bring myself to say *killed*. It somehow sounds out of place in the perfect elegance of the Dean's office.

"Cadet Olson, let me give you some advice." The Dean's voice is calm, only the words come out more accentuated. "Let me say, I'd like to discourage you from wasting time on this matter."

Tom is no longer a young man or human, he's turned into a *matter*.

"We're doing all we can to locate the culprits. We may even find it's someone outside the school. Someone who disliked our establishment. Maybe some war protester..."

The Dean waves a hand toward the window as if he were in the jungle of Vietnam. "We have enemies out there. In any case, I'd like you to concentrate on your schoolwork. I can see from your grades you've made some progress but you have quite a ways to go. Mostly Bs and Cs. You *do* want to graduate?" The question hovers in the air like poisonous gas. I nod. *Is the man threatening to let me fail high school?* A small smile plays around the Dean's mouth. It looks more like a twitch. He opens the folder. "You should consider your future, Cadet Olson. You could join the military and become an officer, move ahead in the world. Sergeant Russel tells me he has high hopes for you."

I nod, unsure what to say.

The Dean gets up from behind his desk. "Now promise me that you'll work on your grades. Finals will be here before you know it." He pats me on the back, his face jovial except for the eyes that bore into my brain. "Enough said, back to your studies."

"Yes, Sir." I click my heels together, smartly doing an about-face as I turn 180 degrees toward the door. At least that part is easy now.

My heart hammers all the way back to the barracks. Did the Dean threaten I wouldn't graduate or am I imagining things? They sure want to forget about Tom. I'll have to be even more careful from now on.

Shouts ring out from upstairs as I enter my barracks. Cadets crowd in the hallway and in front of Toad's room.

"What's going on?" I yell across the throng to Plozett, who stands just inside the doorframe.

"Toad collapsed. We called the doctor."

"What's wrong with—"

"Out of the way, make room," the doctor shouts from behind. Silence ensues as we move aside to let the doctor and two staff members squeeze into the room. I catch a glimpse of Toad, lying on his bed. He seems to be asleep, his face deathly pale. His breath sounds shallow and laborious.

"Maybe he has pneumonia like Tom," someone says.

"A curse," another voice comments. "Maybe Tom returned and gave it to him."

I glance at the ceiling as if I can see Tom's ghost hovering above us. Somehow I have to smile.

"Something funny?" Plozett asks.

"I'm just imagining Tom as a ghost giving us a hard time."

"He sure would kick some ass," Plozett laughs.

"Olson, report to the infirmary."

I try opening my eyes against the cobwebs of sleep. "What?"

"Wake up, you're supposed to report to the doctor."

I rub my eyes and force my groggy tongue into action. "What time is it?"

"Nearly 11:00." The cadet looks impatient. Though he's a second-year and younger than I, he seems to fall in the Muller category. "Can I be sure you're getting up?" the cadet asks. "The doctor made it quite clear…"

"Yeah, I'm coming." I hurl my blanket to the floor. "Can't even sleep in on a Sunday." I want to ask why *I* have to go to sickbay but the cadet has already left.

My stomach cramps as I approach the infirmary. The door to the building looks somehow different, a black hole that swallows boys and spits them out dead. Nurse Mellon walks me to the doctor's office.

I've never been inside, but it looks icy as an artic winter with white walls and a stainless-steel exam table. Smells of disinfectant pierce my nose. I'm suddenly cold and wish to be gone.

"Cadet Olson, please sit." The doctor's face is grave.

First the Dean, now the doctor. "Yes, Sir." I can't figure out what's going on and wonder if the doctor has news about Tom. The metal chair feels chilly against my back.

"How close are you with Cadet Todd?"

The name Todd sounds weird. To me and the rest of the school, it's always Toad. "Not very. Toad, I mean, Cadet Todd, was my best friend's…Tom's roommate. Toad and I didn't really talk."

"I find that hard to believe. Did you harass him in any way?"

I sit up straight. "No, Sir, I didn't even see him much." I silently recall the questions I asked Toad last weekend. "I don't understand."

The doctor stares as if to gauge whether I speak the truth or he should extract something from my mind.

"What's wrong with Toad?"

"That's none of your concern," the doctor says. "He's ill." He pauses. "How do you explain that Cadet Todd is mumbling your name?"

I shrug. "No idea. Is he talking about me?"

"Not talking—he's unconscious."

"I've got no idea, Doctor. I mean, we don't really mix. In class or otherwise." I decide to omit my last conversation with Toad.

The doctor continues to stare. "Fine. When you go back, would you retrieve some of Cadet Todd's belongings? You know, his pajamas and underwear…toiletries. He'll stay with us for a few days."

"Yes, Sir." I straighten.

"Just leave them with the nurse."

I turn and dash out the door. I don't really want to mess with Toad's clothes. Maybe I can ask Toad's new roommate to collect his stuff so I won't have to touch it.

The room is empty. Damn.

I open the metal wardrobe and immediately know which side is Toad's by the size of the shirts and jackets hanging inside. I rifle through the t-shirts folded in neat rows of nine-inch wide stacks, much thicker than my own, wondering where Toad keeps his pajamas.

I grab two pair of white underwear, the same kind I wear but much larger. A laundry bag is lying on the floor inside the closet. It seems heavy as I lift it to look underneath for Toad's slippers. Picking them up with forefinger and thumb I place them with the other items. "Come on, Toad, where are your pajamas?"

"Maybe they're dirty," I mumble and lift up the laundry bag again. If they're not inside, Toad will have to sleep in t-shirt and underwear. I open the strap and the contents spill on the bed, two sets of blue and white striped pajamas, socks, pants and a red fabric shoe sack, filled with something heavy, something jingling.

"What's this?" I pull open the string. Gold glitters inside and I empty the sack on the bed. Three wristwatches, five rings, two necklaces, an expensive looking ink pen, three medals and a pocket watch lie in a heap.

The watch looks familiar. I pick it up, immediately transported back to the bleachers when Tom showed us the watch he received from his father. I open it. Tom's mother, young and pretty, looks at me with a soft smile.

"That pig," I shout, snapping the watch shut and putting it into my pocket. "The damn thief."

I grab Toad's clean clothes and shove them in the laundry bag, throwing the dirty items on the floor of the wardrobe. I return to the stash, Toad's attempt at exerting control over his life. At last, I place the items inside Toad's desk. I'll have to deal with it later.

Nurse Mellon smiles when I enter. I know she remembers Tom. "Hello Andy. You have Allen's clothes?"

"Yes, but I couldn't find clean pajamas. He can wear t-shirts."

"That's fine, tomorrow is laundry day. We'll take care of it." The nurse nods. "You may go now."

"I'd like to see Toad, I mean, Allen."

"I'm afraid that's impossible."

"Please, it's important. I need to speak to him."

"Maybe this evening after dinner. Why don't you stop by and check in with the night nurse? I'll make a note. The poor boy, I'm afraid your friends aren't too lucky." She shakes her head.

"Yeah, I know what you mean," I say. "I'll be back tonight."

CHAPTER TWENTY-EIGHT

Sunday afternoon drags on forever. I contemplate going to town and stopping by Maddie's but am too distracted. Toad's stash is now hidden inside my desk. Before I hand it to Sarge, I'm going to see Toad. Find out why he stole from Tom and get his side of the story. The weather is still horrific and walking to the infirmary, I shiver in the frigid wind. It's nearly seven. I'll have to hurry back for study hour.

The night nurse, a small woman with a lemony smile presides at the desk. Her dark hair with streaks of gray is stretched into a tight bun. I've never seen her before.

"Yes?"

"Cadet Olson to see Cadet Todd." I try a smile, but the nurse ignores me and rifles through her book. The smells of antiseptic and something sweet, like sugar candy, surround me.

"Right this way," the nurse says. She walks down the linoleum corridor, her rubber soles making rhythmic sucking noises. When she stops at a door, I worry it's Tom's old room. It isn't though it looks identical, immediately taking me back to last November. "Five minutes."

I nod obediently and approach the bed. Toad lies under a mountain of blankets, but where Tom nearly spanned the length from top to bottom, Toad spreads wide and square across the bed.

"Toad?"

Toad's eyes open slowly as if reluctant to what they may find.

"Olson," he squeaks but it sounds more like a whisper.

To my great surprise, a feeling of sorrow comes over me. I arrived to yell and scream and smack the guy silly, but all I can think of is how pathetic and lonely Toad looks. It seems that's what the school is best at, making people feel like they've got nobody.

Forcing myself to show firmness, I lean against the bed. "Why did you take Tom's watch?"

Toad's eyes open wide. The color of his face matches the whiteness of the pillow underneath. He opens his mouth, but only a croak comes out. He clears his throat. Then he begins to cry. A dry heaving sound that increases in loudness, reverberating off the sterile walls and scrubbed linoleum. I throw a nervous glance at the door, expecting the nurse to show up any second.

"Toad, please."

"They're going to kick me out," Toad sniffs, his voice even more squeaky than usual. "I couldn't help myself. Can't you keep quiet? I promise to return everything. You can have Tom's watch."

His hands flutter uselessly above the blanket, his voice a babble as he wipes his nose with a sleeve.

"Here." I hand him a tissue. "It's not my watch to keep. It's Tom's family's watch now. Why're you doing it?"

"Don't know, it just happens." Toad blows his nose, inflating the tissue with a flood of wetness. He sniffs again.

"Your time is up," the nurse says from the door.

"Yes, Ma'am." To my relief I hear her squeaking steps move away. I'm not finished. "Why Tom? He really loved that watch." I feel the familiar anger growing.

"I've nothing more to say." Toad turns away his head.

That's when it hits me. The thing that has bothered me all along. "You didn't tell me everything."

Toad shakes his head. "I'm so sorry about Tom," he sniffles. "Please go."

"Your story doesn't add up. You said, you read under the covers when Tom went to the john. You must've left the light on anyway. Tom would've left it on because he was going to return. You would've noticed a light on and you would've seen…" I'm speaking faster, "that Tom was missing from his bed. Even if it was two in the morning."

Toad shakes his head back and forth. "Please understand, I was really afraid." His voice quivers.

"I don't get it." I pause to listen for the nurse and her squeaky shoes. All is quiet. "What does afraid have to do with taking Tom's watch?"

"Big Mike and Tony."

"What do they have to do with it?" I'm tired of listening. Toad is hallucinating. "I'll get the nurse." I walk to the door. "You're lying either way."

"No," Toad says, his voice suddenly urgent, "they threatened to tell the Dean."

I stop at the door. Something in Toad's voice makes me turn. Toad's eyes have a new shine, something insistent and forceful.

I walk back to the bed. "What're you talking about?"

Toad impatiently shakes his head. "Tony caught me in his room once, looking for treasure." Out of Toad's mouth the word treasure sounds giddy, sort of like Gollum talking about precious. "He forced me to open my hand…found a ring I'd taken. He told Big Mike." Toad glances out the window as if he dreams of escape.

I feel brutal. "Why didn't he notify the Dean or Sarge about you stealing?" Something raw is working through my muscles, a wish to grab the bed and whirl it across the perfect lawns.

Toad hiccups. "He said, one day I may become useful." Sweat droplets glint on his forehead and upper lip which are showing the first signs of growth.

"Who said that?"

"Tony."

Darkness brews inside me as I look at Toad.

Toad, getting aggravated, tries to sit. He reminds me of an oversized pill bug thrown on his back, his arms and legs flailing to find traction on the mattress. His face is wet with sweat now but his eyes have dried. The air whistles in his throat and for a moment I'm transported back to the last days I visited Tom and the heaviness emanating from his chest.

"I saw them take Tom. They came in and grabbed one of Tom's blankets while he was in the john. They said I'd better shut up or they'd get me, tell the Dean about my problem and have me expelled."

I'm stunned. I can't get any words out. The rage is so great, I feel it churn through my body like big iron claws. I force myself to remain standing and push the air through my throat to breathe.

"Please understand, I thought they took Tom to another room to play a prank. I didn't know he was outside all night." Toad has new tears in his eyes. "I never meant…"

Visions of Tom bound to the tree return, his blue hands and lips, the way he felt limp in my arms. I'm searching for my voice, my body feeling cold as steel. "But they have an alibi."

"They made a tape with their voices and had a recorder playing in the study room," Toad says. "They'd planned it all."

"Where's the tape?"

Toad shrugs. "Don't know. Nothing matters anymore anyway." He sinks back down and wipes his face with his hand, staring out the window as if I'm no longer there.

I march to the bed and grab Toad's shoulders. "Now listen, Toad, everything matters. You're the most important witness. We'll tell Sarge and ask for a hearing."

Toad shakes his head. "I don't know if I can. I'm so afraid. It doesn't matter now. They'll kick me out anyway." Another sob.

"But you have to—"

"Cadet Olson, didn't I tell you to leave?" The nurse stands in the door, her eyes pieces of black coal that threaten to ignite. "Look what you've done." She marches into the room to take Toad's pulse. "I'm getting the doctor. I shouldn't have let you visit." She runs off down the hall. A bell sounds in the distance.

I leave behind her, my legs mechanical without feeling, my mind daggers, ready to stab anyone who comes near. Still, I don't want to be caught by the doctor. He'll take it out of context and dole out major punishment. I want blood, tear Tony apart, smack Big Mike's spongy gut until he keels over and passes out. I run, ignoring study hour and that I'll be missed.

They planned it all along. Bastards! I run faster as tears roll down my cheeks. I don't know if they're from anger or sadness. My heart beats as if it wants to jump out of my ribcage. Still I run. They murdered Tom and I hold the key to justice. Visions of Tom appear: on his bed, laughing, talking to Eric with his feet on the table, Tom under the bleachers with his new watch.

Toad *has* to tell.

By the time I slow it's dark, the forest whispers around me. I force my steps toward the school and sneak inside. It's past ten and I've probably been written up for missing study hour. I don't care. Tomorrow first thing I'll see Sarge and ask him to question Toad.

CHAPTER TWENTY-NINE

Tom sits at my desk, arms behind his head and legs stretched comfortably like he does when he finishes studying. A smile plays on his lips. "Now that you know, what're you going to do about it?"

The words echo through my mind with the morning bugle. Tom seemed so real. As if he was here just a minute ago. I want to talk to him. A wave of emotion sweeps through me when Toad's confession floods back to my memory. Rage, loathing and grief are competing. I try breathing normally. I can't be soft now, I've got to move fast and find Sarge. Tell everything, set things in motion. I've got to get Toad to confess and interrogate Tony and Big Mike.

First, I've got to see Sarge before lessons start.

At breakfast, I search for signs of Sarge but don't see him. Faculty members take turns overseeing the cadets during meals. Sarge isn't on duty nor is he eating. I swallow my fried eggs and bread without noticing. I want to leave now, but have to wait for the official bell that breakfast is over. Cadets line each table, a low rumble of voices drifting across the room and mingling with the smells of bacon and toast.

At the sight of Tony and Big Mike a few tables down, my hands begin to shake. Big Mike is making his way through a week's worth of scrambled eggs, using a table spoon like a shovel. Tony is talking to a couple of friends, his hands waving like a conductor as he explains—undoubtedly another hero story. Snippets drift across, but the voices near me are too loud and drown out everything else.

I watch Mr. Brown enter and head to the table of faculty, but instead of sitting down, he stands with his head bowed. I decide to move closer and take my plate as if to get a refill.

"...this morning," Mr. Brown says. His voice, deep and resonant and perfect to recite literature, doesn't match his narrow shoulders.

One of the other teachers speaks but I can't hear. I stop and pretend to check my uniform jacket a few feet from the table.

"The doctor felt it best…" Mr. Brown's eyes meet mine for a second. Then he looks down, speaking more quietly, too low to hear.

I move toward the line. The scene from last night returns. Me getting Toad excited, the nurse running.

The bell rings. I throw down my plate and line up to exit.

Outside, the first rays of an April sun burn orange, bathing the lawns in a golden light. Dew covers the grass like watery milk and the air is filled with aromatic smells of lilac and magnolia. It's my favorite time of day but I'm blind to it. Racing toward the infirmary, I take a short cut across the lawns. I'll be yelled at for tearing up the grass. What does it matter? The building is quiet and I brace for the accusatory face of the night nurse.

Nurse Mellon sits at the desk, studying a chart. Her ample bosom heaves in a sigh as she marks a page.

"Good morning," I offer, trying to force my racing breath into manageable gulps.

Nurse Mellon looks up, eyebrows lifted in surprise. "Andrew, shouldn't you be in class."

"Yes, but I'd like to see Toad for a minute."

Nurse Mellon closes the folder in front of her and gets up. "You mean, Allen?"

"Yes, please."

"I'm sorry, but Allen was taken to Evansville first thing this morning. The doctor felt it best that he'd be in the hospital."

My mouth opens. "But…" I'm at a loss for words. Toad is my witness. He can't be gone. "When will he return?"

Nurse Mellon shakes her head. "I don't know. I'm sure he'll be back in a few weeks."

"A few weeks." My voice fails. It sounds like a croak—like Toad. "No, I, he must speak…"

Nurse Mellon moves around her desk. "Are you all right? You look very pale. Maybe I should take your temperature."

I step back. "I'm fine, thank you."

"In that case you better get to class." A small smile appears on the nurse's face. I don't feel like returning it. I spin around and push out the door.

My brain wants to explode and I feel in no mood to study. All morning, I sit in silence, ignoring my classmates, staring at the teachers but hearing nothing. I need to get justice for Tom and no matter what else happens, I'll get it somehow. It's out of the question to wait until Toad returns.

We have three weeks left in the semester. And there is the possibility

Toad won't return at all. Toad has to assume I'll tell about the stealing. He may find some excuse not to come back to spare himself the embarrassment of expulsion. I'm furious with myself for not getting Sarge last night. Without Toad, it's my word against Tony and Big Mike, it's hearsay, one against two. Not exactly a strong case.

But there has to be something I can do *now*. And then I remember.

The tape.

Tony and Big Mike made a tape to fake their alibi. I've got to find it and confirm with the witnesses that they didn't really see the two studying, they *heard* their voices. That's what's been nagging me all along.

I wonder if Tony kept the tape. Maybe he's thrown it out and broken it. Or returned it to the lab and recorded over it. But there's a chance he still has it.

The best time to search Tony's room will be after dinner and before mandatory study time when cadets have an hour of freedom. Tony usually hangs out in the cave where he and Big Mike occupy the most comfortable sofas and smoke *Dunhills*.

***

I chew mechanically, the pork chop in my mouth turning to stale fibers. Ignoring Plozett's and Markus's chatter, I watch Tony and Big Mike. The more I watch, the more disgusted I become. I loathe myself for ever having looked up to them. Even if it was mostly for their athletic accomplishments, what was there to admire?

I jump up when the bell sounds.

"You going to the cave?" Plozett asks. "We received new games and magazines, a donation from an alum."

"Not tonight, got something to do."

Plozett shrugs and turns away.

"Tell me later," I call after him. I'm kind of sorry I never made an effort to become friends with Plozett. Our relationship is one of convenience and familiarity. Still, I wonder if I should've told him about Toad and who got Tom.

I race toward Barracks C. Earlier, I'd asked around for Tony's room number under the guise that I want to drop off a report for English. The barracks are nearly deserted, cadets out mingling and most of the faculty enjoying an hour of freedom to discuss the latest politics.

I saw Sarge from afar, twice during the day outside walking and at dinner, sitting with the faculty. I'll head straight over there once I find the tape. Even if I don't find it.

Room 125 is at the end of the hallway on the first floor. I stride along, my eyes on the room numbers. I have to be quick. Cadets know who lives in their barracks and I'll be recognized as not belonging. For cover I carry an English paper and slowly approach.

If Tony's roommate is there, I'll have to try later. The door stands ajar and I knock.

"Anyone here?" I mumble and push open the door.

The room is empty.

I rush to the first desk, looking for items that identify them as Tony's. Cadets are allowed a personal photo. The black and white portrait of a woman stares at me. It's hard to tell who it is, probably a mother. The other desk also holds a photo, this one of a couple sitting somberly in front of a fireplace. I recognize the features of an older Tony. It has to be his father. The desktop is clean except for a neat pile of books and two folders.

I open the first drawer which contains assorted pens and drawing tools, a metal ruler, eraser and notepaper. Rifling through I find nothing. I move to the next drawer, my ears straining toward the door and potential footsteps.

Folders are stacked inside and I pull them out to look underneath. Nothing. I move to the other side: more papers and a few novels, inside a folder, a Playboy with the cover missing.

Voices drift in from the hall and I pause to listen. Somebody laughs but it doesn't sound like Tony. My heart pounds in my neck. I've got to hurry.

I pull open the last drawer, rummage through assorted papers and throw it shut. The tape isn't there. I open the wardrobe. Neat stacks of shirts and underwear fill the space. I slide my hand in-between to search for hard items, but all I feel is fabric. Closing the cabinet, I look around the room. Toad kept his stash in the laundry bag. Most people wouldn't touch other students' dirty clothes. I yank open the door a second time and inspect the bag on the floor.

It's empty except for two sets of underwear, socks and a shirt. *Damn.*

I close the wardrobe and scan the bed which is an unlikely hiding place since they're often upset by the inspectors. Muller and company love pulling apart sheets and covers during room check, exposing hidden items. I doubt Tony has to remake his bed often, but he'd probably not risk it.

I dash to the door. Time to give up and see Sarge with just the information from Toad. Maybe we can travel to Evansville and ask Toad. The stash is still in my desk. Once I take it to Sarge, it'll be the end of Toad at the school.

I glance around one last time when it hits me. During summer break I watched a movie where evidence was taped behind a toilet bowl. Surely, Tony doesn't have anything hidden in the washroom accessible by all cadets. But if he's stuck it behind the desk…or underneath.

I rush back to the desk and crawl into the leg space between the drawers. I've been here way too long and my fingers shake with nerves.

Groping behind along the backside I find nothing. Then I look up and there in the back corner underneath is a dark lump, almost invisible unless you're close. I pull and a wad of black adhesive comes loose. Nestled inside is a tape. The kind we use in speech lab. My heart begins to gallop as I straighten.

I stick the lump into my pocket and head for the door.

Tony watches me, his eyes hard, his mouth turned into a sneer. How long has he been there?

"Olson, why are you sneaking around in my room?"

I stop, the air stuck in my throat, refusing to bring oxygen to my lungs.

"I was looking for you," I say. "I—"

"Save it." Tony's voice is a low hiss. "Give me the tape."

I stare at the guy in front of me, the captain of the football team who I've played with dozens of times, even admired early on. All I can see now is a man capable of murder. Tony's eyes are cold and I'm suddenly afraid.

I rack my brain to come up with an idea…anything. All I can think of is that I'm in terrible danger. I'm out of breath and feel panic creeping up my spine with icy fingers. If Big Mike is near I won't stand a chance. Even fighting Tony alone would be a losing battle. Tony weighs thirty muscled pounds more than I do. Surprise will be the only way.

I explode forward, my head making contact with Tony's chest, pushing him backwards. The move works, throwing Tony off his feet and against the opposite wall. I jump across his legs and sprint for the exit.

"Stop him!" Tony shouts. And then, "Mike!"

I nearly collide with a couple of cadets rushing into the hallway to see what's going on. Pushing them aside I race out the door. Dusk is settling. I sprint across the lawn. I hear steps behind me as I race even faster. I have to get out of sight and hide if I want to escape because I'll never outrun Tony. He holds the record in the hundred-yard dash and a couple of mid-distances.

I jump across a row of hibiscus hedges in front of the gym, around the corner and so I hope, out of sight. There's no time to stop and check. I dash along the backside of the gym. I've got to hide but where? A steal door appears toward the end of the building. Maybe it's a storage closet I can lock from the inside.

Stopping hard I yank at the knob. The door doesn't budge and I race on, around the next corner. What if I double back on Tony? I feel for the tape which is still stuck inside my pocket. I wonder briefly if I'll have time to hide it, in case Tony catches up to me.

The lawns expand ahead and down toward the lake but I want cover. I turn right, down the path and toward a line of barracks. Maybe I can hide inside one. It'd take Tony a long time to check all the rooms and maybe I'll have time to tell someone or hide the tape.

Barracks E appears. The horsemen live here and I've never set foot inside. I shove open the door. To my relief, it looks the same as my barracks. Momentarily undecided, I hear the door behind me. Tony's red face appears behind the glass of the outer door. I jump down the basement steps, immediately regretting my decision.

If I'd run upstairs the other cadets may help or witness Tony's attack. Down here I'm likely alone. I hurry down the corridor which is identical to the ones on the first and second floor except the doors to my right and left are storage rooms, not exactly a place to hide. There are no windows down here, either. I'm running into a trap and it's closing fast.

Down the hall Tony coughs and holds his sides. Upstairs, a door bangs. "Down here, Mike," Tony yells. "We've got him."

Heavy steps shuffle closer.

"Where is he?" Big Mike heaves. "Leave him to me."

"Why should you have all the fun?" Tony says, his eyes lodged on me.

I quietly walk backwards. There isn't much farther to go. I've made the wrong move by going down here and they'll beat me up or worse. They have much to lose and with Toad out of the way, nobody will ever know what happened to Tom.

Tom. I grind my teeth. I wonder what Tom thought when he was dragged into the forest. And then when nobody came to his rescue and he got colder and colder and then at the end when even breathing required too much effort.

I reach the wall, my hand touching rough concrete block. Next to it, something feels smooth and for a split-second I turn my head. A door. Fifty feet away, Big Mike has caught up with Tony.

I'm trapped.

They stand watching, undoubtedly considering what to do with their prey.

I take a step to my left and feel the knob. Slowly twisting, I hope it will open. The door moves—a grinding sound of metal scraping across concrete.

I quickly turn and jump through the door, hoping it isn't a closet…and immediately know where I am.

The steps into the steam tunnels disappear into nothing before the door slams shut.

CHAPTER THIRTY

I grope for the light, urging my memory to tell me where the switch is. Reluctantly, a bulb springs to life, illuminating rusted stairs leading into the void. Without hesitation, I jump down. Not a moment too soon.

The door behind me flies open just when I reach the bottom. I sprint to my right, hoping I'll remember my way somehow, hoping the corridor doesn't end suddenly. I wish I could move quietly, but my steps echo against the churning sounds of the pipes. I hear movement behind me and continue into darkness. I extend my left hand to the side and straighten the other to avoid running into a wall.

A cloud of heated air comes from my right and I turn. Another corridor. The footsteps behind continue but have slowed. A light comes on in the main tunnel behind me. They're running straight. I pause, forcing my ears to pick up sounds. I hope they'll stop and turn back. Maybe I can wait and sneak back later.

A shadow appears. No such luck. I run ahead as darkness engulfs me. To my left starts another corridor. I'll never find my way back unless we stop soon. Even then, I'm probably lost.

Another opening appears on the right, a black mass of hot air that welcomes me with invisible arms. I shudder, remembering my last visit. I swore never to return. Here I am, running for my life in the worst place I can imagine.

Why hadn't I run to Sarge's office? I would've been safe.

The footsteps behind me are muffled now. It's hard to hear with the steam pipes whistling above me. I continue walking, my hands touching the wall every few feet. The air is black ink.

I stop. I hear nothing except for the blood rushing through my temples and the pipes overhead. My hands grow damp as I imagine Tony attacking, his cold stare. He's going to hurt me. Maybe kill me. This is the perfect place to hide a body.

I made it easy for him. I've got to stop shaking. Leaning against the wall, I force my breaths to be quiet. Still no movement.

I wonder if I should turn back before I lose all sense of direction. Maybe I'm already lost and they'll find me in thirty years, a shriveled skeleton with a wad of black adhesive wrapped around a tape. They'll play the tape and listen to a couple of voices discussing an English paper. So what, they'll say, whatever happened to this guy? I shudder.

I want to live, breathe fresh air and see Maddie again. Most of all, I want justice. For Tom who was right about everything. Regret sweeps through me as I remember my ignorance.

A soft sound reaches my ear. Then nothing. I'm imagining things. There. Shuffling. Wheezing. They're close. I look behind me, but the darkness is complete. Slowly straightening I step away from the wall, carefully placing my feet as I walk farther into blackness, farther away from the sounds. I wonder about Tony's commitment of finding me and realize what's at stake. If Tony and Big Mike are found out, they'll go to prison for murder or at least manslaughter. It'd be worth it to them if I disappeared. For good. The thought makes me shiver.

Until now I've followed a trail like a dog in pursuit of the elusive rabbit. All of a sudden I'm the one being pursued. I didn't think about what it can mean. That they might kill me. Maybe I can hand over the tape. Tell Tony that I got a sudden case of amnesia. Would Tony go for it?

Then I remember Tom. What would he do? I grimace into the blackness. Easy. I can feel Tom standing next to me, telling me to do what I believe is right. That's how Tom lived.

For the fiftieth time I concentrate on sound but all I hear are the pipes. I tread carefully, getting dizzy from the heat and darkness. Despite the threat lurking behind me, the adrenalin in my body is waning, replaced by nausea. The last time in the tunnel I had too much wine and my stomach was upset. This time death lurks behind me.

A draft touches my face. I remember the grates, releasing steam across campus. A faint light shines overhead and I wonder if anyone can see me while I gaze at the sky. I quickly move into the darkness beyond until the glimmer disappears.

My legs are weak and I lean against the wall. About three feet down, a space opens. I kneel to investigate—an alcove, two feet deep and five feet long. Maybe it was used to store tools or boxes. I crawl inside and sit. At least I'm out of the corridor. If Tony and Big Mike don't turn on lights, they'll walk right past me. The steam pipes sound muffled through the stone and I'm drained. I keep listening but hear nothing except pipes and my breath. My throat is dry and scraped raw like sandpaper.

I wake. How long have I slept? Have ten minutes passed or five hours? Even with my eyes wide open I see nothing—only blackness as if I were blind. For a moment I'm paralyzed with fear, but then I remember Tom. Giving up is not an option.

I stretch my legs and crawl into the corridor listening for movement. Nothing.

At last I straighten. Maybe I escaped except how would I know? Tony and Mike got lost last time. Chances are they're still down here. Even if they were gone, I'm stuck with no idea how to leave these tunnels. I slump back down.

I've got to find a way out. And I've got to do it quietly and in the dark. Just in case.

I doze off.

***

When I wake, faint light filters along the corridor. I slept in a fetal position and my legs scream in protest. I carefully look around the corner. The corridor looms empty. I crawl out and walk back the way I came and toward the grate I saw last night. A square spot of sun brightens the floor. I look up and try to figure out where I am. When standing a few feet away, I can make out the school building in the distance. I've been in this spot before—last year—when Tony wanted to sneak up on the teachers.

I briefly wonder if anyone walks near the steam hole so I can yell for help and get rescued before Tony finds me. By the rumble in my stomach it's probably breakfast time. Fat chance anyone passes overhead and hears me. They're all stuffing their faces.

My bladder acts up and I step to the side to pee. As the stream hits the wall, I remember my parched throat. I've read about people drinking their own pee for lack of water. I shudder and lick my lips. Disgusting.

Taking a few steps, I stop and listen. Only the pipes creak. Repeat. I feel suddenly lonely, wishing for Maddie, her softness and warmth. I long to feel safe.

Concentrate.

In my mind the school's campus appears: the administrative building, assembly hall, the gym and infirmary, the classrooms and faculty offices with the faculty dorms behind, the barracks arranged in perfect order on each side. A grid pattern emerges and lays itself across buildings, mapping distances.

I estimate a hundred feet to the classroom building, a hundred feet across the school and a hundred fifty feet to the faculty building. My best chances are the teacher dorms. Someone is always there and even if the door to the tunnels is locked, I can scream and pound against the entrance. I don't care about being punished. All I want is justice for Tom—and escape.

I walk three feet per step. Counting in my head, I stop cautiously at the next intersection. Around the corner all is dark. I decide to risk a light and find a switch up high. The path glows and makes my eyes ache. Beyond: darkness. I warily continue counting.

To my right, a staircase disappears into darkness. I scramble upstairs. The door is locked. I've got no clue where it leads. I must find the teacher dorms. By the time I climb back down, the light behind me turns off and it grows dark again.

My fingers touch stone. A brick wall. The direct route is closed. I retrace my steps to the next cross section, an opening in the wall. Right or left? I choose right and walk until I hit the next intersection. The grid pattern in my mind continues. I've got to be close to the class building. At the next intersection, I turn right again, resuming my counting, three, six, nine, three, six, nine. I risk another light. Rushing along without running so I can count. Three, six, nine.

Even if Tony and Mike are still down here, it'd be coincidence at this point. The classrooms should be above me. I keep going. The path leads straight into the distance. Something glitters ahead—another grate. It has to be between the classroom building and the teacher dorms.

I stop to peer outside. In the distance I make out the edges of a building. It's hard to tell if it's the dorm. To walk faster I risk another light.

I feel the movement more than I see it. It comes from the side corridor. Tony or Big Mike. Without hesitation I sprint away toward the dorms. Footsteps follow and grow louder. It has to be Tony. He laid in wait, guessing my plan of reaching the teacher's building. Or it's coincidence.

My legs feel weak. The lack of sleep, food and drink is taking its toll. Tony seems unaffected and easily begins to close the distance. I risk a glance over my shoulder. The grate has faded. I'm looking for stairs, the kind I saw earlier. What if there aren't any? In the dark I'm likely to miss them. Even if I find them, it'll take time for anyone to open the door. Why haven't I planned ahead?

I can't keep up the pace. Tony is close and I have no doubt I'll be done for. I widen my steps, keeping my eyes stretched open. The shadows deepen into ink. There. A faint glint to my left. Without hesitation I zigzag.

Not a moment too soon. Tony flies past me and crashes to the floor. I grapple air, feeling my way toward the wall. This is another alcove, except it has high walls and looks like a portal to another room. The glint is a shaft of light that squeezes underneath a door above me.

The staircase. I jump two steps at a time, counting on Tony losing a few seconds while getting up.

But Tony is a football player and used to falling. He has quick reflexes trained by years on the field. Steps echo at the bottom of the staircase as I reach the door. Where is the stupid knob? There, I twist. Locked. I pound and start screaming, my voice unrecognizable to myself—an animal in agony. "Help! Open up."

"I finally got you." Tony's hoarse voice is near. "Thought you'd get away." He sounds like a madman.

A hand jerks at my waist, groping for the tape as the other clamps around my throat. I struggle to stay upright, one hand on the stair rail, the other shoving at Tony's hand on my neck.

Fingers made of iron squeeze away my air. Blackness spreads, yet at the same time a thousand pinheads explode behind my eyelids. I can't breathe. Taking hold of Tony's forefinger I pull, bending it back. Tony grunts. For a second the hand leaves my throat. I gulp as a terrible weight begins to pull from behind..

I'm being dragged backwards and down. Away from the door. Into the darkness. Tony is heavier and stronger. I clutch the rusted handrail when I notice a hand groping my pocket. Tony's arm is back around my neck in a choke hold, drawing me down. My hands are slipping.

The bursts behind my eyelids are back. I can't breathe. Tony's arm on my throat squeezes harder. If I fall it'll be all over.

"What the..." Sarge towers in the door, the brightness nearly blinding me. "Olson! White!"

"Help me," I croak as things turn black. My legs give and I sink backwards just as Sarge grabs me by the shirt.

His face is all hazy and I pass out.

CHAPTER THIRTY-ONE

I wake slowly. Everything is white as if I'm swimming in milk. I hear voices but can't make out what they say. Forcing my eyelids open, I see a shape floating near my bed. Maybe I'm dead and this is an angel.

I open my mouth and the air in my throat turns to fire.

"Andy." A huge bosom appears above my face and I recognize Nurse Mellon. "Here, drink some water." A straw enters my mouth and I feel coolness put out the flame.

"Sarge," I whisper. "I need to see Sarge."

Nurse Mellon pats my hand. "He was here earlier. He'll be back at lunch time."

"The tape," I croak. I worked so hard to get the tape. Tony probably took it in the struggle and shredded it into a thousand pieces.

"Shsh," the Nurse says. "He'll be here soon." I drift off.

"Andy?"

I resurface from another dream.

"Olson." Sarge clears his throat. "You awake?"

"Yes, Sir," I whisper.

Sarge towers near my bed, looking grave. "What the heck happened down there?"

"The tape, you get the tape?" As I try to pull myself up, the bed begins to spin. I stare at the window, waiting for it to stop moving.

"What tape?"

"In my pant pocket..." My head back on the pillow, I scan the room in search of my pants.

"Nurse, where are the cadet's clothes?"

"Right in here, Sergeant."

Sarge steps to the closet and retrieves my uniform covered in grime and smelling rank as if I spent a week in it.

"The pants." The pocket is empty except for bits of sticky residue. I slump back deflated. "The evidence."

"What evidence? Olson, will you tell me what's going on here?"

I look at the nurse, then at Sarge, trying to make sense of my thoughts. Scenes flash. Tom in the cave arguing. Tom tied to the tree. Tony shouting on the football field. Toad in bed.

Where can I start? I want to drift back into the embrace of sleep. Forget everything.

Somebody shakes my shoulder. "Olson, pull yourself together."

Reluctantly I open my eyes. Sarge's face is near, his brows knitted into a line of worry. I shake my head. I lost. It's all over.

I tried hard to do the right thing. Get revenge for Tom. I failed. Without the tape my word will be against Tony's and Big Mike's. Tony will say we fought over some stupid thing. That it was an accident. Just like Tom who had an *accident* and turned into an *unfortunate matter*.

I want to disappear and never wake up, but the rage inside me is too large to contain. I open my mouth as if I can release the pressure. I'm choking and crying.

Sarge coughs. "Nurse, would you leave us, please?"

"Sure, I'm just getting the items from Andy's pockets. I put them in the drawer of the nightstand." Nurse Mellon moves to the bed. I follow her arm with my eyes. In her hand appears my red and blue handkerchief—one of Tom's gifts—and a wad of black.

"The tape!" I lunge at it, but my hand comes up short, falling uselessly on the blanket. Tears push through my closed eyelids as the nurse hands me the tape and my fingers close around the sticky bulge.

"Olson?" Sarge's voice grumbles into my consciousness.

I slowly open my eyes. "Better sit down. I've got stuff to say."

CHAPTER THIRTY-TWO

Sarge's face is grim when he leaves my room. I doze off. Things will be all right now.

In my dream Maddie pulls me close and smiles. We're lying on the beach, and I can't take my eyes off the tiny bikini she wears. The sun is blinding and I try adjusting my position.

"Olson, wake up."

I drift back to reality as Sarge's face comes into view. The light on the nightstand glares.

"Sir?"

Sarge gets up from his chair by my bed and closes the door. "We need to have a word. I spoke with the Dean. He—"

"Did you find them?" I try to sit up. "Did you find Tony and Big Mike?"

"We did. But I need to tell you about the Dean's orders. He's asked to keep this matter quiet. At least for now."

"What do you mean, quiet? I thought you'd interrogate them. Did you listen to the tape?" I'm having trouble focusing but something is terribly wrong. "They were ready to kill me because I knew…"

Sarge leans forward. His voice seems quieter than usual as he puts a hand on my arm. "Olson, calm down."

But I'm not finished. "I trusted you. I have all the evidence, Toad's testimony, his stash, the tape. I bet if you ask people if they saw Tony and Big Mike studying they'd tell you they didn't see them, just heard their voices." My throat is closing up on me. "They killed Tom."

"Shhh," Sarge says. "I believe you. But the Dean wants to protect the school's reputation."

"I don't believe this. Of all people, you … I trusted you!" I scream. "You *know* they murdered him. They killed Tom for fun because he didn't want to play their games." Tears run down my face. I don't care. "You always said you believed in justice. That the military is trying to do the right thing, protect the innocent and treat everyone fairly. You…" I feel as if someone punched me in the stomach and sucked the air from my lungs. I try lifting my chest. I can't.

"The military does try but they don't always succeed. Besides, this isn't the military, this is a private institution and it depends on funding and tuition from parents and sponsors."

"You sound like a cheap advertisement." My voice is sarcastic. "Listen to yourself. You should be in politics." I can't believe I speak like this to Sarge, but I don't care anymore. Nothing matters. It's all a complete farce.

Sarge sighs. "Olson, I'm going to tell you something I've never spoken of before. I hope it will help you understand." He leans back in his chair. I remain quiet and stare out the window. I've got nothing left to say.

"A long time ago," Sarge begins, "when I was a child my mother had problems. I didn't have a father, at least none I could count on. My mother had spells. She'd get really angry and throw stuff. She'd lock me in the closet or the basement and forget I was there."

I turn my head toward the bulky man by my bed.

Sarge looks at the wall, his eyes unseeing, and his voice heavy. "One time, I had taken some bread. I was hungry. She caught me making a sandwich. She took the breadknife and cut off my finger." Sarge rubs the scarred stump on his hand. "I know you all believe it's a war injury." He sniggers, but it sounds as if he's being strangled. "She said she'd do that every time I took something. I was eight and scared and from then on I stayed out of her way. I began to make plans to escape. When I turned seventeen I joined the military. They became my family. I had food and a bed and I had friends I could trust as long as I followed orders. They became all I had. They were dying for me and I would've died for them. Almost did a few times."

I stare at the man next to me. It's hard to imagine the pain and fear, the young Sarge went through.

"The military is good in many ways, not perfect. These are good men. They saved me."

I look at the large guy next to my bed and wonder if anything is ever as it seems. I imagine a young Sarge hiding from his mother, running away. "Why did you leave school?"

"Ah, that." Sarge sighs. "I got malaria when I was stationed in Nam. I've had it for years. Sometimes it gets… I have to take a break."

I remember how Sarge looked when he returned. His red eyes and puffy face.

"We thought you'd gone on a mission."

Sarge snorts. "Much more glamorous."

I suddenly feel pity. Even if I'm the one lying in bed. But then I remember Tom. "Sir, you must do something about Tony and Big Mike. I don't care about Toad's theft. He's pathetic but he's not evil. Tony, he's evil."

Sarge shakes his head. "The Dean is adamant."

"But don't you see? If they get away, it'll make a complete mockery of the military. You said they try to be fair, do the right thing, protect the innocent. Tom was innocent. He didn't hurt a fly. All he wanted was to get through school and escape to college." New tears push against my skull and I try to keep my voice steady. "You are the only one that can do something now."

"I want you to get well," Sarge says. "We'll talk again in a day or so. Promise me to stay calm and don't speak to anyone."

I nod.

CHAPTER THIRTY-THREE

Markus stands over my bed, his eyes huge with a mixture of fright and excitement.

"What is it?" I force my eyes to stay open, away from the daydream about me and Maddie lying naked in bed.

"It's about Sarge," Markus says. "He was fighting with the Dean. I thought you'd like to know."

"Why would I care about that now?" I say, remembering how small Markus was when I first saw him. He's grown a foot and there is strength in his voice.

"They talked about you and a tape."

I'm suddenly wide awake. "Tell me everything."

Markus slumps into the chair by my bed. "I was reporting to Sarge about a paper when the Dean barged in. I mean he didn't even knock, just burst in. He was really mad."

"Go on."

"Sarge threw me out right away, but I...sort of hung out for a bit."

I smile. Markus is getting brave. "It wasn't hard to hear because they were yelling. 'I thought I'd made myself perfectly clear,' the Dean shouted. 'I waited for the tape but it didn't arrive.' Sarge tried to say something, but the Dean cut him off. 'I don't want any trouble, least of all from you.' He hissed like a viper. 'You were always reliable. The cadets like you. I must have the tape.'" Markus takes a breath. "Sarge sounded really weird, like he was furious and scared at the same time. He said 'Sorry, Sir, I already gave it to a cadet from the search detail who's supposed to drop it off to you after class. And I spoke with Olson.'

'That boy has a vivid imagination,' the Dean said, but Sarge yelled. 'I know Olson is telling the truth. He has no reason to tell stories, besides I saw White in the tunnel. And I know when someone is lying.'"

Markus leans forward. "The Dean's voice got really creepy when he asked about White. Sarge said that both Stets and White were filthy and sweaty as if they'd been running a marathon. White said they got lost in the tunnels searching for you, because you stole a tape with music from his room."

Two red spots glow on Markus's cheeks. "At that point the Dean's voice dropped, so I sort of stuck my ear on the door. 'Can you imagine what this will do to our school?' he said. 'Our parents and sponsors will think we're running a prison where crimes are committed. Funding will dry up.'

'But these are serious accusations,' Sarge yelled. 'We must at least get to the bottom of it. There were crimes committed. Tom Zimmer lost his life.'

'According to Olson,' the Dean said dryly. 'I know you like the boy, but he's been less than reliable. Sergeant, I expect absolute secrecy in this matter. You're no stranger to secrets. *And* a man of your word? I'll handle it from here.'"

Markus's eyes flash. "I heard steps and dove around the corner."

"I'm proud of you," I say though I'm feeling murderous. I finally have proof that the Dean is hushing things up.

"Does this have to do with Tom?"

"Yeah, Tony and Big Mike did it."

"You mean they…"

I nod.

"But they have an alibi."

"A tape with their voices."

Markus gets up slowly. "The Dean is going to call the police."

"He won't," I whisper.

Inside me something breaks.

CHAPTER THIRTY-FOUR

I wake. Judging by the light outside it has to be afternoon. I feel better until I remember Markus's story about the Dean, the argument with Sarge. The only guy left, the only person I thought I could trust turned on me. Everything will be forgotten, despite my efforts, despite Toad's confession. I swore justice for Tom and I lost. I'll graduate and move on. I failed at the one thing I promised to do. The pain hits me then, a void in my middle that spreads to my bowels and up to my chest.

Tom died for nothing, a terrible waste and the people who did it, stupid bullies who jerk others around win. I sigh. I thought I could finally make a difference, do something right, somehow show Tom that I learned to do the right thing. I gaze at the ceiling, my eyes wet.

"I'm sorry," I mumble.

I realize I'd thought that if I could find Tom's murderer I'd feel less guilty. Guilty for abandoning Tom in the cave, for not believing in him. If I'd only stood by him, been strong, he may still be...

I crave his forgiveness, which will never come. Rolling to my side, I pull up my knees.

I feel dead inside.

The only brightness left in my life is Maddie. I suddenly have the urge to see her. It's so strong that my legs and arms ache and I want to jump out of bed to run into town.

Yeah right. So what if I go to see her. I'll sneak out after dark, make a lump in my bed with a blanket and hightail it into town. Tell Maddie and Eric what I found out. Maybe Eric has an idea. I also want to discuss the latest news I saw on TV. Four students at Kent State got shot by the Ohio National Guard during an anti-war rally.

I chuckle to myself, the sound of a crazy person in an asylum. Before Tom died I hated Eric. Now I enjoy his company, our discussions. Before

Tom... after Tom. I wish he could see me now. A tear squeezes through my eyelids. Too late.

The shrill sound of sirens tears through the peacefulness of my room. I jump out of bed. Ignoring my burning legs I yank open the window. Several police cars, their lights flashing a sharp white and red, are coming up the long drive toward assembly hall and stop in front of the registration building. I stretch my neck, but can't see past the hedges and trees. I notice Sarge hurry up the path and disappear behind the bushes. Several cadets out on errands stop what they're doing and inch closer to the building.

I pull on slippers and head outside. A crowd is gathering in front of the administration building. I feel awkward in my housecoat, an older vintage too short in the arms and lose threads hanging from the hem, but I care more about what's going on.

"Olson, what're you doing up?" Mr. Brown waves at me through the crowd. "Get back to bed."

"I will," I say. "Do you know what's going on?"

"No idea, but I'll find out. I suggest you all go on and finish your projects. I don't want to see anyone by the time I come out," he yells at the gathering throng before ducking into the building.

"Maybe we should go inside," someone says. "What would be a good excuse?"

"No way, they'll give us all Extra Duty," another voice laughs.

A car door slams and a policeman in uniform appears behind us. "You boys better leave," he says. He reminds me of the secret service that shields the President, tall and gray with a chiseled chin, sunglasses and earplugs. Except this guy's ears are free of technology.

The door of the administration building opens and Sarge muscles into the crowd, his chest like an icebreaker digging his way to Antarctica. He looks grim, his eyes narrowed into slits and his breath loud and heaving as if he's having trouble getting air. He ignores everyone and heads down the path when he glances over and sees me.

"Ah, Olson, I was looking for you. Come in here for a minute." Sarge steps closer and puts an arm around my shoulder, a blatant violation of Palmer's no-touch rule.

I'm too stunned to speak and follow him. Whispers ensue around us. "Wonder what he did," a voice says. "Maybe they'll arrest him."

Sarge closes the door with a clunk, drowning out the murmurs outside. Several people stand in front of the reception desk, the hall and the door to the Dean's office.

"In here," Sarge says. He sounds gruff, but the arm on my shoulder pats softly. "It's okay," he mumbles before he shuts the door behind us.

I find myself in a conference room. I recognize the Commandant standing in one corner, an old guy with gray hair and a huge nose. The

Dean sits at one end of the long polished table and several men and one woman line the sides. A chair has been placed at the other end opposite the Dean. It's empty.

"Andrew Olson?" The man in the middle of the table straightens. "I'm Detective Frazer from the Evansville police. We have several colleagues here, Ms. Tilling is taking notes and you know Commandant Riker, the Dean and Sergeant Russel."

I nod.

"Have a seat. May I call you Andy?"

"Yes, Sir."

"We received a call from Sergeant Russel regarding the matter of Tom Zimmer who died here last year. Is it true that you have information about the cause of his death?"

I nod again. The Dean's eyes drill into my head from across the room.

"I need to tell you that you have the right to have your parents present. If you wish for them to be here, we will postpone this hearing. But you are here as a witness and not a suspect."

I shake my head. "I'm fine. I don't need my parents."

"Now tell us what you know. From the beginning."

All eyes turn toward me. I take a breath, turning my thoughts inward, away from the Dean's icy stare. Nobody moves as the silence expands.

I push my back against the chair to gather strength. "To tell you everything I must start with Tom, my best friend…" I swallow, "who was murdered."

The men around the table lean forward, the woman types.

About half way through the story when I find Toad's stash and go to ask him about it, the door opens. A uniformed policeman enters. Ignoring everyone he walks directly to the Detective and whispers into his ear.

"Let's stop for a moment," the Detective says and leaves the room.

I notice the Dean has shrunk into his chair. His eyes shine like galvanized steel as he gazes at me.

Frazer reenters, leaving the door open long enough for me to see movement in the hallway. Tony White and Big Mike are standing surrounded by uniformed police.

"Okay, let's continue."

When I describe the chase in the tunnel, one of the men gasps. By the time I finish, the room has turned into a mausoleum.

"Thank you, Andy," the Detective says after a pause. "I assume you can produce the stolen items you took from Cadet Todd?"

"They're in my desk."

"You have the tape, Sergeant?"

"Yes, Sir," Sarge says. "Right here." He places the tape on the shiny table, covering one hand with the other to hide the missing finger as if to shield it from the Dean. The Dean sits motionless, his face gray marble.

One of the detectives gets up and drops the tape in a bag.

"I'm sending a policeman with you to your room, Andy. Please give him the items for evidence."

"Yes, Sir." I jump up. I'm suddenly drained and long for my bed.

"You did well," Sarge whispers as I leave the room.

I grin to myself. Tom would've considered it hilarious to see me in my housecoat in the admin building.

The throng in front has thickened. Dinner started, but it looks as if half the school is out waiting for news.

"Look, he's getting arrested," a high voice says. "The policeman is taking him now."

I smile. I'm famous.

A siren sounds, not the drawn-out wail, but short spurts intended to spread apart the horde of cadets. I turn to look over my shoulder and recognize Toad, dressed in jeans and a red shirt that looks more like a tent, as he leaves the car. He looks foreign like a strange visitor without his uniform.

"You better return with me," the policeman says after bagging Toad's stash from my desk. Even more people have gathered by the time we return. A path forms as we approach, cadets pulling apart to make room for me.

To my disappointment neither Toad nor Tony or Big Mike are visible inside. I slump down and wait. My stomach rumbles, a reminder that I haven't eaten since breakfast. The hallway is deserted except for a couple of plain-clothes policemen standing in front of closed doors. I wonder what's going on behind the walls, whether they're asking Tony and Big Mike about Tom.

The phone rings. Once. Twice. Its shrill sound echoes across the room, but nobody picks up. The secretary who also functions as receptionist, an older woman related to the Dean, isn't around. Nor are any cadets pulling office duty.

The phone stops, leaving behind unnatural silence. I wonder why I can't hear anything and contemplate passing by the doors to eavesdrop. Surely, the men in the hall won't allow it.

I look around the room, remembering my first visit here. How scared I was of the Dean and this place, the rigidity and the threat of punishment, of disappointing my parents. I'd felt out of control and thought my life was finished.

I no longer care what the Dean thinks or if I get along. I'm taking back control and doing things my way. My parents have their lives, I've got mine. I decide I'll forgive them and to my own surprise break into a smile.

It's nearly seven when the door to the Dean's office opens. The

Dean's voice sounds angry and shrill as he yells into the phone.

"You'll have to speak to the police about your son…no, I can't discuss it…repercussions, yes, I'm aware…it's out of my control…"

"Andy?"

Sarge towers above me. For the first time since I entered the school, he's addressed me by my first name. The bench sags under Sarge's weight as he sits down next to me.

"You did well today," he says. "The truth is coming out at last." He sighs. "I never imagined this kind of thing at a school. Here I left the battlefield only to find bloodshed in the Midwest."

"Sir, what happened? You said you had to obey orders. You said the Dean was going to…"

Sarge waves an arm. "I was wrong. I called the police."

"*You* did that?"

Sarge nods. He suddenly looks old. "You were right. It came down to obedience versus truth. I may be out of a job for disobeying orders, but it was the right thing to do." He leans against the wall and wipes his forehead with his sleeve. "You did the right thing, too. It almost cost you your life."

"Tom would've done the same. If I could've said…" I shake my head, my throat too thick to go on.

"Listen, Son." Sarge pats my knee. "Promise me to forgive yourself. It wasn't your fault. None of this was." His voice lowers into a whisper. "For many years I felt guilty about my finger. I thought I'd done something to deserve it. It took me a long time to recognize I was not the one swinging the knife."

I nod numbly. With a pang I realize that all this time I was afraid to offend someone. Because when I did growing up, my family sent me away. They taught me not to have an opinion, to shut up. I wanted acceptance, even love from guys like Tony and Muller. By playing along I'd only enabled them and belittled myself. Guys like that have nothing to give, only to take. Tom had known that all along. Just as he understood the war and the wrong it's been doing to the people, civilians and soldiers.

Tom knew the real truth. Tom, my smartass best friend.

A chuckle escapes me and all of a sudden I can't stop. I'm laughing so hard, my jaw muscles ache. Sarge glances at me curiously. Then he smiles. Still I laugh until my vision blurs with tears. Sarge's shoulders begin to tremble as he joins in. I realize I've never heard him laugh before. And for the first time in months I get the feeling that things will work out.

Behind one of the doors, somebody wails like he's been stabbed. At first I think it's Toad, but then I recognize Big Mike's voice except it sounds like a different person, not the mean and domineering guy, who frightens young cadets. More like a trapped animal fearing for its life.

A commotion starts down the hall as several doors open at once and people spill into the corridor. In their midst walks Big Mike, his face streaked, tears dripping onto his massive chest. His hands are cuffed behind his back, followed by Tony, his face pale and impossible to read. He's handcuffed, too. Then comes Toad. He looks relieved, his face relaxed as if he's been sleeping.

The doors slam behind them.

The Detective stops in front of me. "We don't have anything else for you right now, but you'll have to testify in court. Probably not 'till the fall, though. Make sure to leave your address."

I nod, realizing that my new life is about to start.

"You should feel better now," Sarge says. "You helped find Tom's murderers. It won't bring him back but…Tom would be proud. What're you going to do with yourself? I mean after school lets out."

Somehow it's all clear now. I've him-hawed and labored over the right decision. But there it is, obvious and not at all difficult. I realize it's me and me alone who's going to determine my path. Not my parents, not my classmates, not Sarge nor the school. Just me. Knowing that feels good.

I smile. "I do."

"Not a military career, I take it."

"No, Sir."

CHAPTER THIRTY-FIVE

"Can you believe this?" Maddie folds up the newspaper. "The Dean was asked to step down."

"I wonder if he'll ever work again," Eric says.

"He should've gone to prison like Tony and Big Mike." My mouth tastes bitter. "Even Toad is in jail, though probably not as long. The trial won't be 'till December. In a way the Dean is worse—he tried to cover it up."

We're sitting in front of the ice cream counter at the store, Eric behind us, his hair much shorter, his beard trimmed close to the skin, revealing chiseled cheekbones. His eyes are clear as he rearranges jam jars on the bottom shelves.

"I'm glad it's over," I say. "Tom's father stopped by."

"The mean one?" Eric asks.

"Yeah, except he wasn't mean. They called him to discuss the case, tell him about the murder and give him Tom's watch. You know what he did?" I stop for effect.

"No," Maddie and Eric say simultaneously.

"He gave *me* the watch." I pull it out of my pocket. "He said Tom would've wanted me to have it. He only kept the mother's photo. He seemed pretty mellow."

"Tom brought out the best in us," Eric says, his eyes serious. "He was just a neat guy. I miss him."

I swallow the lump in my throat. Not a day goes by that I don't think about Tom. "At first I hardly knew how to go on, but then I got so busy trying to find the murderer." I rub the watch with my forefinger and clear my throat.

"I've decided what to do," I say quietly. "After school."

Maddie looks up. "What?"

"I applied to the University of Evansville and I'm pretty confident I'll get in. It's not a school in high demand and they're interested in football players. After finishing Palmer, it won't be a big deal. I'll stay in the dorms and on the weekends I'll come up here to visit and help."

Maddie flies off her chair and into my arms. "I'm so glad. I was worried you'd leave me." I place my arm around her waist. "Your parents will be angry," Maddie says. "They're expecting you to join the military."

"They'll have to get over it. It's my life and my future."

"I wish Tom could hear you," Eric says. "He'd be impressed. I'm glad you finally came to your senses."

I look at Maddie who looks amazing in a pink and white shirt and navy blue shorts. "You ready to go?"

Maddie picks up a bag. "Ready."

"Wait a moment," I say as soon as we're outside. I run back in.

"Forgot something?" Eric asks.

I lean across the counter and place a box with six shotgun shells on Eric's palm. "I don't think you'll need them anymore."

Eric stares for a moment. Then he grins. "You're right. Thanks, man."

I nod and hurry to the door.

"Be good!" Eric shouts after me, but I can tell he's smiling.

"I'd like to put your photo into the watch," I say to Maddie as we're walking toward the forest. "Maybe we can take one sometime."

"I'd like that," Maddie says. "I'd feel very special being placed in Tom's watch."

The fishing hole sparkles below us when we spread the blanket. We didn't bother to take poles, neither of us being in the mood to deceive. The May sun has real strength and it's warm despite the shady spot and the coolness from the water below. I trace Maddie's cheeks with my forefinger. "You're so beautiful. I don't know how I'll survive without you."

"Maybe when you visit you could sleep over," she says with a grin. "Except I don't know if Dad will let you. Maybe in the office behind the curtains."

"I'd sleep in the broom closet to be near you."

She pulls me close and opens her lips, our breaths joining, quickening, until the blood is rushing through my head like currents in a fast-flowing river. I undress her slowly, her pink and white shirt with the tiny buttons, kisses in-between on bare skin revealed inch-by-inch. Maddie murmurs softly as I pull off her top, revealing a pink bra with a tiny white bow on the breastbone. I kiss around it, the cleavage above and the smooth white stomach below.

Unhooking her bra, I carefully lift it. "The sun feels so nice," Maddie whispers. "Like a thousand caresses."

"Better than my caresses?" I tease.

"Mmmh, no, yours are magical."

I chuckle and snuggle my face against her breasts, finding her nipples with my tongue, swirling around each tiny rosebud until they're hard and she begins to moan. Her hands have found their way under my shirt and I rip it off impatiently. My crotch pushes against the fabric of my pants.

"You want to go on?" I ask as I finger the button on her pants.

"Mmmh."

"Maddie? I don't want to stop if we take all our clothes off."

"You have protection, right?" Maddie leans back on her elbows. "I could probably get something in the store but my dad might find out."

"Got condoms," I say, pulling out a packet I traded Plozett for a box of my mother's cookies. I look at the girl I love. "We can wait until later."

"I know but I want to do it with you. It'll be something to remember during the summer."

I smile. "I just want to make sure you won't regret it later and blame me."

"It's my decision. I'm eighteen and I can have sex. Millions of young people have sex every day. All the hippies in Haight Ashbury have sex. Why not us?"

"Right, why not."

I lie back down, unbuttoning her pants. She lifts her hips and wiggles out of them. My hand wanders lower to touch the dampness between her legs. I pull aside the fleck of fabric and touch her. She moans again, pushing against my hand. I borrowed a book from the library last summer and studied it for months. I learned where things are and hope I'm doing it right. Maddie's moans grow louder.

"Tell me if I'm doing something wrong," I whisper, kissing her open lips.

"Good, it's good," she says, her voice throaty now and so sensual that I want to rip my pants off and mount her. But I've waited this long and I'll wait just a bit longer. I keep touching, one finger probing the tender opening, more rubbing. Her breath comes fast now, her legs spread wide and she's lifting her hips toward my hand.

"Just a little more," she breathes. And I continue feathery light, fingers fluttering. Her climax comes fast and hard and she shudders.

"Mmmh," she says, looking at me. "Your turn."

I'm ready to break through my pants when I feel her hand on my zipper, slowly moving it down.

"Relax," she says, groping to release me into the air of the sunny afternoon. I yank down my pants and lay back, closing my eyes. I feel suddenly embarrassed, never having been naked in front of a girl, but the urge in my middle is stronger and pushes away all thought. Her hand feels soft and pliable against me as she moves up and down. I want to explode and then it happens. I come violently, the energy of the last weeks releasing.

"Damn," I say, but Maddie laughs.

"I've heard about that happening," she says. "We'll just have to do it again until you can wait long enough." She lies back giggling and opens her arms to catch more sun.

I take a sock to wipe myself and move next to her. "You're wicked." Then I grin. "It was great anyway."

The shadows grow longer as we lay caressing each other.

"You know," I say, looking into the sky, "we should wait for the real thing until after the summer. It's something to look forward to. And it's precious." I roll to my side and look at her. "I'd be totally cool with that."

Maddie shields her eyes against the low sun, which bathes the air orange and creates sharp edges along trees and bushes.

"Okay," she says.

I know she's pleased and I place my hand on her stomach. We stare into the sky. My path is clear: college and being close to Maddie.

In a few years, I'll take her away—away from this town into the future.

The End

EPILOGUE

The smoke from thousands of joints clouds the air as the crowd sways. Giant peace signs, banners and flags hover above the heads of more than 500,000 protesters assembled near the White House and the National Mall. They have climbed trees, sit, stand and lounge to listen to the speakers and musicians.

Peter, Paul and Mary sing *Blowing in the Wind*, their voices distorted by microphones and crackling loudspeakers. It's cloudy and cool, a typical spring day in April 1971, but the crowd doesn't seem to care.

Near the wall of the reflection pond two people stand hand-in-hand. Maddie looks at the man next to her. Now over six feet tall, Andy scans the crowd. He's grown a beard and brown curls cover his ears. Maddie likes twisting her fingers into them, especially when they make love.

Andy is studying at the University of Evansville, but will transfer to Purdue in the fall. He likes the freedom of organizing his days, running or walking without being stopped, eating when he's hungry and studying when he wants to. After the hard training at Palmer his grades are better than expected.

Tony and Big Mike, both eighteen when they attacked Tom, have been convicted to twenty years in prison. Toad received two years on accessory charges. With luck he'll be out in the fall. Sarge retired. He wrote a letter to Andy, inviting him to Florida where Sarge built a cabin and leads fishing tours for tourists. Andy can just imagine how well organized his boat is.

Palmer has a new Dean. Plozett attends Harvard, so does Muller. Thanks to the G.I. Bill, Eric studies political science at the University of Wisconsin through long distance courses. On the side he helps at the store. He stopped drinking and is writing a book about his experience in Vietnam. He even has a girlfriend and seems much happier. Maddie will join Andy in the fall at Purdue. She received a scholarship and now that Eric is at the store, she's free to go.

For the past year Andy and Maddie have saved every penny—waited for an opportunity. Now they are finally here in DC at the largest anti-war protest in two years. Andy looks at the girl next to him. She raises her arm making a peace sign against the banner they hold between them.

It says *PEACE* and below *For Tom & Eric*.

Andy smiles. Sarge was right. Tom would've been proud.

FROM THE AUTHOR

Thank you for purchasing A DIFFERENT TRUTH. My sincere hope is that you derived as much entertainment from reading this book as I enjoyed in creating it. If you have a few moments, please feel free to add your review of the book at your favorite online site for feedback (Amazon, Apple iTunes Store, Goodreads, etc.). Also, if you would like to connect with other books that I have coming in the near future, please visit my website for information on upcoming works, recent blog posts and to sign up for e-news: http://www.annetteoppenlander.com.
Sincerely, Annette

ANNETTE OPPENLANDER

Annette Oppenlander is an award-winning writer, literary coach and educator. As a bestselling historical novelist, Oppenlander is known for her authentic characters and stories based on true events, coming alive in well-researched settings. Having lived in Germany the first half of her life and the second half in various parts in the U.S., Oppenlander inspires readers by illuminating story questions as relevant today as they were in the past.

Oppenlander's bestselling true WWII story, Surviving the Fatherland, received multiple nominations/awards. The recently translated German version received the silver Skoutz Award 2020. Uniquely, Oppenlander weaves actual historical figures and events into her plots, giving readers a flavor of true history while enjoying a good story.

Oppenlander shares her knowledge through writing workshops at colleges, libraries, festivals and schools. She also offers vivid presentations and author visits. The mother of fraternal twins and a son, she recently returned to her home, Solingen, Germany where she lives with her husband.

She was inspired to write *A Different Truth* after interviewing her husband, a cadet at a military prep school in the late 1960s.

AUTHOR NOTES

The Vietnam War was a complex and long-lasting endeavor that morphed into horrific tragedy for many Americans and the Vietnamese people. There were many sides and as President Richard Nixon said, the Vietnam War is neither easily explained nor understood. Below are just a few facts to spur discussion.

Facts about the Vietnam War
While the Vietnam War lasted from 1954-1973, the U.S. had the largest military presence and dominated between 1965 and 1968. In Vietnam it is known as the American War.

The U.S. supported the Republic of South Vietnam against communist forces that included South Vietnamese guerrillas, Viet Cong units (VC), and the North Vietnamese Army (NVA). Because U.S. involvement failed, South Vietnam was taken over by the North in 1975.

More than 58,000 U.S. soldiers and civilian personnel died, over 150,000 were injured. Nearly 2,000 are still unaccounted for today. Of those killed, 61% were younger than 21. These numbers don't include men who suffered physical and emotional injuries that surfaced later and last a lifetime. South Vietnam suffered much higher casualties, both military and civilian.

2,709,918 Americans served in uniform in Vietnam.

Vietnam Veterans represented 9.7% of that generation.

Facts about the Anti-war Movement
Also known as the peace movement, the anti-war movement began with small groups of left-leaning students on U.S. college campuses.

In 1967, as American troop numbers reached 500,000, with 15,000 U.S. soldiers dead and nearly 110,000 wounded, more and more average citizens became disillusioned. More than 40,000 young men were drafted into service each month, adding fuel to the fire of the anti-war movement.

With the public's increasing discontent, demonstrations skyrocketed, including people from all parts of life, housewives, students, men and women alike.

Along with demonstrations grew confrontations between protestors and police, leading to arrests and killings, even on college campuses.

Civil rights leader Martin Luther King Jr. spoke publicly about his opposition.

By 1968 fifty percent of the population opposed President Johnson's handling of the war. Vietnam vets began to join anti-war demonstrations.

In 1968, newly elected President Nixon promised to snuff out protests and rioting, stating that the "silent" majority of citizens was in favour of the war.

This he followed with the instatement of the draft lottery in December 1969. Tensions escalated, men fled to Canada as the country divided itself further.

Mass demonstrations with hundreds of thousands became common, so did violence against demonstrators.

In 1971 details of U.S. involvement and misconduct in the war came to light through the "Pentagon Papers," a 7,000-page compendium of historical analysis and original government documents, causing even more people to question the government and military establishment.

Pressured by antiwar sentiment, Nixon finally announced the end of U.S. involvement in Vietnam in January 1973.

www.ingramcontent.com/pod-product-compliance
Lightning Source LLC
Chambersburg PA
CBHW070456120726
47910CB00003B/1057